A Dark Holme Publication

Ethereal Nightmares

The Second Sleep

A Publication by
Dark Holme Publishing
Edited by Kerry Holmes
Cover design by Lena Ashford

First Edition

Paperback ISBN 978-1-0686164-9-5
Hardback ISBN 978-1-0686164-8-8

www.darkholmepublishing.uk

Contents

A word by our Founder

Get ready to plunge back into the depths of terror with *The Second Sleep*, the next volume in the *Ethereal Nightmares* anthology series. In this collection, the horrors don't just return—they evolve, creeping into your mind and twisting your perception of reality.

The Second Sleep is a relentless exploration of fear in all its forms. Each story is a carefully crafted descent into the unknown, where dread builds slowly, leaving you feeling unsettled and vulnerable. The chills range from subtle unease to gut-wrenching terror, ensuring that no matter where you turn, there's no escape from the creeping horror that awaits.

So, pour yourself something strong, turn the lights low, and brace yourself. These aren't just stories—they're nightmares brought to life, and they're waiting for you in *The Second Sleep*. Are you ready to confront what lurks in the shadows?

Kerry Holmes

Bleed For Me

W.H. Vigo

The vampire's blood on the bathroom tile crept up Nanyamka's leg.

She flicked a finger, and a fountain of crimson poured from the mouth of its corpse laying in the empty tub, its face locked in surprise.

The blood snaked over the tub's edges and spiraled in neat circles towards her toes, as she imagined how good it would make her feel. Nanyamka opened her bathrobe and let the creature's liquid essence slither up her thighs and stomach, then fork into two streams, just as she wanted.

The small slit between her breasts opened, sucking in the fluid, while the rest flowed into the corners of her mouth, thick and bitter, she swallowed it down. Unlike human blood, it did little for her hunger. Rather, it produced unique effects.

The creature's body swiftly flaked to dust.

Nanyamka waited. Then, the hallucinations began.

She stumbled out of the bathroom down the elegant corridors of her mansion, humming happily as the cream-colored walls melted into technicolour rays of light, that flashed like lightning through her skin. Giggling, violet pixies in dandelion dresses tickled her brown cheeks with kisses. They grabbed her long braids, lifted her from the ground, then flew Nanyamka to the bedroom. When her feet touched the transparent floor, Nanyamka threw off her robe and flopped onto the bed. She tossed and turned through its sheets, laughing as they morphed into sparkling, black ocean waves that swept her out to sea, towards an emerald sun dominating the horizon.

What a trip! she thought to herself, *that bloodsucker must've been really old for a high like this!*

"Nanyamka," the sun called, in a chorus of angelic voices, "Destroy them all!" it boomed, "Spare no one! Take the world into your mouth!"

"I will!" she cried joyfully, licking at her teeth as they vibrated and chimed in her head. "Give me inspiration! Take me with you!" she begged.

Nanyamka felt her body rise as though evaporating from the galactic waves into the rainbow-colored sky, through a gelatinous atmosphere, then into space. She opened her arms, flying between thousands of glowing pearls, looping around red planets that screamed and bled, the emerald sun at her heels. The slit in her chest filled with light, and she felt invigorated with hundreds of lives, human and vampire alike, her mind and body overwhelmed with euphoria.

Then, she closed her eyes.

**

Nanyamka's cell phone chimed and vibrated across the nightstand. She jolted awake and found herself on the floor, tangled in bed sheets. Nanyamka scrambled onto her feet and snatched up her cell phone. Panic flared in her eyes when she saw the name on its screen.

"H-Hello?" she said, clearing her throat, "Romulus, how are you?"

A male voice sighed gruffly.

"Why haven't you been answering your phone?" he demanded, his voice grating with anger, "I called you a dozen times last night!"

"I-I was trying to...t-to finish what I was working on," Nanyamka stammered. She hobbled over to the window and threw aside the curtains, letting the fresh sunlight warm the sleep from her face.

"I told you I was coming to look at the sculpture, did you forget? You never came to the door. I know you were home; the lights were on!"

"Well, uh...the things..."

"You're slurring your words. Were you getting high on vampire blood again?"

Nanyamka swallowed hard.

"...Yes. I got stuck...just wanted some inspiration."

"Inspiration?" Romulus hissed, "You can't accomplish anything in a bumbling stupor! Nanyamka—the Prince's Awakening is in five days. If you need inspiration read a book or go to a museum. Do something reasonable—"

"But I did."

"Do not interrupt me! Everyone else has done their part for the celebration except you. And you were only asked to do one thing. If you've nothing to contribute, the others will think I've been an incompetent guardian. Haven't I been good to you all these years?" he asked mournfully, "Looked after you. Done my utmost to give you the best of everything. Sheltered you in a bubble of luxury and adulation. Even today, I house and clothe you. Now, you will bring shame upon me."

"I'm sorry! Please forgive me!" Nanyamka begged in Twi, their shared tongue from Ghana, hoping its soothing melody would smoothen her apology. "I swear I will not bring shame upon you and will finish on time! C-can I tell you about my latest draft? Please?"

A pause came, followed by a long sigh.

"Quickly."

Phone still clutched to her ear, Nanyamka bolted from her room and down the hall, past the dust-filled bathroom, and into a dark bedroom. She flicked the light switch and started to describe the contorted sculpture on the bed.

"I have the nude, pale, corpses of a man and a woman, split in half from crown to navel," she began, "They are next to each other in a seated position. The man's left half has been removed, and the same has been done to woman's right. An intricate bridge of blood hangs between their torsos—a snowflake pattern was my intention, but it appears more like a half-finished spider's web. The man's free hand reaches for the ceiling, in a priestly manner, while the woman's gestures at the floor."

"Interesting. What's wrong with it?"

"It's not quite what I envisioned. May I please have them disposed of?"

"...Very well. I'll send one of my assistants to pick up the corpses. But do not let perfectionism get the best of you," Romulus chided, "In three days, I'll will arrive with a pair of judges to evaluate the piece. Finish something. If you do not, I shall take back all I've given you and put you to toil among our people as a servant."

Nanyamka crinkled her face as though Romulus' words had poisoned her.

"You...you mean I'll have to work?" she whimpered.

"Indeed."

"But—"

The phone line clicked.

Nanyamka folded her arms and pouted, examining her failed attempt at gorgeous carnage on the bed.

"Three days..." she echoed, "Prince Ageaboye...I wish you had more time to teach me hemamancy. I would've been able to control the blood better. Command it with my mind to become sharp as a sword or hard as a chisel. Peel skin from flesh like plucking petals from flowers. Truly create something worthy of you."

She thought back to the wonderfully fearsome things the prince had created with his mastery of hemamancy. Scarlet forests of weeping flesh, twisted and screaming, composed of thousands of lives. A true artist.

"Look at you both!" she snapped at the corpses, as though they had somehow misbehaved in their stillness. "Not even symmetrical! I could've used your blood to slice you apart properly if you hadn't saturated it with vodka!"

She walked around the bed, entered the bathroom, then slammed the door.

Nanyamka filled the bath with hot water, stepped inside, and let herself stew as dried blood lifted from the soles of her feet. She traced her fingers down the thin opening in her chest.

"I'll finish something, You're Highness," she said to herself, "I won't be useless, like on the day we lost you."

Nanyamka sniffled and closed her eyes, as her thoughts rewound to ancient times...

***

In a village one night, Nanyamka was tearing the neck out of an old man with her teeth. Two sudden bursts of pain took her by surprise, one through her arm, then another in her thigh. Overwhelmed, she collapsed, stunned by a fiery torment she'd never experienced. Her skin sizzled and smoked, its odour rank as a wild boar. In an instant, she was surrounded by shouting men brandishing swords and torches.

As her vision blurred, a strange silhouette appeared and waved an arm.

The men's yelling cut to silence.

Nanyamka opened her eyes to the sight of warriors' heads laying on the grass. Some of their torches still were alight, casting shadows over their faces still clenched in anger.

A nude young man stood above her, with iron claws and sparkling silver eyes like her own. He had woolly white hair and seemed barely old enough to take a wife.

"Do not be afraid," a voice whispered in her ear, cool as morning air, "I'll help you."

The boy snapped his fingers. Every arrow ejected from Nanyamka's body in a spurt of blood that was so quick, she felt no pain. The boy picked one up, its tip twinkling red and yellow in the moonlight.

"Beware of gold," he cautioned, although his lips did not move. He threw the arrow into the bushes.

Starting with her arm, the boy ran his tongue over every wound, which closed right away. Still in shock, she let him finish.

He helped her to her feet then stared into her eyes with an absorbing gaze.

"I'd heard rumours that a new one of our kind was in this area—what is your name?" he asked.

"Na...Nanyamka."

"'God's gift'—a charming name. I am Prince Ageaboye. You taste fresh. When did you change?"

"I...don't know."

"What can you remember? Tell me."

"Th-there...was a fire in my village. I tried to escape through the forest with my sister...but something attacked me—a large, grey beast with metal teeth. It took me into the trees...at dawn, my sister found me outside the forest..." She opened her mouth and touched her trembling claws to thick, iron fangs. Tears streamed down her face. "But I tore her apart with these. Now I can't stop killing...no matter how hard I try. Why can't I stop?"

"I'm sorry for your loss," said the prince. "But it is your nature now." He wrapped his arms around her, his embrace warm and comforting as that of a lover. "It pains me to see the women of our kind suffer, for there are so few among us. Nanyamka, I shall give you a gift and teach you to do wonders with it. No human shall ever harm you again without deep regret."

The prince looked at a large hole in the centre of her tattered robes.

He reached a claw inside, carved a line down her chest, lowered his head, then slipped his tongue into the wound. Nanyamka felt it flicker across the bone, rough as a crocodile's hide, as shivers rushed down her spine and nestled between her legs. She would've fallen in ecstasy had he not been holding her. He kissed her on the cheek.

"It is done. Come, meet the others. We all look after each other."

He took her by the hand and led her away.

From then on, Nanyamka's life was renewed. A new family. A nomadic lifestyle offering new lands and fresh blood. A life of captivating beauty and thrilling terror.

A century later, what her people called the *Oseye Kesse*—
'The Great Destruction'— claimed the prince.

That day, a small troupe led by the prince was passing
through a valley to bathe in a river. Nanyamka and a few
others kept watch from atop the surrounding cliffs.
An abrupt seismic crash knocked Nanyamka off her feet.
From the many caves and caverns lining the cliff, came
thundering drums and chimes, the voices of men and women
chanting in a language she did not understand.

"Run!" an Elder shouted, "Sorcerers are here!"

Nanyamka tried to clamour down the cliff—if she could see
these sorcerers, she'd destroy them! —but an Elder grabbed
her arm.

"Let me go, Akibu!"

"It's too dangerous!" he yelled, "You will die!"

He dragged her away, kicking and screaming.

That night, in an underground cave, the walls echoed with
the weeping of Nanyamka's people. The prince lay on a bed
of grass and flowers. His body was covered in dark holes
weeping blood, which instantly reopened every time they
healed. A flame-covered woman knelt by his side, frowning.
She held his hand and whispered into his ear like a mother
soothing her child.

Nanyamka stood by Akibu, sobbing into his shoulder. "Is he
dead?" she asked.

"No, he sleeps," Akibu replied, "In a futile battle between
death and regeneration. The sorcerers know he is too powerful
to be killed, so they've cursed him instead. The Adzé rescued
him," he said, gesturing at the burning woman. "She will work
her magic for as long as it takes to revive him, and we will
wait. Keep your distance—she is *not* of us but a shapeshifting
being not of this world. She and Prince share a history
spanning eons."

Nanyamka covered her face with her hands. "What will become of us?"

Akibu sighed. "We will continue looking after one another. Nine of our young were killed today. The Elders have decided that all who've seen less than two-hundred rainy seasons must have a guardian," he placed a hand on her shoulder. "And I will be yours."

***

The doorbell rang, snatching Nanyamka from the grip of her memories—the assistants had arrived.

Romulus was reliable as always.

***

Night fell and Nanyamka stepped out of the back of a taxi in her tightest, shortest black dress. It was easy to blend in with mortals—with one thought, she could make her fangs and claws appear as human teeth and nails. The only thing she couldn't hide were her crystal eyes, but Nanyamka thought this was beneficial as mortals found them alluring.

She took in the pulse of the street, racing with activity. People drinking on patios; groups of young people rushing in and out of clubs; couples strolling under neon lights. Finding the right material to sculpt was paramount, so she decided to try a new venue in hopes of new flesh. Somewhere calm and mid-upper scale, away from the slurring drunkards who stank of cigarettes and sweat in dive bars, or the prepositions of wealthy fat men and sexually audacious couples in exclusive dining clubs.

She found a spot that seemed to fit the bill, and went inside. Amber lighting, quartz counter-tops, and dark wood cabinets with matching chairs. Music low enough to hold a conversation. She took a seat, ordered a chocolate martini, and the game began: cat and mouse.

The first set of hitters wouldn't do, with blood either too old or too young and alcohol-filled to manipulate.

"Oh, I'm waiting for my boyfriend," she'd say, or "My friends'll be here soon."

Nanyamka took a sip of her drink, then stared out the window at the passers-by. Sometimes, looking disinterested drew interest. Out the corner of her eye, she caught a man with auburn hair in a neatly pressed jacket staring at her from across the room. He took a step forward.

She shifted in her seat, looked down, then frowned, as the zesty scent of cologne grew stronger.

"Hi."

Her gaze wandered up from polished shoes, blue jeans, a sweating mug of beer, and a tie covered in smiley faces, then met with a pair of green eyes.

"Are you alright?" the man asked, somewhat shyly, "You look a little sad."

"I'm okay," she answered, then let her voice fall, "I was waiting for someone...but got stood up."

"Stood up? No way!" he protested, "How long have you been waiting here?"

"Two hours."

The man shook his head. "What a jerk. Can I pay for your drink, at least?"

"No, that's all right. I'm gonna finish it then go home."

"Oh. Want some company? No pressure though, I'm not trying to be a creep."

Nanyamka examined him closely. Adequate height, healthy skin and eyes, strong build and pulse. Definitely good material to work with.

"Sure. What's your name?" she asked.

"Justice." He stretched out his right hand, thick gold rings circled his middle and index fingers. "What's yours?"

Nanyamka nervously twisted the napkin in her lap. "I'm Nikki."

She lifted a hand to meet his, and subtly brushed her knuckles against the martini glass, tipping it over.

"Sorry!" she blurted, tossing the napkin over the mess and wiping it away. "I'm clumsy."

"No problem. I can help y—"

"'Justice'. Interesting name. I like it," she said.

Justice sat down across from her, and the cushy seat creaked.

"My parents were interesting people, so I blame them," he joked. "Circus performers. They travelled all over the world."

That's new, Nanyamka thought to herself. Bankers, priests, politicians—she'd met tons of boring people before.

"Cool! Were either of them contortionists?" she asked, wondering if some natural flexibility would enhance her art.

"Fortune-telling. Bit o'magic too," he said with a chuckle. "They even got me and my siblings into it, said we were 'gifted'."

Nanyamka leaned forward. "Do you think magic's real?" she asked playfully.

"Nah. I wanted to be a clown."

"Is that why you're wearing that funny tie?"

"What funny tie?"

Nanyamka giggled.

Justice beamed. "You have a beautiful smile. Nice eyes, too. The tie's definitely nerdy but I like having a bit of a quirk. I like being *creative*. Helps me survive at work—the competition can be pretty killer. Anyway, I think it's better than being boring."

Nanyamka smiled. "I agree," she raised her empty glass, "to being creative!"

"To being creative!"

They clinked glasses and laughed.

The pair chat for a while, Nanyamka mainly listening, surprised at how interesting Justice was. He worked at an archive and specialized in ancient cultures and languages across Africa and the Middle East. Justice mentioned all sorts of things she had never heard of before and she couldn't help but ask question after question, astounded by his detailed responses each time. He travelled often, lived alone, and had no children. Coincidentally, his two siblings did the same kind of work he did but lived in different countries. When Justice asked her questions, Nanyamka answered with her typical, canned responses.

"2AM folks! Last call!" the bar man shouted, clapping his hands.

Nanyamka gasped. "Already? Did we really talk for three hours?"

"We did. How are you getting home? Need a ride or a taxi?"

"Can I get a ride?"

Justice paused as if he hadn't expected her reply. "No prob. What area are you in?"

Nanyamka rattled off the name of some common place.

"But I'm not ready to go home yet," she added, "I'd rather spend more time with you, if that's okay? No pressure though, I'm not trying to be a creep," she said with a wink. Justice grinned.

"Let's get out of here," he said, jutting a thumb at the exit.

***

The drive to Justice's place was much farther, and quieter, than Nanyamka anticipated—they had left the city entirely, to a more rural area where the houses were generously spaced apart. His demeanour had changed somewhat, still friendly, but his replies were shorter, his enthusiasm lukewarm. They stopped in front of a modest house shrouded by trees. Justice exited the car, walked over to her door, and opened it.

"Hope I didn't seem too out of it while driving," he said, as they walked up the short driveway. He yawned. "Long day."

"No worries," she reassured, as Justice unlocked the front door.

The home's interior was large yet simplistic, to the left, a long corridor filled with swollen bookshelves, encased statuettes and trinkets, and bizarre masks. To the right, more bookcases, and an eat-in kitchen. The dimly lit living room had a long, yellow sofa, resting on mismatched antique rugs, papers feathering the floor and coffee table. A shiny, flat-screen television was seemingly the only object from modernity.

Justice rubbed the back of his neck, blushing. "Wasn't expecting any company tonight. I'll tidy up the living room a bit. Feel free to look around."

Nanyamka watched him briefly as he fluffed the pillows on the sofa and adjusted its cushions. She turned left and started down the hall, reading the spines of books about ancient history, mythology, world cultures, and the occult.

"You have tons of books," she said.

"Half of them belonged to my parents," Justice replied, "They left me the house after they died. Loved to read."

"Oh. Sorry for your loss."

Nanyamka continued down the hall, peering into small display cases. A multi-headed dragon carved out of jade. A fossil containing a troglodyte. A bronze statue of a bat-winged beast standing on its hind legs, hooks for feet and hands, another at the end of its tail. It had a strange face, a combination of a human, jackal, and bat, and its mouth agape baring large, silver fangs. She leaned in closer and grit her teeth, wishing she could hammer the thing into oblivion.

The scent of cologne tickled her nose.

"Looks weird, huh?" Justice asked.

"Yeah. What is it?"

"It's an Asasabonsam," he replied, "from West African mythology. Specifically, the Akan peoples from parts of the Gold Coast—modern day Ghana, to be precise. They're semi-vampiric creatures—or spirits—that lived in forests. Some of them ate humans, some didn't. Some were considered caretakers of nature and most even had families. The whole narrative about these creatures got turned inside out by Christian missionaries who lumped them in with demons. But in the traditional stories, they're as just as diverse and complex as people are."

"How'd you learn all this?"

Justice shrugged a shoulder. "Going to talks at various universities by professors who specialize in African religions. Reading books on Akan spirituality. Interviewing people willing to share folk stories. I'm actually in the middle of developing a new research project. Wanna hear about it?"

"Yeah!"

Justice cleared his throat. "Well, during my research, I came across folktales featuring *derivatives* of Asasabonsam—*Adisa,* they're called. People who'd been attacked, either by accident or on purpose, but survived. They become immortal and live off human blood."

Nanyamka snorted. "So, African vampires?"

"No. Blood-drinking and immortality are the only things those two have in common. Adisa have none of a vampire's weaknesses. They're masters of adaptation, and each possesses unique abilities," he said, an air of showmanship in his voice, "But there's still a lot to learn."

"Got any research grants yet?" Nanyamka quipped.

Justice smirked. "A few. Anyway—" As he tugged his tie loose, Nanyamka noticed that he no longer wore his gold rings. She licked her lips. "Why don't we go sit down, Nikki?"

"Okay. I'd *love* to pick your brains some more."

The pair went and sat on the yellow sofa, making idle chit-chat, Justice drinking from a thick mug. As he talked about some obscure conference, Nanyamka put a hand on his lap. He stopped mid-sentence and squeezed a hand over hers. Nanyamka could hear and feel his pulse quicken.

"You really made my night," he said, leaning forward.

Nanyamka laid back onto the sofa and slightly parted her legs.

"Come closer and I'll make it even better."

Justice's eyes grew wide, and he hastily emptied his cup. He pressed himself on top of Nanyamka, and kissed her passionately, oblivious to the grinning slit beneath his heart. Nanyamka thought about how hot and slick his blood would feel inside her mouth and between her fingers. All the wonderful ways she could use it to sculpt him.

Come to me, she commanded, imagining the fluid racing through his mouth and into hers. Her prey opened his mouth, and Nanyamka felt something fly down her throat.

She shoved the man off as her throat tightened with molten agony, then tumbled off the couch gagging and convulsing, gripping at her neck. Vomit surged from her mouth, followed by her fangs and a gold marble. As the skin on her throat melted over her hands, fresh terror rose within her and surged through her thoughts with a catastrophic vengeance.

Justice smirked. "Gotcha. Told you at the bar: *I'm creative.*"

Nanyamka tried to crawl away as Justice tossed the couch cushions to the ground.

A heavy, sharp pain slammed into her back. The slit in her chest went numb.

She looked at him: face splattered with blood, and an axe in his fist, its edge glimmering with gold. He lunged at her.

Nanyamka raised an arm to shield herself, but it sailed across the room in a foul mess.

"What's wrong?" Justice asked stonily, tightening his grip on the axe's handle. "Scared? My parents were scared too when one of you Adisa assholes ripped them apart!" Nanyamka roared as the gold tore through her flesh and claimed her other arm, leaving behind a smoking stump.

"Killed three of you in Ghana last year," Justice growled, wiping blood from his face with the back of his hand, "One of them was a slut, just like you—thought she was clever, too. I dunno why you parasites are suddenly crawling into this city, but I'm ending it!"

Nanyamka kicked, and her heel crashed into her attacker's knee with a sickening crunch.

While Justice howled and cursed, Nanyamka tried to concentrate, to call his blood again, but was thumbed to the floor with pain. Unbearable pain!

Not like this! She couldn't end up dissected on some mortal's dirty carpet! Not when she was so close to seeing the prince again. Not when she still had to make a masterpiece for him.

Justice raised the axe, the shadow of its blade drawing a line across Nanyamka's neck.

"I'll put your head in a fucking jar!" he roared, "Just like the others!"

Eyes glowing red, the Adisa flared her nostrils. Throbbing veins and a bullish determination strangled the softness from her face. Nanyamka took a sharp breath and a stream of blood spurt from the corners of Justice's eyes and onto her face. She licked every drop from her lips.

The slit smirked.

Stunned, her opponent fell onto his back howling, and the axe clunked beside him.

Nanyamka turned onto her stomach and forced herself onto her knees. Her dress torn and body covered in blood, she crept over to him like the *Venus de Milo* of death.

A dazed titter escaped her lips.

"Wow...you could've killed me!" she cried, letting out a dazed titter. "I thought I'd forgotten fear. But my heart was *racing* and my whole life flashed before my eyes." She grinned. "What a high!"

Nanyamka collapsed onto Justice's chest and the slit inhaled, sucking in blood as he howled with pain. Raw bone and muscle sprang from her missing limbs and cobbled themselves into silky arms. New fangs broke through her gums, and she sank them in the terrified man's neck.

The Adisa quickly withdrew and ran her tongue across the wound, sealing it.

"I want you," Nanyamka cooed into his ear, basking in the afterglow of violence. She met his rage-filled gaze. "This look on your face—overflowing with hatred and the will to live. Gorgeous. Devastating. *Inspiring*."

Nanyamka straddled him and flicked her wrist. The veins in Justice's arms and chest swelled and exploded into threads of blood that flowed into her hands and wrapped around her fingers. She tugged and pulled at them, Justice's limbs and body flailing in rhythm as he screamed. Pieces of flesh and fat pummelled the old bookcases and furniture, Nanyamka panting with excitement.

As the sun rose, she admired her creation, hands clasped together, blood and teeth as her crown.

Nanyamka's eyes glittered and smiled to herself, triumphant as an artist receiving a prize.

***

Three days later, Nanyamka paced by the door of her mansion, awaiting the arrival of Romulus and the other judges. At the first chime of the bell, she pulled the door open and saw Romulus standing alone, his black suit and long hair impeccably neat, his posture erudite. The large man had a nervous look, his lips tightened together and eyes unblinking, like a mouse caught in a cat's glare.

"Good afternoon, Romulus. Where are the other judges?"

"Ah...they have been re-assigned to other duties."

"Really? By who?"

Romulus stepped aside. Behind him, a cloud of white hair, fresh brown skin, and a charming face with a warm smile.

"Prince Ageaboye!" Nanyamka cried.

She went onto her knees and touched her forehead to the ground. "I didn't know you were already awake!"

"No formalities, please," he said gently, helping her onto her feet. "I woke up yesterday. Only Akibu and the Adzé know. I'll surprise the others later." The prince hugged her. "How are you, Nanyamka?"

"I'm grateful to see you," she answered. Smiling, she wiped tears from her eyes.

"Do not cry, sweet Nanyamka. All is well and I am happy to see you. You were the last young one and hemamancer before I was cursed." He turned to Romulus. "Thank you for caring of her, Akibu."

Romulus bowed. "My pleasure, You're Highness."

"Now, my dear protégé, is it true that you have a surprise for me?"

"I do!"

"And it's wonderful, *isn't it?*" Romulus asked through a tight-lipped smile.

"It is! Right this way, please."

She led them down the hall and into a small, white room. In its centre, a high marble podium hosted something tall, gurgling beneath a red curtain. Nanyamka grabbed a corner of the fabric.

"You're Highness, I humbly present you with this token of appreciation. My latest piece…"

She pulled the curtain away, revealing a naked, masculine figure in a ballerina-like pose, its nose swollen scarlet, a skeletal leg tucked behind the other in a triangular shape as though dancing. The skin on its chest was flayed into an open vest, and the cap of its skull spread open like a lotus flower. Red, transparent balls floated in its upturned palms and over its head, like a juggler performing.

A bloodshot green eye stared at the art admirers. A hoarse rattle escaped the sculpture's throat.

"I call it, 'The Clown'!" Nanyamka announced.

"Oh my," Romulus remarked, "Is it still *alive*?"

"It is," Nanyamka answered with a hiss, admiring her work through narrowed eyes. "Should last several months—or even *years*."

Romulus stroked his chin and sniffed the air. "Those floating balls are made of blood. How did you accomplish that?"

Nanyamka giggled. "That's a secret!"

Prince Ageaboye, stared at the figure; expressionless, silent. Romulus turned to him.

"Thoughts, You're Highness?"

The boy threw his head back and broke into thunderous laughter, clapping his hands.

"It-it reminds me of th-that time—!" he cackled hard, and slapped Romulus on the back, "she tried to command the blood out of a monkey and its head exploded! This is *exactly* what I needed after a millennium—a good laugh! It's *so* silly and whimsical and has a fascinating sense of movement. The figure's expression is executed beautifully: fear, hatred, *passion.* Well done, Nanyamka! You've put your gift to good use."

Nanyamka bowed, overwhelmed with joy.

"Thank you!"

Such Noble Rot

Odin Meadows

I

In between the mashed potatoes and peas, Morgan scratched at the ceramic plate like she was digging out a grave. The tines made those little grating squeaks of metal against glass as she dragged her fork. Her shoulders were slumped over like a bodily frown, her dark hair hanging like a funerary veil. She had been like this since Emily, their infant, died of SIDS. Hudson let out a sigh.

"What?" she said, throwing the word like a stone, glaring up from her plate.

"Nothing," he sighed again.

"No. What is it?" Her brows furrowed like she was either confused or about to start an argument.

"It's nothing, really," he didn't mean to, but he could feel himself shaking his head.

"No. Tell me what it is. I'm tired of you sighing and groaning and *nothing* this and *nothing* that. Just tell me what the fuck is wrong."

"Nothing is wrong—"

"Bullshit!" She looked like she was about to cry, yet he remained stoic, almost cheerful. "You keep looking at me like something is wrong, like you think I'm pathetic."

"Well—" he started but even *that* sent a pang of hurt across her face. He rolled his eyes and continued, "it just feels like you've given up."

"Given up? What is that supposed to mean?"

"It's like one bad thing happened and now you've just given up. There's no hope or whatever."

"I never said that."

"You didn't have to."

"Our baby *died*! She is dead. She hasn't even been dead a month and you think that I've just given up? I'm grieving."

"Okay," he said and went back to eating his dinner.

"Okay? What do you mean *okay*?"

"Okay as in, obviously you're struggling or whatever, but you can't just let it consume you. You're using it to excuse everything. You've just given up on us, on yourself, on having a family."

"Just because you have a weird thing with death doesn't make *you* the normal one. You know, Hudson, that people *do* grieve, and it *is* normal? I knew you shouldn't have taken the job at the farm; it's warping your mind."

"Now *that's* bullshit. My job has nothing to do with this."

"Oh," Morgan laughed and set down her silverware, "it has everything to do with this. It is not normal to be surrounded by dead bodies all day."

"It's important research."

"Oh, who gives a fuck! *Important research* for who? For some dead body that doesn't give a fuck if it's been properly dated? No, it's for the fucking police to pat themselves on the back and for you to play with your dead bodies and come home smelling like shit."

"So, it's the smell that's bothering you?" he said like he had it figured out.

"No, Hudson. I mean, that is not what *was* bothering me, but it does bother me, you know. It does actually bother me that you come home smelling like shit, and you don't touch or even look at me. You bring the fucking smell home and it's here. I can smell it."

"Honey, there is no smell," he said, and she stood up, crying.

"Stop it," she said through gritted teeth.

"Babe, I'm telling you, I don't smell anything."

"How! I don't know, maybe you've just gone nose-blind to it, but *I* can smell it. The fucking stench, it's every day now. It's just everywhere." She picked up the block of meatloaf on her plate, smelled it, and dropped it in the floor, "It's... in the fucking food, Hudson."

"Morgan, you need to calm down."

"Stop! I am not being unreasonable. Why does our food fucking smell like rot, Hudson?" She paced around the dining room before walking into the kitchen, Hudson following closely behind. She opened cabinets and stuck her head inside, inhaling deeply. "Something smells awful. There's something in this house."

"You're starting to act a little crazy," he said gently.

"I am not crazy!" she screamed, balling up her hands against her temples. She opened the fridge and smelled inside. She dropped to her knees and stuck her head in the cabinets under the sink. She pulled her head out and looked around, her eyes frantic. She dropped her face down into the floor and sniffed the tiles. "It's coming from underneath the house," she said and darted across the kitchen, through the living room, out the front door.

"Morgan, stop!" Hudson yelled out as she pried off the cover to the crawl space. "You're going to hurt yourself."

She didn't stop. She crawled through the small opening, and instantly the stench of rot and decay flooded her nostrils. She shined the flashlight of her phone around and let out a cry. The ground was covered in the rotting bodies of animals. It looked to be mostly roadkill: smashed possums, mangled racoons, and an entire deer propped up against a support beam. The skin around its skull was gone; maggots crawled out of the eye socket. Covering her mouth with her sweater, she crawled in further and, leaning against the back wall, was a human skeleton sitting on top of a throne made of rotting animals.

"Morgan," she jumped when she heard her husband right behind her. "I'm so sorry," he was crying. "I wanted to tell you, but I didn't know how to explain." She looked into her husband's eyes and felt like she was staring at somebody else. He was upset but was it just because he'd been caught? Without saying a word, she pushed past him, crawled out from under the house, got in her car, and drove away.

Hudson sat, crying with his hands in his lap. "What do I do?" he asked the skeleton, looking into the hollows of its eyes for an answer. He brought his hands together as if in prayer, "Please, what do I do now? This isn't what I wanted."

The bones of the skeleton rattled as it shifted forward, its head tilting towards the carcass of a raccoon hanging from a floorboard behind Hudson. He turned around and dug his fingers into the raccoon's body. The rotting flesh gave away easily, and he pulled out a folded-up piece of paper. Wiping off the grime, he unfolded it and saw it was the deed to an apartment building on the other side of town.

II

He tried to convince her to move with him. He called her several times after she left, but she didn't pick up until late that night. He started to explain everything, but she hung up as soon as he mentioned the skeleton. It's understandable that she would be weary. He too thought he was going insane when it first spoke to him at the farm.

Being surrounded by decaying bodies has a way of getting to you and the first whispers were faint. It called out to Hudson, begging him to take it away from the farm. At first, he tried to ignore it, then he tried telling it no, but that only made it more persistent. Then, the day after Emily died, the skeleton proposed a final offer: if he took it home, it would bring back his daughter.

Granted, Hudson was sceptical at first but there was just enough desperation for him to cling onto any hope flung his way and, when it was dark, he snuck back into the death farm, loaded the skeleton into his trunk, and stuffed it in the crawlspace. He wasn't sure how it would work but it whispered to him, begging to be brought decaying flesh. Again, Hudson was sceptical but still desperate, he went out the next night and collected a trash bag full of roadkill. He scattered the bodies at the feet of the skeleton, and it was pleased.

The next night, it called him down to the crawlspace and told him to reach into a bloated possum. He gagged as his fingers punctured the skin, releasing the noxious fumes of decay, but his fingers found something soft. He pulled it out and it was a pink beanie with a little bow glued on it. Even through the grime, he recognized the hat Emily wore on her first night home. His heart shattered. Sitting in front of the skeleton, he sobbed.

From that point on, he was devoted to the mission and spent almost every night collecting roadkill for the skeleton. The smell built up slowly, but he did his best to keep Morgan from noticing, lighting candles, spraying air freshener. By the time she left, however, the crawlspace was nearly full, and the smell was undeniable. Maybe he should have told her sooner. Maybe then she wouldn't have left.

Either way, he was determined to get his daughter back and if that required moving into this apartment building then he was all for it. The apartment building was on the outskirts of town, completely abandoned as were most of the buildings that surrounded it. The streets were quiet. You could only hear the faint noise of traffic from the highway.

It was a two-story building with eight units and a spacious attic which the skeleton claimed. Hudson found a fancy wooden chair and propped it up to where it was looking out the window. He then claimed a unit on the first floor and moved in his necessities. Morgan still wasn't answering his calls, but he texted her that he was moving out and invited her to take the house.

He asked the skeleton if he should bring the roadkill, but it told him no, that they would recuperate the loss in the new apartment. Before Hudson could go hunting for dead animals, however, it called him up to the attic.

It needs to be human, it said.

"But… the roadkill seemed to work fine. Why does it need to be human?" Hudson fell to his knees like laity and looked up at the skeleton.

If you want Emily, it needs to be human.

Working at a death farm and living in a death farm are two different things and, while Hudson was no stranger to rotting corpses, he wasn't thrilled at the prospect of living with them nor did he want to hunt for human bodies. It was hard enough finding roadkill. He considered murder, even stalked in the tree lines of the local park for a few hours, but he couldn't bring himself to hurt anyone. Instead, he spent the nights cruising through the more derelict, rundown parts of town. It was getting cold, and he knew just as well as anyone else that the homeless population would start dropping like flies. All he had to do was find one and scoop them into his car before the police showed up.

It took nearly a week before he found one. The skeleton had grown frustrated, berating Hudson at all hours of the day, demanding to be brought bodies. He was about to give up for the night when he noticed a bundle of clothes bunched up at the bottom of a dumpster. It wasn't moving but was vaguely human shaped enough to make him stop. He got out of the car, walked over to the pile, and kicked it. It didn't move so he peeled back the blanket and saw the face of an older woman, her face frozen in agony but frozen, nonetheless. She wasn't very large, so he picked her up, blankets and all, and tossed her in the backseat. When he brought her up to the attic, the skeleton was pleased.

Hunting for dead vagabonds wasn't an easy job but, eventually, Hudson learned enough to better his odds. He learned where the homeless population *actually* congregated, not just the locations where he assumed they lived. He learned their patterns and how to spot a dead body out the corner of his eye. The unhoused population, however, also learned of him. After collecting a handful of bodies, he noticed that homeless people would run when they saw his car turn down their street. It didn't bother him. If anything, it made his job easier. If they could run, they definitely weren't dead.

Over the next few months, Hudson found a total of twenty bodies. The skeleton, at first, was pleased but, over time, demanded more and more. Now, it was berating him again, questioning why he was incompetent and unable to procure bodies at a higher rate. It didn't seem to care much about the ethics, telling him to make bodies if he can't find them. Hudson never outright refused but instead danced around the topic, assuring him that he will find more bodies; but Winter was soon to give way to Spring, and he knew pickings would be slim.

He was driving around after a flash freeze, one of the last forecasted for the season, and found a body slumped against the underside of an abandoned bridge with a needle sticking out of his arm. His clothes were filthy, soiled. Drool and vomit leaked out his gaping mouth, but he was still warm.

He must have died only moments before Hudson found him and, while he normally would wait until the body had frozen stiff, it had been a few weeks since he found anyone and knew he couldn't waste the opportunity. The man's joints were loose, and his body flopped around as Hudson dragged him to the car. He struggled to stuff him in the backseat but eventually was able to get him in and drive away.

The smell from the man was awful and almost made him gag as he drove back towards the apartment. He pulled onto the main road but, when he looked in his backseat, he could see that the man was breathing. His breaths were shallow, but he was still breathing.

He stopped at a redlight and sweat rolled down his forehead as other cars pulled up around him. The man was beginning to convulse but nobody seemed to notice. The light turned green, and he turned off onto a side street and pulled into an abandoned parking lot. He watched through the rearview mirror as the man's body lurched violently. He winced as he spewed vomit over his leather seats. The man's head bounced against the door and his arms twisted around themselves. He moaned something that sounded like slurred speech, but Hudson couldn't understand any of it. He almost started crying but soon, it was over, and the man went limp once again.

Hudson wiped his eyes and drove the body back to the apartment. He stuffed it in one of the upstairs units and went to bed. The next morning, he woke up and left the apartment like normal but as he was locking the door, the homeless man came walking down the stairs.

"Hello," he said, making Hudson jump. He turned to look at the man who was now well groomed. His beard was trimmed neatly against his face, his hair was clean, and his clothes looked nice, almost business casual. He walked up to Hudson and held out his hand.

"Hello," Hudson said and shook the man's hand, but he clenched his hand and jerked it down, causing Hudson to stumble forward.

"Nice to meet you," the man sneered, "I'm the bloke you let OD last night. Name's Ezekiel but you can call me Zeke. Looks like we're neighbours now." The man patted him on the back and walked out the front door. Hudson ran upstairs to the attic.

"What is this?" he asked the skeleton.

What?

"That guy. Who… why did you… what… why is he alive?"

We made a deal, much like you.

"What kind of deal?" The blood rushed out of his face.

I saved him and now, he'll save me.

Hudson nodded his head and left the apartment. He didn't go out searching for bodies that night and, instead, watched out the window waiting for Zeke to return. Late that night, a sleek red car pulled up and Zeke stepped out, went around to the trunk, and dragged the body of a woman to the front door. She didn't look homeless. She looked young and Hudson could tell that her clothes were stained in blood. The skeleton was elated.

Zeke killed indiscriminately. Over the next few weeks, he averaged between one and three bodies a night: men, women, elderly, young, rich, poor. It didn't seem to matter who he targeted. Hudson couldn't sleep. The skeleton no longer demanded bodies from him but still, he felt somehow responsible. He walked up to the attic to confront it.

"I don't like what this has turned into," he said.

It hasn't turned into anything. It is what it always was.

"I want the killing to stop," his voice quivered.

No.

"Yes. The killing needs to stop."

No.

"Yes. Now! I am no longer going to participate—" The skeleton's bones rattled as its head snapped towards Hudson.

No! It screamed.

"If it doesn't stop, I will go to the police, and they will come in here and end this whole operation. They will take away your bodies." The skeleton's empty sockets stared into Hudson. He felt cold; his mouth went dry. For a moment, he thought he saw it smile, and then the floor fell out from underneath him.

He fell from the attic down to the ground floor and landed on his back. He could hear and feel his spine snap upon impact; the searing heat shot through his body and blood sputtered out of his mouth. He screamed in agony but, when he looked up, the skeleton was leaning over the hole in the ceiling, the darks of its eyes boring down.

Are you going to the police now?

Hudson shook his head.

Are you going to stop Zeke?

Hudson shook his head again.

Are you going to cooperate?

Hudson nodded his head and the hole in the ceiling closed. He could feel the bones shift around in his body. Ripples ran through his skin but, after a few seconds, he was healed. He stood up, limped back into his apartment, and locked the door.

III

It was nine months since Hudson had moved into the building. He barely left the apartment anymore as the rest of the building had been taken over by Zeke and his new gang of cohorts. He had accrued five followers so, now with six nightly murderers, the house did not take long to fill. Other than Hudson's apartment which remained clean, everything else was covered in some kind of decaying matter or layer of filth. Walking through the hallways, you had to trample over the corpses, now piled on top of each other, covering the floor like a carpet. Everywhere you looked, there were bodies in various states of decomposition: piled in the corners, hanging from the stairway banisters, stuffed into the cabinets. Innards hung on the walls like streamers. Heads were mounted on the banister posts. The house had been consumed by decay, but Hudson didn't care. He stayed barricaded in the apartment, waiting for Emily.

Finally in the middle of the night, he heard the skeleton call out to him for the first time in months. He pushed his door open and treaded carefully over the rotting corpses. He climbed up the stairs, stepping on shoulders and skulls. When he made it to the attic, however, the skeleton was not alone. Zeke stood to his right and, against the far wall, was a body wrapped in a white sheet laying on top of a gurney. Judging by the way the sheet bulged around the stomach, it seemed to be the corpse of a pregnant woman.

"What is this," Hudson said, barely over a whisper.

It is time. You have been a worthy disciple, and now it is time for your reward.

A pit formed in the bottom of his stomach as Zeke put his hand on his shoulder and guided him to the woman on the table.

"Who is it?" he asked.

Do not worry about such details. Hudson swallowed and nodded his head.

"Reach in," said Zeke, smiling.

Hudson continued to nod his head, but he felt far away. The whole thing seemed surreal, but he reached into the white sheet, his fingers puncturing first the fabric then the skin. The flesh squelched as he pushed his hands through until he felt something warm and soft. He wrapped his hands around it gently and pulled out an infant girl. She was covered in grime but as soon as she left the stomach, she began crying.

"Thank you," he whispered, and patted her on the back. Tears rolled down his cheeks as he carefully brought her downstairs to his apartment.

At first, Hudson was overwhelmed with happiness. He washed her off in the sink and held her while sobbing for what seemed like hours. She giggled in the same way, she had the same chubby cheeks, but something kept gnawing at him. He tried calling Morgan again but now the line was dead. He tried to tell himself that she just changed her number, but he kept thinking back to the woman under the sheet. She couldn't have been pregnant before she left, right? She would have told him if she was pregnant, wouldn't she?

He began to wonder if the baby was even Emily. He compared the infant to her baby pictures, but he couldn't discern any major differences. Still, most newborns looked similar. He tried to push the doubts out of his head and just focus on taking care of his daughter. A part of him didn't care if it was really her; believing it was enough.

He kept trying to get a hold of Morgan so they could be a family again but even her extended family was ignoring his calls and messages. A few months passed, and he grew more and more concerned. He even asked the skeleton directly if it was Morgan under the sheet, but it just told him that such details are unimportant. Again, he shoved down any doubts and took care of Emily. He noticed she didn't seem to grow or develop but, then again, it had only been a few months.

Otherwise, everything was well, and he enjoyed being a father again. Zeke and his cohorts continued the murders but, squared off in his own apartment, everything was almost normal. He even began making plans to get a job and a house away from this place. He was grateful but it wasn't a good environment to raise a child in.

He was in the process of applying to jobs when the skeleton called him again. He laid Emily down in her bassinet and climbed up to the attic but, when he went up the ladder, he was greeted by Zeke and his cohorts. The skeleton was seated at the end of a large banquet table, Zeke sat to his right, and the rest of the gang surrounded them. The table was full of food: breads and pastries, fruit, sliced cheese, turkey, lobster. It was a feast.

Zeke raised up a gilded chalice and they all cheered when he walked in. He was wearing luxury clothes, his hands full of rings. Every member of his crew had expensive jewellery: watches, chains, necklaces, and bracelets. They were all stuffing their faces with food.

Hudson, welcome, the skeleton said.

"What is this," he said, eyes surveying the room.

We're celebrating the beginning of a new era.

"What do you mean?"

Ezekiel and his friends here have been so successful, we're now going to branch out. We're going to take over the surrounding buildings, expand our influence.

"Oh… I'm not sure I want to be a part of that," he said, backing away.

That's fine. You were the original, the first believer and for that you will always hold a special place in my heart. But for now, I just have a small favour to ask you: I need you to bring Emily up to the attic.

"Why?"

For the banquet! See, Zeke and his friends here want to taste the flesh of an innocent. Zeke's smile grew to a monstrous grin.

"No."

Hudson, I thought you said you'd cooperate.

"You cannot have her."

I told you not to worry over such trivial things. I can make you a new daughter but a celebration like this is once in a lifetime. Surely you understand.

"No," he whispered and ran to the opening of the attic. He jumped down to the second floor and ran. He could hear Zeke yell, and the rest of his cohorts chased him as he slid down the stairs. He fell through the flesh, covering himself in grime and filth, but he made it to the bottom, burst through the door, and locked it behind him. They banged their fists against his door, but he scooped the baby up in his arms and climbed out the window.

He made it halfway across the yard before his ankle twisted and he stumbled. He tried to stay upright on his legs, but his knees buckled underneath him. He twisted his body as he fell to not land on the baby and hit the ground with a thud. Zeke and his gang surrounded him. He tried to resist as Zeke grabbed the baby out of his arms, but he could see that his own flesh had decayed nearly down to the bone. He had no strength, and he lifted her out of his arms. He couldn't move. He could only listen as Zeke lifted the baby above his head and his cohorts cheered. They all returned to the apartment as Hudson could feel his body disintegrating into the dirt. He looked up at the window to the attic and the last thing he saw was the hollow of the skeleton's eyes staring back at him.

The Festering Filth That Sloshed Inside

Mathew Gostelow

Jamie felt like someone had cracked his skull wide open, filled his brainpan with agonising sludge, then nailed it shut. His eyes would only open halfway, and daylight sent painful jolts through his temples. It was the kind of hangover you could photograph from space, but, as he staggered through the door into his flat, Jamie was determined to hide it from his fiancée, Kellie. Put a face on. Front it out.

"You're back! Did you have a good weekend?"

Her shrill enthusiasm shot through Jamie's ear like a knitting needle. Kel kissed him, wrinkled her nose. He knew he stank – desperate for a shower, a change of clothes, about 18 hours of uninterrupted sleep. He felt jet-lagged, even though he'd only been overnight in Liverpool with the lads – stag do, organised by his best mate and best man, Johno.

"It was good, yeah. What about you?"

Deflect. Distract. Put the ball back in her court.

Kellie was looking alright. Spa-fresh skin glowing, nails done. No make-up as usual – shame she didn't take care of herself with a bit of slap. Still a bit chubby, but the wedding dress diet was definitely helping.

"It was amazing," she grinned. "Sue booked Heaven Salon – we had treatments, massages, saunas. The whole works. Oh, and dinner was so lush. I had one of those lava cakes, with the gorgeous oozing chocolate inside."

Jamie was guzzling water by the sink, stomach churning at the mention of rich food.

"What about you, Jay? You okay? You look a bit worse for wear. Johno didn't make you do any drugs did he?"

She laughed, but her eyes were serious, forehead creased. Always an open book.

"Fuck's sake Kel, of course not. Jesus! Give me some credit."

Jamie scratched his forearm – he'd been itchy and irritable since he woke up.

"Alright Jay, alright. Well, what *did* you get up to?"

The lies came easily – half-truths slipping oily from his lips.

"We went to a bar, had a few drinks. Then a casino, a few more drinks. That's it. All very classy. I don't know why you have such a problem with Johno."

"I just don't think he's a good influence on you, that's all. Look, forget I said it. As long as you had fun, my love."

Kellie put her arms around his waist, gazed up at him. Jamie caught his own stale stink biting through Kel's fresh perfume, pulled away, put his glass in the sink – unable to look her in the eye.

"I need a bath."

***

Even after a good night's sleep, Jamie felt rough arriving at the showroom. But he wouldn't let the punters see it. If you want to sell cars you have to keep up appearances. It's all about the image. People don't buy the car; they buy the man. So, his suit looked sharp, his aftershave was strong, his hair was slick.

Still though, on the inside, Jamie felt fucked. Head pounding. Mouth dry. Skin on his arms still itching – sore, worse than before – the back of his neck too.

He did his best to shake it off. *Keep it together. Front it out.*

Jamie's phone rang as he stalked the forecourt, eyeing a couple who seemed serious about buying – timing his approach.

It was Johno, screaming down the line.

"Woy-oy saveloy! How's the fucking head?"

Jamie pinched the bridge of his nose.

"Sore. You?"

"All good, all good. But then I'm not the one getting married in a week's time. You fucking mug! Nah, you're a legend mate. Good stag though, wasn't it? Did you enjoy yourself?"

"It was amazing Johno. Honestly, you did me proud. Thanks for everything. And I mean everything."

"No problem Jamie-boy, no problemo at all. How was the …"

His voice changed gear, conspiratorial.

"How was the private session?"

Jamie's face flushed at the memory.

"Honestly, it's a bit of a blur, but what I remember was fucking amazing."

"Well, it doesn't have to be the last time, you know. What Kel doesn't know won't hurt her."

"Nah, Johno. I'm turning over a new leaf."

Jamie squared up, trying to believe the hollow words as he spoke them. Johno just laughed down his ear.

"'Course you are Jay, 'course you are. Never bullshit a bullshitter."

"Alright mate. I've gotta go. Customers."

Jamie scratched under his collar. Some sort of rash? Allergic reaction? No time to dwell on it. He had to focus, get his game face on. Cautiously, he closed in on the couple who were now inspecting a second-hand hatchback. The car was a shitbox – cosmetically fine, bodywork sound, paint job pristine, but under the bonnet she was a dog. The engine would shake itself apart within six months.

Shifting this one would take every trick in the book. Jamie made one last check, admiring his reflection in the metallic paint of a nearby car, running a hand through his hair. *Looking good. Now make this fucking sale, yeah?*

"This one caught your eye, did it sir? A very good choice..."

***

Kellie called in the afternoon, while Jamie was at his desk, catching up on paperwork. He could hear the background bustle of the cold storage where she worked.

"We had a batch of easy peelers come in this morning. Clementines. Gorgeous they were, shiny, plump, beautiful colour to the skins – but we opened a few up and they were horrible. Bitter, manky. I think we're going to reject the entire batch."

She was always so passionate about her work. So engaged. Jamie couldn't bring himself to care, but he went through the motions anyway. Smile and nod. Keep her sweet.

"Hmm. That's good."

"I miss you Jay."

"Yeah, well, I'll see you after work Kel. It's not like we're –"

"I still miss you though. Not long now "til the big day. Are you excited?"

Jamie watched Carol, the receptionist, walking over to Steve's desk. She was a bit older, 35 maybe, but she clearly took care of herself. Cracking arse. Tidy body.

"Yeah, me too, Kel. Me too."

"Jamie? Are you even listening? Is this a bad time?"

"Not a bad time Kel, I'm just finishing some paperwork, that's all."

He watched as Carol bent over to deliver a message to Steve.

"Thing is, I want to ask you something Jamie. And I want you to answer me honestly."

Jamie gritted his teeth. *Oh, here we fucking go.*

"Thing is Jamie, I need to hear it from you. Is this really what you want? Us? The wedding. All of this?"

"Because it *is* what I want. You and me. And our future together. That's everything to me. But I worry that it's not enough for you sometimes."

Carol sashayed back to reception. Jamie gave her a wink as she passed his desk.

""Course Kel. Of course it's what I want. Look, I'll see you tonight."

He shook his head, hanging up the phone, absently scratching the sore patch on his forearm.

Kellie was too soft. Too open. She needed to grow thicker skin, put some barriers up against the world. Or else people would just keep taking advantage.

*   *   *

Driving home, Jamie thought back to his stag night. Fleeting memories drifted behind his eyes, where the hangover ache clung on stubbornly.

Johno and the boys. Beers. Shots. Lines racked up on porcelain cisterns in the bogs. Swaying by the roulette wheel. Going bust over and over again at the blackjack table. Bouncers having a word after the gang got too rowdy. A club. Dry ice and strobe lights. Snogging some slapper, then spewing his guts out in the toilets.

A 2am cab ride back to the hotel. Stevie and the boys saying goodnight as Johno dragged Jamie into the bar for one last round.

At 3am, another cab ride, this time back out to a strip club. Just Jamie and Johno. More cisterns, more lines, more drinks. The room was a swirling whirl of blue and green lights, beautiful girls spinning round chrome poles. Eyes and lips, hips and tits. Voices muffled by overloud music. Patent stilettos shining on the stage.

A memory of Johno shouting at the dancers, waving handfuls of fivers.

"My mate's stag do!"

Jamie grinned at the memory. His best man was right. What Kel didn't know couldn't hurt her.

***

Over dinner, he stayed quiet, staring at his plate, distracted by the itchy patches on his neck. The skin was peeling, revealing layers underneath that were rough, dry, unyielding. And even though the area was irritated, Jamie felt nothing when he scratched – like it was someone else's flesh.

It was the same on his arm – skin flaking, sore patches growing larger, tougher, losing sensation. Strange bumpy ridges were forming, a blueish tint faintly visible on the skin. And still the constant pulse of pain throbbed behind his eyes.

Kellie chatted as she cleared plates, no longer curious about his stag night. She always accepted what he told her. Trusting, that was the word. A bit naive maybe. Too sweet for this fucked up world. That was the thing Jamie found most attractive about her.

He went to bed early again, hoping to shift the headache, but his sleep was fitful – and he woke frequently through the night, troubled by anxious sweats, incessant tickling itches that skittered on his skin like tiny sand crabs.

***

At work the next day Jamie kept his sleeves rolled down, paranoid that someone would spot the blue-green tint now visible on both arms. He felt rough. Tired. Clammy. Fuzzy headed. Generous palmfuls of aftershave couldn't hide the sour, meaty reek of his own body – like a ham sandwich left too long in a hot car.

Carol swung around to his desk in the afternoon, leaned down. Even with a headache, Jamie enjoyed the opportunity to take a good long look at her cleavage.

"You okay Jay, love? You look a bit peaky."

For just a moment, Carol pulled a face, berry-red lips puckering as she caught the stink of him. She made excuses and left Jamie scratching at the back of his neck, where the newly-revealed skin was turning tough, textured – like the dashboard of a car.

He walked outside, phoned Johno.

"Fuck's sake mate. I'm not feeling so good. What exactly were we taking the other night? You didn't dose me with something, did you?"

"Oooh, memory a bit hazy, is it Jamie-boy? Don't worry, what happens up north stays up north! You had nothing but the finest Bolivian marching dust, mate. And whatever you got up to in that back room is between you and … What the fuck was her name?"

"I don't know Johno. All I know is I feel like shit. I'm going home early."

***

Jamie got back before Kellie. He showered – desperate to feel fresh, shake this scuzzy, prickly, filthy feeling.

Examining his body in the mirror afterwards, Jamie pushed tentatively at the discoloured patches on his chest, noticing an oily sheen – petrol puddle rainbows. The crusty areas were growing, spreading, peeling like sunburn. And the skin beneath was dead, hardened – more like dry clay than flesh.

Running fingers over the back of his neck, across his shoulders, Jamie felt lines of rough bumps. Along his arm he saw small stubby spines in the hardened areas. He tapped his forearm and felt nothing – rapped it with his knuckles, heard a strange shell-like hollowness.

When Kellie came home, she could see Jamie wasn't well.

"Oh Jamie, sweetheart, you're burning up. Your skin… Can I get you anything? Heat up some soup, maybe? Call the GP for you?"

He couldn't face it – her affection, her care – it made him sick in his stomach. His lies festered inside. Knowing he didn't deserve her, knowing he had betrayed her trust over and over, knowing that he'd do it again.

Jamie made excuses and went to bed, but he didn't sleep. He tossed and writhed under the covers, sweating, head aching – unable to lie comfortably with the new lumps and growths pressing out from his skin.

When he finally drifted into shallow, feverish slumber, Jamie dreamed – troubled visions of his stag night. Johno pressing a handful of twenties onto a stripper's fist, yelling something about 'the full works', before she led Jamie by the hand into the sea-green depths at the back of the club.

They entered a small, dark room. A leather armchair, mirrors on the walls. She pushed Jamie into the seat, said something he couldn't hear. His head swam, eyes rolling, loins throbbing vaguely, too much coke and too many shots coursing through his veins.

Jamie caught his own face in a mirror – red, leering, disgusting. He looked away.

The rest was snatches, fragments. Electric pink lights on spray-tanned skin. Black suspenders, lace knickers, push-up bra. Smokey eyes and hot red lips. The click-clack of heels on vinyl floor. A smell of stale cigarettes, sweat, and perfume. The dancer ran through her performance, rolling and swaying in front of him like an eel surging through neon waters. She swept low, pushing her breasts into his face, before turning, bending, flaunting a perfect round arse. Jamie gave a slow blink, and the room spun like a whirlpool.

The stripper straddled him, her crotch grinding against his own – rhythmic, urgent. Her long, scarlet nails clawed at Jamie's chest through his sweaty shirt. His own hands explored the lines of her body. Any 'no touching' protocol seemed to be waived in the strange bubble of this private room.

In the mirror, he glimpsed a tattoo on the girl's shoulder – a coiled snake, beautifully detailed, forked tongue extended, tasting sweat and desperation in the air. Above it, his own face loomed – flushed, bloated, sweaty. As Jamie watched, his features shifted, morphing, stretching, becoming freakish, discoloured – skin splitting to reveal a dark blue skull, eyes like tiny black jewels, two-pronged insect jaws stretching from his mouth, mandibles dripping gelatinous spittle down the dancer's back.

***

Jamie woke with a start, legs kicking, gasping for breath. Kellie was still, next to him, breathing gently. The clock said 2am. He slipped from the covers and quietly crept, on aching limbs, to the bathroom. Memories of the stag night raced through his mind. He remembered going back for a private dance, but that weird shit with his face? *Just a dream.*

Splashing water, Jamie rubbed his eyes, looked blearily into the mirror, head thumping with deep pulses of migraine pain. The skin of his face had a sickly green tint, an oily sheen, like spoiled meat. There were rough patches on his cheeks and forehead – hard, unfeeling, cold, covered in tiny bumps.

The infection on his arms and neck, his chest and back, was spreading – patches of toughened skin grown larger, dappled with deep inky blue stains, completely numb, while the peeling skin around them was sore, flaky, scratched raw.

He couldn't go into work like this. He couldn't let Kellie see him, not with this fucked-up sickness, whatever it was. Not so close to the wedding. *Shit, the wedding.* It was just two days away. Jamie needed time and space to make a plan, to work out what was going on, to get some antibiotics or something, to fix things. As quietly as he could, he dressed, sneaked out, and drove to the motorway hotel on the edge of town.

There, Jamie struggled through an awkward, sweaty check-in conversation with a sleepy-looking receptionist. She eyed his discoloured face with a blend of curiosity and boredom.

Finally, in the privacy of the anonymous beige room, he stripped to his boxers and collapsed on the bed, resting his aching limbs, pressing hands to his forehead, trying to ease the fierce thump behind his eyes.

In dreams, Jamie found himself back inside that stuffy, airless room, his face shifting in the glass, becoming alien, freakish, as the room seemed to spin – caught in a kaleidoscope. Each time he looked at the mirrored walls, watching the stripper's body gyrate against his own, Jamie's pleasure was interrupted by the vision of his own horrific visage – insectoid, crustacean features, black soulless eyes, and glutinous drool oozing from his chitin maw.

The dancer, avoiding his eye, seemed oblivious to Jamie's fearful metamorphosis and he moaned a blend of fear and pleasure into her breasts as her hands moved to his belt, his flies. A flurry of fumbling left his trousers down around his ankles, and the woman straddled him once more. He gasped as she rolled a condom onto his hardness, guiding him inside her, pressing him back into the seat and starting to roll her hips.

Looking down, Jamie saw his body transformed. A shining carapace covered his torso – deep blue-black, like mussel shells – his soft flesh replaced by grotesque angles, spines, and claws. And at his groin there was an opening in the shell, two plates split apart, revealing a freakish organ – anemone tendrils squirming around a pale, slug-like tube of rubbery flesh, pulsating rhythmically inside the sheath, where it entered the stripper's body.

Jamie wanted to cry out – shocked and sickened by his own anatomy – but his throat was choked, only producing muffled clicking sounds. On top of him, the dancer writhed and bucked, eyes closed, until his terror and confusion were overwhelmed by a surging wave of orgasmic release – blood rushing to his head, the room swirling into empty dark.

Nothing then. Quiet. Blackness. Pressure in his ears, until Johno shook him awake, pulled him up. Staggered with him, towards the door.

"What the fuck mate? Sleeping is cheating. Was it good though? She looked fit! Come on wedding-boy, let's get you back to the room."

***

Jamie woke groaning. Everything hurt. He looked around – vision blurry, mind slow to recall the events of the previous night. Daylight glowed around unfamiliar curtains. And then it came back to him. The haunting, confusing dreams of the strip club. The sickness. The state of his face. The secret escape to this shabby hotel.

He checked his phone. It was afternoon already. Eight missed calls from Kellie. Three from his manager at work. Messages that started concerned, became impatient, and finally dissolved into passive-aggressive lines of question marks.

Slowly, tentatively, Jamie tottered to the bathroom. His body felt alien, awkward, sore. The hardness was all over him now – legs, stomach, chest. His left forearm was huge, inflamed, misshapen, skin split wide to reveal a hard chitin limb beneath. His hands were the same, knuckle joints stiff, skinless, flesh encased in a rough, unfeeling exoskeleton.

Jamie stared into the mirror, aghast, sickened by what he saw. His hair had fallen out. His face was transformed, dappled deep blue-green, eyes dark, glittering oily in deep sockets. There were lines of spiny lumps and bumps across his forehead, his cheeks. Jamie's jaw dropped involuntarily, mouth stretching wide. The gums inside were red and bloody, several teeth missing, fallen out while he slept. Jamie moaned, distressed.

And then a splitting sound came from deep inside his throat. A squelching of flesh torn, as a pair of claw-like mandibles slid painfully from dark recesses of his mouth. The new appendages twitched and clacked as they pushed inexorably outwards.

Panicking, coughing blood, Jamie slammed a hand down onto the fake marble of the bathroom counter. There was a sharp crack. A strange new sensation of pain. Looking down, he saw a dark split in the outer shell of his fist. A slow ooze of thick yellow matter seeped from the wound. Stinking pus.

Jamie began moaning softly to himself, unable to form words with the fresh mandibles jutting between his old jaws. He couldn't live like this. He couldn't get married like this. He couldn't even go to the doctor like this. The world couldn't see this face. This body. Nobody should see the stinking yellow bane that filled the space inside him. Not even Johno would understand.

An urgent agony exploded in Jamie's forehead, and through the mirror, he watched in terror, as a rapid transformation took place. With a series of creaking, cracking sounds, his skin split open, the shell beneath shifting upwards, his entire head now formed of interlocking plates – hard, thick, senseless. Craggy with spiny lumps.

Jamie cried out, afraid of the freakish beast, the unfeeling monster looking back from the glass. His mind whirled with bewildered terror. And then, without thinking, he slammed his head down, butting the edge of the sink with terrible force. Pain arched through his face, his neck. Again, he slammed into the white porcelain, the cold, hard counter.

Teeth scattered; splintered shards of shell flew. A yellow spatter of reeking milky liquid exploded across the clean surface. In the mirror, Jamie saw a crack splitting his grotesque visage. The pain was intense, threatening to overwhelm him, but he pushed through, determined to end his transformation.

Again and again, Jamie slammed his head into the sink. Sick, poisonous custard sprayed, as angular chunks of his shell crust fell away. The mandibles clacked and cracked until one snapped, shearing off, tearing the soft flesh of his gums. Blood flowed then, mixing with the foul yellow goop.

More and more he crushed the shell of his face, wanting to see it destroyed, loathing what he found beneath, revulsed by the festering filth that sloshed inside him. Fireworks of pain exploded behind his beady black eyes, obscuring his vision, and still he butted his head, over and over on the hard surface, breaking himself apart, piece by piece.

Eventually, overcome by waves of unconscious black, Jamie tumbled to the bathroom floor, limbs twitching weakly, oozing goop pooling in foetid puddles around the shattered remains of his face, blood flooding the tiles, as his final breaths came in wet, choking rasps.

Coffin Girl

Josh Roach

1

The two men sat on the tailgate, a cooler full of beer between them. Both men had something to say, when they were ready. For now, they sat drinking, watching the sun go down.

Mike's truck rested atop a hill overlooking a valley of farmland. Wind whistled unseen, weaving amongst hay bales that dotted the landscape. The smell of dried grass and the cold end of a day lingered in the air. A sky the color of bruises and hurt painted the horizon. Shadow stretched long and deep below.

Mike drained his beer, tossed it into the bed of his truck, and cracked open a new can. He took in his friend next to him, saw him now no different than when they'd met twenty years ago. His build, even then, sharp, and angular, like his silhouette was carved with a boxcutter. Austin was staring into his beer, legs swinging back and forward, one after the other. The old truck creaked with each swing. He occasionally lifted the can to his lips. taking down his beer in a few large gulps. Austin never even looked up at the falling sun.

He'll talk when he's ready.

Mike wore a brave face for his friend, soft eyes firmly held. He spent the better part of the last hour quietly watching him. He was no tough guy, but he knew when it came to emotions, the kind that drew from deep in your guts, men like Austin needed time to stew. Otherwise, they would boil over, and that was always messy, and sometimes violent.

But now, Mike's attention was elsewhere. He watched a spider on the outer rim of the truck box. It shone an inky black in the twilight. He hadn't seen it scuttle over. It just appeared there, as spiders do. Mike stared at it, and though it was hard to tell, he felt very much like all eight of the spider's eyes were staring back.

"Don't kill it," his scout leader used to say. *"Spiders are good luck!"*

A pair of headlights sprung to life a half mile out into the field, cutting through the grass, bobbing along through the dark, drawing Mike's eye.

When he looked back to the spider. It was gone.

2

Austin saw the sky – its beauty nothing more than a painful reminder that the universe is cruel. They had been there long enough to track the afternoon sun move across the sky and dip west, and he would stay until it was gone, and any beauty that lingered from this horrible day would be gone with it, eaten up by the night.

A light flickered off the metal of his can.

Austin lifted his head, saw headlights; an unnatural brightness made the world around them appear darker than it was.

Trespassing.

Though this wasn't his land, Austin had come to think of this place as his. He had brought Mike many times. It was where they came to talk, to get away. Or just to drink. It was a nice gesture for Mike to bring him here, and that he bought the beer. Like old times. But as time moved on, things, feelings, slipped away. Trying to get them back was impossible. Austin was beginning to understand that. It was something that happened when you lose the one you love.

He wasn't sure if what he was feeling was sadness. What he knew as sadness hadn't come, instead there was a new feeling. It wasn't overwhelming, but something beyond that. In the way that being overwhelmed feels as though some great force is pressing down on your body, this new feeling felt sharper, a pressure that grew from within. He felt cold, no matter where he was or what he was wearing. A steady pain punched his chest, and his stomach was upset whether he ate or not, which is why he took up his friend on the chance to chase beers. It couldn't make him feel any worse. He was in immense pain all the time, and yet there was a numbness to it all. It wasn't that he didn't believe she was dead, he had seen her body, knew for a fact that she was gone. He had looked down upon her and saw there was nothing behind her eyes, and Jess had the most vibrant blue eyes, like the first colours of a sunrise before dawn, endlessly full of life. He never realized how much he depended on it, her eyes lighting him up, breathing life into him as if his own lungs belong to her. Now the only thing he felt when he breathed was pain.

There were plans, even before he bought the ring, to do it here, at this time of day, during magic hour. He would tell her all about this place, about how it was his, and how he wanted it to be theirs. Then he would get down on one knee and ask her.

It didn't work out that way. Instead, his proposal was desperate, clumsy. He was leaving for a work trip the next day. She was so worried, he could see it crawling over her face, hiding behind those eyes, her fear that he might not come back, that he would find someone else or find some other way to fuck it all up.

The night before he was set to leave, they fought and went to bed with the embers of anger still hot. He lay next to her, heartbeat whacking against his breastplate. She would later tell him that she thought he was just nervous about work, could feel his pulse thrum while lying next to him. He did it then, grabbing the ring from the pocket of his pants, walking around to her side of the bed in the dark. He fumbled for the light switch on the base of the lamp next to the bed and ended up knocking it over. Jess turned on the light, and what she saw was not a man scrambling for what pitiful romance he could muster, but the man she loved, down on his knee, a velvet box in his grip. She cried. Then he did.

Jess had a saying, life's unpredictable and that's half the fun. The other half is getting drunk enough to forget the first part.

Austin drank. He felt his eyes grow hot and wet.

"What the hell's he doing?" Mike said.

The headlights were gone. In their place stood the silhouette of a truck, an older model domestic with a white canopy over the box that glimmered in the gloom of the dying day. He had forgotten for a moment that they weren't alone.

A man lumbered around to the box of the truck out in the growing dark. The shadow man grabbed a shovel from the back, carried it five feet before he jammed it into the earth and dug

They both watched, silent, focused on the sight and sounds of the man digging. They could hear him grunting in the distance, the cut and thunk of the shovel slicing into the ground and tossing back dirt was soothing.

Austin grabbed a new beer from the cooler. Mike's hand flew onto the lid.

"What are you doing?" Austin asked.

"He'll hear you."

"So?"

"He doesn't see us. He doesn't know we're watching."

Austin didn't understand why, but he set the beer down and watched silently.

The man dug for a half hour until a sizable hole lay before him. He let the shovel drop, went back to his truck and reached under the canopy, yanked out a long crate then dragged it over to the hole and set it down inside it. It dropped out of sight. He lifted the lid off it.

The man went to his truck again, this time grabbing something from the back seat. He slung it over his shoulder and struggled his way back to the hole. The thing bobbed and bounced with the man's step. There was something familiar in the way it moved that made the beer in Austin's gut roll over.

And then Mike said it.

"That's a body."

3

The body flailed, long hair floating freely as though it was drifting through a deep ocean and not jerking with the steps of a man carrying another human to a grave he just dug.

It was a woman. Mike couldn't see clearly from this distance, the low light rendering those below to just shapes and shadows, but he knew. It was in the air, whispering to him as the hot summer breeze turned cold.

The man dropped the body, the woman, into the hole. Her legs went in first. Then the shoulders. The man set her down inside the coffin, put the lid overtop and stood, glaring down at the grave. He pulled out something from his back pocket, dropped to one knee and swung. Hammer strikes ripped through the night, one after the other, like gunshots.

"What in God's name…" Mike couldn't finish. His brain felt like a soaked rag wrung out, soggy.

The scene below, with its long stretching shadows and bruised palette of colours swathed over the prairie field, looked like a painting. The man below was both subject and artist.

When the hammering was through, the man shovelled the dirt back to where it belonged, working quick, tossing it in with wide, swinging shovel arcs.

"Should we do something?" Austin asked. He kept his voice quiet.

Mike imagined the two of them barging down there, his truck galloping along the field like a war steed. They would put a halt to whatever misdeed the man was committing. There would be yelling, maybe things would get physical. It was two of them against one, and Austin was bigger than the man below from the looks of it. They could detain him and call the police. They would be heroes.

But another thought popped into Mike's head. On the ride down, the uneven rumble of his truck would alert the man far before they were close enough to do anything about it. They would demand the man to stop. He would, long enough to go to his truck and pull out his Mossberg pump action. The first shot would take out Mike. In his mind, he took the lead. The shot would tear through him, the pellets breaking him into pieces like his bones were made of glass. He wouldn't die right away, he would die looking up at the sky, star gazing until the world went dark. There would only be one more shot, maybe two. Austin would have time to run. He might make it into the truck, might manage to fire up the engine, but Mike doubted it. More likely was that the next shot would hit Austin in the back, knocking him onto his belly. Then, the man would hobble over to Austin, who pleaded for his life. The man would take aim. The second shot would explode Austin's head, painting the grass the same colour as the twilight sky.

Mike stayed quiet.

4

By the time the man finished, the sun was gone and the world around them was bathed in a blue glow. The man looked down upon his work. Then walked back to his truck and drove off.

Austin pushed off the truck and hit the dirt hard. The booze swooshed around inside him, nearly knocking him over.

"Easy there, buddy," Mike said. He hopped off the truck to steady his friend.

"I'm okay. Just buzzing a bit."

Austin marched to the edge of the hill and stared out towards the grave, which would be impossible to see if you didn't know it was already there. Mike stood to his shoulder.

"We have to go down there," Austin said.

"We're both drunk, we don't really know what we saw--"

"I'm not that drunk. And I know what I saw. You know what you saw, and if you don't, you feel it." He looked out towards the grave. "I'm going down there, and I need your help."

"Why don't we just call the cops?" Mike said.

"And tell them what?" Austin's words came out sturdier now. "We're two drunks that watched a guy bury a girl in the middle of nowhere. I know how cops work around here. We call em, we're likely to get pinched."

"I'm not doing it."

"That girls buried out there. Who knows what that man did to her." Austin paused. "No one deserves to be dropped out in the middle of nowhere like that. To be left all alone."

"What the hell you wanna do then?"

Austin glanced back at the truck. Mike followed his gaze and then stared at him. He nodded, then grabbed the shovel from the back, and the two men made their way down the hill towards the unmarked grave.

5

They stood, staring down at the pile of dirt, at what lay beneath.

Mike glanced at his friend, could smell pain radiating off him, stronger than the booze, almost like burnt grass. Mike held the shovel in his hand. It felt heavy in his grip.

"I'll do it," Austin said.

"No, it's okay." Mike stuck the shovel into the dirt. It came loose with ease.

Mike could feel his friend's stare burning through him as he tossed out heavy shovels full of dirt. He could hear his own laboured breaths as he dug.

Austin dropped to his knees and dug up dirt with his hands.

They worked quickly. The two of them together.

"I know we don't get into this kind of thing, but you can't just keep it down. You can let it out. I'm here. That's the only way to fight through it."

"Fight what."

"The pain."

Austin went on digging. Mike looked at him.

"I'm fine."

"I know you are. Just wanna say I'm sorry this happened to you. And, I didn't say it before, but I'm saying it now. I love you, alright?" Mike dug out more dirt. "Christ, maybe I am drunk," then he laughed.

"It's not me you should feel sorry for. I'm still here."

"I know that. It's just, I'm sorry, it's something you gotta live with."

"Yeah, well, maybe I don't."

"What the fuck's that mean, man."

Mike's shovel struck something hard below. A heavy thud filled the night air. They exchanged a single, brief glance.

They dug on until they had room to free the thing. The coffin was made of cheap, hardware store plywood and ran close to six feet in length, wide enough for a body, but only just.

Austin tried the lid, but it was nailed shut.

Mike handed him the shovel. They hadn't discussed it, but there was something in the way Austin had gotten down on his knees, sunk his own fingers into the dirt, that made it feel as though Austin should be the one to do it.

Austin jammed the shovel under the lid, wrenched on it until the nails popped open. The plywood whined as it bent and then snapped loose. The jolt caused Austin to lose slip, but he caught himself, showering dirt all around. Austin chuckled.

Then the night around them was silent.

Together, they lifted the lid and opened the coffin.

It was a girl. Her face freckled with fresh dirt cluttering soft cheeks. A few speckles dotted her closed eyelids. She had a round, delicate, youthful face. Her skin smooth and pale, almost grey. Long dark hair dyed red brown from the blood and dirt. Her arms lay across her chest in a wonky X-shape. She wore a white dress that was stained with dirt, like the rest of her. Her jaw hung slack, wide enough to expose two front teeth that hung down further than the rest. It made her look young, too young to be lying here in a grave.

Mike thought she looked cold.

"What should we do?" Mike asked.

Before Austin could answer, the girl's eyes flew open, and she and she sucked in a deep, violent breath.

"Get the truck," Austin said.

6

The truck's engine rose like the sound of a crashing wave.

Austin could feel the wheels sliding through the loose dirt road. The truck kicked up gravel and the world behind them was shrouded in dust that burned an angry red in the glow of the taillights. It was as though a storm cloud was chasing them, and he knew it was only a matter of time until they'd be caught up in it.

Austin glanced into the rearview.

"She's not doing too good," Mike said, straining his voice over the roar of the engine.

Mike was in the back seat. The girl lay across him, her head placed carefully in his lap, swimming in and out of consciousness. Austin suspected that sooner or later that swimming would turn to drowning, and she'd be gone.

"She needs a hospital," Mike added.

Austin had hopped into the driver's seat of Mike's truck and drove. He did not remember starting the engine or pulling onto the highway. He found himself driving down an old country road he'd forgotten the name of. Hadn't thought about where they were headed.

"Austin. The hospital."

"No," a voice said.

It came from the girl. Her eyes fluttered. Her frail chest rose in short shallow bursts.

Still swimming, Austin thought.

"No hospitals," she gasped. Her voice grated – words forced through a rusty cage.

"You're hurt," Austin said. "You need a doctor."

"Please," she said, her voice clearer now.

Austin slammed the truck to a halt. The truck idled at a cross intersection. He knew the right-hand turn led to town, where the hospital was, but his eyes looked beyond, into a great field being eaten up by the gathering dark. How had it gotten so late? He expected today to never end, or if it did, to just sort of fade away, abrupt, and unclear, like the ending of a dream.

"Austin," Mike called out. "Where we going?"

Austin knew the day was not over. He knew then where they needed to go now. And though he wasn't certain, he had a good idea about what he needed to do as well.

Austin took his foot off the brake. The truck rolled on straight through the intersection.

No hospitals.

7

They pulled up to Austin's farmhouse ten minutes later. Mike jerked forward, as the truck lurched to a stop, holding tight to the woman in his lap, her eyes danced behind her eyelids. She hadn't woken up since her blurted request. Her breathing slowed to an unsteady wheeze. He could feel his own blood pumping hot in his chest.

The truck door flew open.

"Help me lift," Austin said.

They carried the girl out. Mike held her shoulders and watched her head bob with the beat of their steps. Her features seemed alien from his upside-down viewpoint. He watched to see if her eyes were still dancing. They weren't.

They struggled up the porch steps. The faded, old wood winced under the weight of them, crying out in warning.

Austin balanced the keys and the girl's legs in a messy panic as he shouldered open the front door. They moved into the dark house. He could hear only the heavy thud of their boots against the floor as they moved through the house, passed the walls and furniture which mixed in with the dark seamlessly, a maze of shadows.

"Set her down here," Austin said.

Mike felt the side of a couch with his hip. He guided her head as he lay her down.

A light clicked on. Mike jumped as he saw the girl's face. It darkened under the dim orange glow, her soft features turned mean in the lamplight.

Austin moved past him.

"Where you going?"

"I'm going to get help."

"She said no hospitals," Mike said.

"I'm gonna go find a doctor. Just stay here and watch her, alright?"

Mike glanced over at the girl and then back at his friend. "Aren't you a little…" He held off that last word. "It's been a long day. Can't you call someone?"

"I'm fine," Austin said. "I'll be back soon. Stay here and look after her, alright?" Austin met Mike's eye – a hard look gleamed off it in the dark.

"Hurry back."

Austin was out the door. Mike stood, the sounds of the truck grinding against the gravel rose and then fell as the purr of its engine was lost into the night.

He stood alone with the girl in the electric quiet of the house.

8

Austin drove to town, but only because he had nowhere else to go. He wasn't going for help. That much he knew.

Main Street was brightly lit and busy, a small collection of electric fireflies buzzing against a backdrop of blackened farmland. The town had a life to it that only existed on Friday and Saturday nights. A long line queued at the Dairy Queen, families and kids and couples stood waiting. The Chevron, with its bright white LEDs, dragged his attention as he passed, it always did. There was a girl there talking on the phone, pumping gas into a new model Taurus that looked ghostly under the lights. Hal's restaurant stood down the street, only a few cars parked in its narrow lot. Too late for dinner now, and there were better spots to get drunk around town.

And that's where Austin would check.

He drove passed the Bamboo Pub; a rickety wood building painted a heinous green. He could practically feel the heat from its red neon sign as he passed. The parking lot of the Bamboo was busy, a few vehicles he recognized, others sat in darkness away from the lot's single light post that stood a giant above a sea of gravel. Dave Mercer's new yellow mustang stood out like an angry, screaming child in the middle of a mall. It suited Dave well.

The Bamboo was the last stop before the town gave way to a stretch of highway that offered nothing but dark. Even in the daylight there was only sun-parched grass painted across rolling prairie with the only the occasional farmhouse breaking up the spareness.

And while Main Street was full of life now, the town itself was filled with nothing but death and loss and Austin could feel it wearing down on him as he drove through it.

He hung a left as Main Street ended and drove up through a residential street, it too sat in dark, then came back around to the mouth of Main and drove down it again.

This time, his eyes fell upon the people. The ice cream line was smaller by half, the time for cold treats running out, the crisp chill of night bearing down on the town more and more as the night moved. The people looked impatient and angry. The girl in the Taurus was Ryan Garrison's daughter, he ran the hardware store. She was done pumping gas. Austin passed her on the road, her phone held up to her mouth as she screamed into it. They made eye contact, but Austin made no attempt to greet her. Neither did she.

Austin cast another look into the lot of the Bamboo, his eyes skipping over that ugly yellow Mustang, skipping over most of the cars he remembered from his first go-around, seeing into the darkness. He hit the brakes.

He wondered if he had missed it the first time, wondered if it was there at all.

The truck was parked just beyond the lamplight, a white canopy glowing in the dark.

He pulled into the lot, fitting into a parking spot three cars down from the truck, and got out. There was a group of people standing out front near the exit shrouded in a cloud of cigarette smoke. When he thought the coast was clear, he slid over and took a closer look at the truck.

The canopy was more tattered than it had looked from up on the hill, and it was a Ford, like the Garrison girls. Austin cupped his hands around his eyes and peered through the dirty canopy window.

Inside was dark but glinting in a thin strip of moonlight that seeped in, was a shovel.

It was here. *He* was here.

Austin headed for the entrance of the Bamboo pub, unaware that he walked with his hands balled into tight, angry fists.

9

A low moan came from behind him.

Mike turned. He could see her in outline, a mere silhouette on the couch. He heard the rough sound of skin rubbing on fabric as she writhed. She was awake.

"Hi," Mike said.

She flinched at his voice, clinging to the couch as if she expected it to wrap her up and protect her. She had a haunted face in the shadowed light. Her eyes were wide. They took in the lamplight like two greedy black holes.

"It's okay," he said. "I'm not gonna hurt you. You were in a…" Mike paused. He wanted to say accident, but that wasn't right. Whatever happened to her was far from an accident. It was an evil act. "Do you remember what happened to you?"

Her huge bulb eyes lit up, then shimmered. Her skin was slick as oil and shiny with sweat. Her mouth hung open, wordless. Her gaze broke, and she took in the room around her.

"Was I attacked?" She tasted each word as it came out of her mouth. Her voice rough. It didn't fit her. It belonged to someone older, someone battered and beaten mean. But, beneath the dirt and filth was a frail, pretty girl, a flower trying its best to bloom out of a mound of bad soil.

"Yeah, you were." Mike said. "But not by me," he added. He hadn't considered until this moment that the girl might think he was her attacker.

She took him in with a steady look. "You… saved me?"

"I did," he said. "Me and Austin – my friend. I'm Mike."
He let that settle into the air. "What's your name?"

Her mouth hung open again and she stared into the space past Mike's shoulder, then up to the ceiling, searching, but she stayed quiet. Her eyes welled up.

"It's okay," he said. "Do you remember what happened to you?"

She looked off into the darkness again. She spoke as the memories came to her, slow and gooey, clinging to somewhere at the back of her skull, somewhere hard to reach.

"I was walking in the woods. I walk in the woods sometimes when the weather is nice. I have Fridays off usually, and I didn't have anything to do."

"You were attacked on Friday?"

"Yeah." She said. "It's not Friday?"

"It's Sunday."

She bit her lip, and the tremors came back at once. She tried to steady herself, taking in and letting out rattling, raspy breaths, slower and slower until the shaking subsided.

"You're alright now." He stepped closer to her, leaning against the couch.

She flinched. Mike stepped back. She looked up at him, and then relaxed some, shuffling further down the couch. Mike sat on the arm furthest away from her. The couch was her safe place and Mike wanted to keep it that way.

"Do you know who attacked you?"

She shook her head. They sat in the quiet dark. The girl grabbed at her stomach, curling up in a pained way.

"You okay?" Mike asked. He inched closer to her. Cautious.

"I'm…" She paused, then looked up at him. "I'm really hungry."

"I'll get you something to eat. Just rest." Mike smiled. He got off the couch and made his way to the kitchen.

The poor thing, he thought. *She was so brave.*

10

The place was packed, but it had a depleted, worn feel to it, like someone drained it of any life it once had, used it all up and then forgot about it. Wood panelling lined the walls, muting everything around it to a drab oaky brown. Low hanging lights cast a harsh dusky glow over the place. Had it been brighter, he might not have found the man, but in the low light, the people at the bar in shadow, the man's silhouette was unmistakable.

Austin felt anger spider through him. He swallowed, felt his breath shorten high up in his throat. He sat down next to the man but would not dare look over at him.

A wiry bartender sauntered over; face partially hidden under a jungle of starchy purple curls. Austin knew her and the heavy perfume that wafted off her. He ordered a beer. She gave it to him. He stared straight ahead, could see the man out of the corner of his eye, smell him too, the sour stench of old beer and smell fresh dirt.

The beer went down hard, his throat dry, draining it in two gulps. The buzz horse-kicked him. He felt the stool wobble beneath him.

Austin turned; hand gripped on his beer. He took in the man in profile. Under the harsh bar light, he looked less like a man than any person Austin had ever seen.

"I know what you did." The words came out shakier than he'd hoped.

The man didn't react. It took him a moment to realize Austin was talking to him, staring at him. The man turned his gaze onto Austin. His face was slack. Dead still.

"I know what you did," Austin repeated.

"I heard what you said."

The man's face was burlap. Tiny, dotted scars poked holes in his skin, old scars from old wounds. His jaw jutted out at a sharp angle; short, shadowy hairs bristled from it. Thin lips stretch wide across his face. He had deep, sunken eyes, with sockets that closed in on themselves, giving him a look of a man who was permanently squinting. His hair was messy, parts of it glued against his shinning forehead, others sprouted wild, cut jagged, as though chopped with a knife.

"I'm gonna go to the police," Austin said.

"That's your prerogative." The man's voice was dusty, cracked like desert rock. He turned away from Austin and sipped his beer. "What do you plan to tell them exactly?"

"I'm gonna tell them…" Austin stopped. He looked down at the end of the bar. The bartender was watching them out of the side of her head. "I'm gonna tell them what you did."

"Uh huh. And what did I do?"

Austin kept his voice low. "You buried that girl out there. I saw you. You hurt her."

The man tensed, his beer bottle hung mid-air, lips pursed and dried, thirsty. "You don't know what you saw." He drank.

"Don't you try and intimidate me. I'm not afraid of you. I saw what you did and you're not going to get away with it. You can't just hurt people like that."

The man tipped his beer bottle and stared straight down the neck of it. The dark brown glass glistened wet, reflecting the bar lights.

"She was better off. Trust me there." He was cooked. Piss drunk.

"You piece of shit," Austin said. Anger boiled up inside him. He tried to muster more words but couldn't. There was only anger, red hot, filling his brain.

"That's how the world is, son. Some things belong here, and others, well, it's best we put "em in the ground."

"She's alive, you fucking asshole. I dug her back up and I saved her. You fucked her up, probably for life. She'll still have a life. But you won't. You'll spend the rest of it behind goddamn iron bars, or if you're lucky, the chair. I'll see to it."

"You stupid son of a bitch." He said calmly. "You have no idea what you've gotten yourself into. No goddamn idea."

"I saved a girl's life."

"You shoulda never dug her up."

"I'm calling the police now," he rose.

"It's Austin, right?"

Austin hung in the air for a moment, halfway out of his seat.

"How'd you know that?"

He was still staring into the black hole of his bottle. "I'm real sorry about Jess."

Austin's stomach ran cold. A blizzard in his guts. "What the hell did you just say?"

"You were her husband, right? Took me a minute there, but it's you."

Austin fell back down onto his stool.

"What the fuck are you talking about. How did you... Don't you talk about her."

"I knew her."

"Don't you fucking lie to me."

"We worked together. A few floors above me, of course. Coroner always gets the basement. Part of the job. I'm not naive enough to call her a friend. We sometimes sat together in the cafeteria. Sometimes we played scrabble. She didn't deserve to die the way she did. Left in a ditch, abandoned after some son of a bitch whacked her with his car. No, sir." He took another sip; Austin couldn't take his eyes off the man. "She was a kind person. Knew how to make me laugh.

She reminded me of…" The man paused. "I'm sorry for your loss."

"No. You're a liar." He was shaking.

"I'm not. Funny how things go. You and I meeting like this." He drank.

"You're insane".

"Maybe." The man said. "But what was that Jess always said?" He looked deep into his beer bottle. "Life's unpredictable and that's half the fun. The other half is--"

"Getting drunk enough to forget the first part." Austin finished. His eyes were hot and his jaw quivered.

"That's the one." The man set down his beer. It clanked empty against the hard bar. "Do me a favour," the man got up, dropped a few bills on the counter, "and put that fucking thing, whatever it is, back in the ground."

11

The fridge light flickered and then went dead. Mike stood in the kitchen with only the tiny bulb from the stove lighting the room. He scrounged together two slices of bread and some luncheon meat. Mike was generous with the mustard and grab a handful of crushed chips from an old bag and piled them on the side. He grabbed the plate, a glass of water, and headed back into the living room.

He had expected to see her where he left her, seated on the couch, but she was gone. He glanced around the room, saw only shadows here. As he approached the couch, he saw her there, her frail frame laying across the couch cushions, curled up.

But something was wrong. What lay on the couch was not the girl.

Her clothes were there. It was as though she had slipped out from under them, left them there where her body was supposed to be. But not just her clothes. Nestled amongst the fabric was a wrinkly brown material, the colour of thin leather, almost translucent, coiled up in the shape of a sleeping girl like some weird ghostly image.

It took a moment for Mike's eyes to adjust to the darkness, it took his brain a moment to adjust to what he was truly looking at on the couch.

It was her skin.

Mike recoiled. The plate fell from his grip, the sandwich hit with a soft splat and then the plate rattle against the hardwood, keeping whole as it did.

The house felt much darker now.

Mike glanced at the doorway to the kitchen. That feeble light above the stove had gone out, there was only darkness there now. The shadows of the living room furniture felt sinister. Every creak and wince of the house shifting, the rumble and electric crack of the fridge in the other room, was like screams in his head.

He turned and called out to the empty room. "Miss?" He felt stupid saying it, and no response came.

His feet stuck to the wood floor, like he'd grown roots. He stood there and listened to the haunted sounds of the house. He had to remind himself that these were normal sounds. It was an old farmhouse after all. But there was something there, layered in beneath the breathing of the furnace, or the wind outside. It was a ticking. Not like a clock, not at all. It was irregular, unpredictable, and organic.

Not a ticking, he thought, but a click, like a short, sharp rap against the wood. Cat claws clacking away against the wood floor. But even that wasn't right. It was too quick.

He moved for the door, and heard the clicking grow closer, coming from somewhere in the dark entryway. He froze and listened. The clicking stopped. He could feel something just beyond his vision staring at him.

Eyes in the dark. Many of them.

He backed away, his eyes on the entry for his first cautious steps and then turning, his stride long and quick as he moved to the kitchen.

Click-clack-click-clack.

There it was again. Coming from the kitchen now. Following him. Trapping him, and it was then that he placed the sound as it clicked against the laminate kitchen floor.

It was scuttling. Something crawling across the wood floor somewhere in the shadow.

Something big.

Then there was quiet again. Mike did not move.

Click-Clack. Getting closer.

He thought of the day, of sitting on the tailgate, the cold beers, watching the hot sun pace across the sky. He glanced out the window and found only night.

Click-Clack-Click-Clack.

A crisp cold gripped his spine. The sound was close. He knew now where it was. He could feel the thing's presence.

It was above him. Scuttling along the roof.

He looked up. The thing was bulbous, and jagged, like a child scratched it with black marker right into existence. The thing had a glow gleaming off it, darker than the shadows where it hid, like black light.

Mike braced. He would fight. He wanted to be brave.

But what he didn't know is that bravery and fear tasted the same. And the thing came down on him vicious and hungry.

12

He wanted to get out of there, away from the brightness, and the warmth, and the stench of booze and sweat. With his keys in his grip, the smell of the bar fading away, he found himself looking to the night's sky, moonless and barren. The large overhead light that hung over the parking lot buzzed in uneven bursts, like an overlarge firefly perched above.

Austin scanned the lot. There was no sign of the dirt-stained truck with the faded white canopy, no sign of the man either.

Main Street sat empty, lineups and traffic gone to bed. Even the lights, halogens, and neon, seemed faded.

He saw no cars on his way home. All was dark.

He pulled up to his place, put the truck into park and sat listening to the engine cool.

What a goddamn day.

There was a time when Jess, the grief she brought with her, had left him, but it had crept back now, the man at the bar had insured that. He grabbed his keys and got out.

His boots clunked against the porch wood and echoed in the empty air. At the top of the stairs, he halted and listened as the last footfall was sucked into the quiet night. There was no croaking of frogs from the pond around back, or the orchestra of the cicadas singing their song in the fields. There was only the muffled howl of the breeze.

Austin looked up and saw his house was dark.

Once inside, he flicked on a single unsheathed bulb stuck out from the ceiling in the entryway. It cast its light into the small room, but not much beyond.

"Mike?" Austin called out. The house, and the dark, ate up his words. When no answer came, he stepped out of the light, into the dark living room.

He twisted the knob on the lamp near the couch and it sparked to life. The cushions were bare and empty. The place smelled like fresh cooking, thick in the air, like meat fried in grease.

A shadow lurked behind him, lingering in the dim light of the entryway. It held there, lording over Austin, its monstrous form grotesque, even in the dark.

Austin turned, and the thing scurried silently away, hiding in the deep dark.

Must have taken her to the hospital.

He was okay with it. Austin was done with the day. It beat him from sunup until long after the sun fell. He was ready for it to end, so he moved on upstairs.

At top of the stairs, he flicked on the hall light and stood, glancing up the hall one way and down the other, the open doors leading only to more darkened rooms.

"Mike?" He asked. They were gone.

He walked down the hall, stopped at the only closed door and gripped the handle, the metal cold against his palm. The old brass wined against his grip.

It was his bedroom. Only, he didn't think of it as such, not anymore. It was hers. It had been hers the second she moved in, the second he'd brought her home that first night and she slept. It was hers, and he was allowed in only because she let him. It was hers like he was hers. She had him, every bit of him. And now she was dead.

Austin stepped into the room, not bothering to turn on the lights. He couldn't bear to see it. He could handle it in the dim light slipping in from the hall, but only barely. He sat on the bed and, felt the weight of it all, the weight of her, bear down on him, collapsing his entire world.

Austin sobbed until he choked, tears thick, painful, as grief usually is. He swallowed, sucking in a deep, cold breath. He just wanted it to be better, to be okay.

He sat with his back to the door. Had he sat on the other side, he might have seen it coming, but he didn't, because that was her side. The thing, hazy and fat, limbs like serrated blades, black in the dim light, crawled up the side of the stairwell wall, leaping across the hall, a silent image. It slipped its way into the dark of the room.

Austin looked to the stairwell. He called out for his friend, and no one answered.

The bed creaked behind him, and he felt a weight drop down onto it.

Austin turned and faced the thing sitting next to him at the edge of the bed. In the night, in the shadow, he saw the silhouette of a woman soaking in the darkness, still and picturesque.

For a moment, he thought it was her, and wanted to call her name, but couldn't, the words clogged in his throat. He stopped breathing and only stared.

Jess, he thought. And he reached out to her.

The shadow woman shifted in the dark, and he saw it, in the blink of light, its long, greasy black hair pressed to its skin, skin darker than shadow and oily, almost burning in the night. Four elongated legs sprouted out. Its black faceless head looked down at him, it snarled from somewhere deep within it.

Austin lurched back, but it was too late.

It snapped at him. Its long, crooked teeth red with fresh blood.

Austin screamed. Pain seared through Austin's hand and shot up his arm as the thing bit into him. Austin felt the thing's teeth tear through him. He fell, flailing backwards, hitting the small of his back on the wood bedframe and toppling to the floor.

Austin held his hand up saw just his thumb was left, fingers on his left hand gone, torn off in jagged strips. He clutched at the wound, hot blood oozing out, and sprawled to his feet, pedalling with his good hand and feet towards the door.

He heard it race along the bed, tearing at the bed sheets as Austin bolted down the stairs, two-three at a time. He went for the front door, grabbing the handle, turning in time to see the shadowy thing leap from up on the wall towards him.

It whacked against the front door as Austin dashed out of the way.

A burst of pain exploded in his knee as it collided with the bottom stair. He gasped, eyes bursting wide from the pain. A pair of sneakers sat on the floor in the living room lamplight. They were covered in gooey black blood, ankle bones jutting out, ripped of any flesh.

Austin got to his feet quick, used the stairwell to drag himself up, his wounded hand clutched tight to his chest. He followed along the wall, tracing along until his hand rattled a doorhandle he knew would be there.

Click-Clack-Click-Clack. The thing raced across the floor to him.

He threw the door open and jumped through, slamming it behind him, closing him off into full darkness. The thing hit the door, the sound of it nearly knocked Austin over. Hurrying, he took a step and found the stair he expected was gone and he fell, reaching out into the dark, smacking four sharp angled wood stairs before he caught the railing, steadying himself. He hobbled downwards until his feet hit soft dirt.

Bang. The thing hit the door again, the crack an explosion in the dark.

His right leg was stiff and flared hot with pain. He could feel it swelling, hugging tight to his jeans. His left hand throbbed like pulsing lava. He waved his good hand through the air, blindly searching. He swatted a chain hanging in the dark, caught it and yanked.

Light lit cement walls in a ghostly grey. For a second, Austin thought that the thing might rise from the black dirt that lined the basement floor.

He could see now how bad he was bleeding. His sleeve-stained charcoal with his blood.

The thing hit the door once more, and he heard it splinter.

Austin moved to an old wardrobe along a wall, yanked open the drawers, searching.

The thing burst into the basement, sending a blast of wood rattling down the steps.

Austin opened another drawer, pilfering through the linens until he found the empty bottom. He moved on to the next.

Click-Clack-Click-Clack. The thing scurrying along the walls, rushing fast.

Austin drove his good hand into the bottom drawer. He felt cold steel beneath his grip. He drew it out, spraying old blankets out onto the floor.

The sounds grew louder, and he saw it closing in on him.

Click-Clack-Click-Clack.

Austin turned and readied the gun.

The thing launched at him.

Bang.

The shotgun blast erupted, and it flew out of his grip. A horrid wail burst out from the thing. The flare of the muzzle blast illuminated it, glowing a grim dark purple, its wet, hairy body, its muscles palpitating below black, translucent skin, mouth wide, rows of razor teeth blacker than night and dripping with his blood.

The thing hit the floor with a wet splat.

And it was still. As was Austin.

Pain coursed through him. Breathing heavy, he grabbed the gun, struggled it into his grip. He readied another shot, balancing the thing with his thumb, pressing the barrel against the open wounds of his fingers.

The sound of its wet, gurgling breaths rose and fell in the room, huffing gasps of death-stenched air. The glow of the black light that gleamed off it was dimming. He watched as its form was shifting before his eyes.

Its hairy, inky skin brightened, turning the colour of flesh. The limbs cracked and popped as they slunk into its rounded body, becoming the girl they had dug out of the earth only a few hours ago. He could see the face now, the eyes, forming, staring up at him.

He fired again.

13

He drove along dark roads, steering with one hand, the other bandaged heavily. He had almost blacked out searching for the first aid kit. He had searched for Mike as well but found no sign of him. Only his shoes remained.

Austin turned onto an off-road trail, felt the weight of the thing, now a mostly a girl, slide across the box of Mike's truck and thud against the side.

He drove on.

The hill looked different in full dark, but he found it without trouble. He drove slow, tires scraping against the grass, unbroken headlight beam guiding him.

The truck skidded to a stop. Austin left it running, jammed it into park, and stepped from the vehicle. He dropped the tailgate and looked at the thing. It was a girl now, more so then when he had left the house. Remnants of its other form, the inky shine of its skin, the roughness of its form, still lingered. It was bound by thick rope, a heavy chain, and duct tape for good measure.

She hadn't woken, and he was thankful. But whatever it was, was still very much alive.

He dragged her out by the feet, letting her body hit the ground with a heavy thud. The shovel was there, hidden behind her, shining in the moonlight which beamed down on him like a spotlight.

Dragging her was hard work. She was heavier than she looked. He brought her to the grave that the man had dug. The coffin was still there.

He dropped the thing down into the coffin and waited for her eyes to open.

But they never did.

When he felt enough time had passed, he closed the lid, pulled a hammer from his belt loop and pounded it shut.

He shovelled the dirt back onto the grave, burying the thing below.

When he was finished, he looked down at his left hand. Blood was staining the bandages. His next stop was the hospital. The thing had taken all the fingers, including the wedding ring he and Jess had picked out. He thought briefly about going down, ripping through the thing's stomach to find it. But it was better this way.

The day had begun with death, and he thought about dying himself enough today as well, nearly had died. Austin understood now, about burying things, and about how things never stayed buried. He knew the thing buried there wasn't dead. He doubted it could ever be dead, but he would finish what the man started. He hoped that he'd done enough.

Walking back to his truck, Austin saw the sky to the east was a vibrant blue, the first colours of a new dawn kissing the sky. The darkness from the night before was gone.

He thought of Jess.

The Ice cream Man

Tom Johnstone

I thought I'd really landed on my feet when I moved into the flat in Sharman Heights. At last, I might be able to move on after Anne-Marie. But there were signs even then that things weren't quite right there.

It wasn't that the people there were unfriendly. In some ways the opposite was the case. There was a nice community feel to the place, with a very active Residents' Association, but still licking my wounds as I was, I didn't respond well to their overtures at first. As the weather grew warmer in the summer, my reserve began to thaw a little.

There's a grassy area outside the flats, where people go on long, warm evenings, some drinking cans of cold beer, young families sitting around disposable barbecues. The shouts and cries of children echo off the walls. The meaty charcoal fumes prickle your nostrils. A metallic jingle wafts over on the breeze. There's a squealing hullabaloo as the kids get excited.

There's an ice cream van a few streets away. Breathless whispers as the children wonder when it will pull up on this street.

But it was the arrival of one of these one Friday evening in September that told me things were a bit... off there.

Usually, when it turned up, playing the sprightly theme from *Match of the Day*, that was the cue for a stampede of small, excited feet towards its shiny, pastel-coloured flank, decorated with bright, garish pictures of the array of treats on offer.

This time was different.

The ice cream van wasn't playing *Match of the Day*, but something else, something slower, sadder. Like the usual tune, the jingle sounded vaguely familiar from when I was a kid, but I couldn't quite place it. As it echoed through the canyons of the surrounding flat blocks, there was still that sense of anticipation, but it was an uneasy one this time. As the tinny jingle grew louder, heralding the arrival of the van, many of the children looked uncertainly at their parents' tense faces. Already some of the adults were packing up their picnics and ordering their kids inside, glowering at the sound.

Maybe they were just weary of shelling out for ice creams all the time. That's what I thought at first. Sharman Heights isn't the kind of place where you go to live if you've made it big. In any case, despite the Indian Summer weather, the sun had dipped behind the flats. The area was suddenly quite chilly in the shade, so no need for a frozen treat to cool you down. Though Anne-Marie and I never had children, I could sympathise with the parental feeling of annoyance at an ice cream van rocking up right now, just when things were supposed to be winding down before bedtime. There were a few whines of protest from the younger ones, but for the most part the exit of these families took place without much incident.

When it finally arrived, it looked different too. Unlike the gleaming van that came most days, its dark purple paintwork looked shabby, peppered with rust, and what looked like millions of jagged little white flecks dotted around where the paint must have peeled off, like snowflakes but nasty biting little shards, not soft fluffy blobs or ornate crystals. The pictures of the ice creams on offer were faded and the brands were ones I remembered from years back.

But no one returned my wry smile at these retro varieties. The remaining families followed the others back into the block, stony-faced. It really felt like a signal that summer was over, another one without Anne-Marie, or indeed anyone else to warm my bed or my heart.

It was just then that I saw someone I hoped might do at least one of these things: Penny, a single mother who lived on the same floor as I did, joining the exodus, hustling her seven-year-old son Sam indoors. She was usually more friendly. Sometimes I even thought I saw a twinkle in her eye when we passed each other on the echoey stairs. Not this time. Maybe it was because I still hadn't got around to prising off the redundant wedding ring from my finger.

Looking down at the discarded cans, foil trays for disposable barbecues, even clothes some had abandoned in their hurry to get inside, I said, "Seems like no one really fancies ice cream today."

She nodded, tight-lipped, distracted.

"Maybe those brands are a bit too outdated for them," I suggested. "Or maybe they're boycotting it for undercutting the usual one."

I looked pointedly at the sorry state of the vehicle. Maybe its lower overheads did indeed enable it to charge less than the more familiar van.

"Something like that," was all she said.

She seemed irritated at my trying to continue the conversation, probably because Sam was now looking longingly back at the ice cream van, but I persisted.

"Still, not everyone's giving it the cold shoulder," I pointed out.

At that, she spun around, her eagerness to get indoors momentarily forgotten.

"What?" she said, her eyes wide, her arms enfolding Sam as if to prevent any move on his part to run over to the van. The dimples on her elbows as she did this looked cute, as did the ones in her cheeks when she smiled, not that she was doing so now. Her expression suggested she was in no mood for me to make any overtures. She was staring at the two little girls, a five-year-old and an eight-year-old I guessed, whose dad was buying them ice creams. He seemed pleased with himself that everyone else had disappeared, leaving him and his offspring a clear path to the van without any need for queuing, but I noticed him shivering when he was next to it. For a moment, I even thought I could see his breath – that of his little girls too, wafting from their mouths like ghosts.

I couldn't see the seller in the van, who was in shadow, but I could just about hear his voice asking, *What can I do for you?* It sounded oddly tinny, rather like the jingle that had announced its arrival. I didn't recognise the kids or their father, so they must be newcomers to the estate like me – even more recent arrivals by the looks of things. I still felt like an outsider here myself and probably would do for some time yet. Neither they nor I had got the memo about the campaign against this upstart ice cream van.

"No," Penny said, almost a cry of pain.

If it was meant to stop the transaction, it came too late. Maybe she wanted to save the man and his daughters from any possible reprisals for their flouting of whatever unwritten rules put this ice cream van beyond the pale around here, but the two girls were already smearing their faces with what looked like Mr Whippy, reminding me of mine in the morning when I smothered the lower half of it in shaving foam.

Penny's response did seem a bit much to be honest! What was this? The Sharman Heights version of the Ice Cream Wars? Would the poor man get his arms and legs broken for buying from the wrong seller?

But before I had a chance to ask her these questions, she'd turned and gone inside, avoiding any contact with the broadly grinning father and his sticky offspring, or me for that matter. All I could do was shrug. It was getting dark by now and I still couldn't make out the ice cream vendor's face, as the blueish light from within the cab lit him from behind and he was shrouded in icy vapours anyway. Somehow, I didn't want to go and get a closer look. Maybe I was afraid of my fellow tenants looking out of the window and spotting me fraternising with the enemy or something. That's what I told myself.

I did notice one thing though.

As the evening light faded, making everything seem that much darker for having been so bright a short time before, I saw that what I'd taken for scratches in the dark, purple paintwork seemed to glow faintly. They weren't just patches of the metal bodywork showing through after all. They were stars painted on in luminous paint to give the impression of night sky.

As the van finally pulled away after what must have been a very poor day's business, I heard the desolate chimes of its jingle, and it suddenly struck me what the tune was. It was from the musical *Singing in the Rain*, but not one of the big lavish production numbers. The love-duet between Gene Kelly and Debbie Reynolds: "You Are My Lucky Star'.

***

It wasn't until the following June of 2014 that the battered purple ice cream van appeared again. But I'd forgotten all about it by then. I'd begun seeing more of Penny, trying to take things slowly. I had finally taken off the wedding ring, telling myself it was time to put Anne-Marie behind me.

Gradually we were getting closer, I thought. Sam called me 'Uncle Peter' now, and Penny trusted me to look after him when she needed a bit of time off. It gave me a much-needed sense of purpose to play the role of a surrogate father-figure. To him, that is! I had a few years on her too, but not to *that* extent, I liked to think. It didn't bother me that I was doing the job that rightfully belonged to another man, whoever he might have been. I didn't ask too many questions, not wanting to look a gift horse in the mouth.

As the weeks went by and spring turned to summer, Penny started going out more and more on Friday nights, asking me to babysit. I didn't mind. It gave me a chance to see her dolled up for her night out, briefly anyway. She'd get back a little worse for wear, but Sam was always still awake, so nothing ever happened between us.

He was a bit of a mother's boy I thought, having grown up without a father. I often used to buy him an ice cream to distract him from her departure, but always from the shiny, pastel-coloured van. She had some sort of faddy notion about not letting him have anything sugary after about 7pm at night, so I told the boy to keep mum about it.

That Friday was a hot one, and so was she when she came to the door to let me in. She looked stunning in the red dress that set off her strawberry blonde hair, but she didn't need to wear such things to impress me: I'd have been happy to see her in her usual T-shirt and jeans.

"Who's the lucky fellow?" I joked, hoping she'd scoff and make it clear this was just another night out with the girls, but her secretive smile told another story. So that was all I was to her after all: Just an unpaid babysitter.

I felt a lump in my throat and a sharp, sick sadness in my chest and stomach as she said, "No one you'd know," her voice scornful, dismissive even. Then she tottered down the switchback staircase, leaving me alone with her son and the echo of her clacking red stiletto heels on the concrete steps, the brash, sweet scent of her perfume in my nostrils.

I've always been unlucky in love.

I don't really believe in chance though. You make your own luck. But someone else's had run out by the look of the blue lights flashing outside Sharman Heights later on. Sam and I watched the drama from the window, wondering what could be happening. The ambulance left, but the police were still there for a while afterwards, searching the area, going door to door, asking about a missing six-year-old. A little later, when things had quietened down, the sound of sirens was replaced by the tinkle of an ice cream van, but not playing *Match of the Day* this time. It was the shabby purple one, not the shiny pastel-coloured one.

"Off you go then, son," I said, pressing coins into the little boy's hand.

I didn't mean 'son' literally of course.

"You're not my dad," he said. I flinched. "Mum says I'm not supposed to," he added, rubbing it in.

I sighed at his solemn little face staring back at me. We'd been over this hundreds of times. But remembering her reaction to the purple van, I sensed he didn't just mean her objection to late night sugar rushes. Well, if she thought the van was somehow ill-starred, I decided I'd have to over-rule this ridiculous superstition.

"It's okay," I said, feeling some misgivings of my own, but quickly overcoming them. "Tell you what. It's a bit dark out, so I'll come with you as far as the front step if you want."

Despite the remains of the summer heat in the darkening evening, I shivered as I watched him approach the van, where the ice cream seller stood, his face in shadow, his tinny voice saying, *What can I do for you, young man?*

***

The next day, the police were back, organising a search of the estate and the nearby scrubland for the missing six-year-old, one of the little girls whose dad bought them an ice cream from the purple van. Her older sister had been rushed to hospital with meningitis, resulting in septicaemia and the eventual amputation of all her limbs. Due to her unconsciousness or delirium for much of this ordeal, it hadn't been possible for her to tell anyone she'd locked the younger one in some disused storeroom in the rarely-visited basement of Sharman Heights as a prank. They didn't find the child's emaciated corpse, blood on the little fingernails and ingrained in the scratch-marks inside the door, until much, much later.

I didn't dare tell Penny I'd sent Sam to the van.

***

It could all be coincidence of course.

But now it's Friday 13th March 2015, and Sam's come down with Measles, even though he's had the MMR jab. It's got a ninety-three per sent success rate I've heard. But apparently, he's one of those seven per cent for whom it fails. The doctors say he might not pull through – that would make him one of the two in a hundred who die of the virus, even in this day and age. Doesn't sound like much, but it is if you counted up the numbers and statistics don't matter if you happen to be one of the unlucky ones.

I knew the van would come back today, because the last time it did was June 13th, also a Friday, in 2014, and the time before that Friday 13th September 2013. Maybe that was why it took two that time.

It sounds ridiculous, but I expected it, and there it was in all its rusty, purple, star-specked glory, looking like the type of ice cream van a Goth or a New Ager would drive. But he was neither of those, just a man with a face you couldn't see because the light was behind him and the vapour concealed his features.

What can I do for you, sir? he asked me in his metallic voice.

"Take me," I said. "If you must take someone, take me. He's just a boy with his whole life ahead of him. I'm a nobody, with no future. I had my chance, and I blew it. Several chances. Haven't even got any kids of my own who'd miss me. She doesn't love me. I'm just the sad sack who sometimes babysits for her. And this is all my fault. Not hers. Not his. This is the least I can do for them. The very least...

"So please, take me."

The ice cream van man just stood there, considering my offer as he held up a wafer cone to catch something that oozed and swirled out of the machine in his van. He held out the cone that gleamed pale and sickly green in the blueish light from the van and the yellowish light from the streetlamp. I noticed his fingers looked frosted with specks of ice; the tips blackened. I wondered briefly if he suffered from frostbite, on account of spending all day handling iced goods, but the time for such down-to-earth thoughts was long past.

Very well, sir.

"You mean you'll do it?"

His head moved a little. It could have been a nod. It had to be.

"That's fantastic! So, Sam's going to be alright after all! I'll go and tell Penny right away!"

But as I turned to leave, his cold, iron voice stopped me.

Wait.

I knew it. There must be a catch.

Don't forget your ice cream, sir.

"Oh, yeah."

I grabbed the cone from his icy grip without thinking. As I did so, whatever it was that iced his fingers and blackened their tips seemed to pass into mine. I felt the cold spreading from my hands, up my arms and into my body.

Now, I can feel it sitting at the heart of my being, as icy as the vacuum of space depicted on the side of that shabby, battered, mysterious old van, the vast, empty, airless, heatless space between those points of light.

It won't be long now.

Why didn't they tell me? It seems as if everyone on the estate knows the secret of the Ice Cream Man, except me and that man with the two girls. Maybe it's something you find out about if you've lived here long enough not to fall foul of him -- before you know to steer clear of him. If you approach him unawares before you've done some unspoken probationary period, then tough luck.

Despite the warm, early spring evening, my fingers felt almost too numb to grip my ice cream. Yet somehow, I made myself hold it, not even noticing it melting, because of the heat of the air -- not that of my hand, which no longer had any. The ice cream seemed my last link with the world of the living. So, I kept my grip on it, even though I couldn't even feel the sticky drip of it on my hand.

I know I'm a dead man walking, an ice cream man like him.

I turn and run up the switchback steps to Penny's. As I approach her door, foolishly thinking to tell her the good news, maybe get in her good books for my sacrifice, I hear the faint sound of the phone ringing from within. My fist freezes at the point of knocking. Better to wait. I hear the faint sound of her voice answering the call, silence as she listens to what the caller says, then muffled sobs. My ice cream melting, raspberry sauce staining my hand, I creep away from her door to my own flat at the other end of the hall, starting to weep frozen tears myself as the truth hits me.

The ice cream man agreed to take *my* life. But he didn't agree to spare Sam's.

Summer Friends

Mia Dalia

For Chelsea...

I was twelve the summer I killed my best friend.

And yes, we weren't friends for long, and I know that everyone said it wasn't my fault, but none of those things mattered. Then or now. I had relived it every day since, regretted it every day since. But the thing is, I'd do it again if I had to. In a way, you see, I never really had a choice.

That summer started like any other—with my birthday. I hated having a summer birthday; everyone I knew always seemed to be away. My parents tried to put together a small party that back then I would have described as sad and now, with the perspective and vocabulary of intervening decades, as desultory. A few kids came, some family members showed up.

There was an unmemorable selection of tone-deaf presents that had nothing to do with me at twelve.

My family was always big on aspirational gifts—things one can evolve into, from oversized sweaters to hobby-specific objects I never developed an interest in. That year, it was a microscope. What I wanted was a telescope. Maybe a pair of binoculars. To look at far away things, not focus on minute details of the ones at hand.

The cake took a beating on the ride home from the bakery and, as a result, sagged on one side like old Mr. Reynolds' face after his stroke.

I didn't express any of my disappointment out loud, of course. I was a well-mannered kid, a proper Midwesterner in the making. I thanked my parents, ate the saggy, soggy cake, and smiled like a game show host. Went to bed sugar-high and downhearted.

The next day, Arms moved in. First, there was a motorcade comprising a giant moving truck, a wood-panelled station wagon, and a black sedan. Then, a procession of cardboard boxes was hauled into the house next door by large sweaty men. Were they family or hired help?

Eventually, I got tired of watching them and returned to my book. I had discovered King the previous summer and was steadily working my way through his back catalogue. It gave me nightmares, but I didn't care—the stories were too thrilling. My parents didn't approve but prided themselves on being too liberal minded to raise objections. "At least, he's reading," they'd sigh.

And I was. Books offered me the sort of companionship I had never quite found with other kids. I wasn't an oddball, not really, but I didn't fit in and was all too aware of it. Not athletic enough, not funny enough, not brazen enough. Not even a proper nerd. No clique would have me.

Ever since Jake, my neighbour and pal since age six, moved away two years before, I'd only had casual friendships, nothing of any meaning. Jake's parents got divorced, and, when his mom remarried to a lawyer in New Jersey, he went with her. We promised each other we'd write and visit, but the communication died out slowly and steadily over six months, and that was that. He never visited. Neither did I.

New Jersey felt unimaginably far. Almost as far as Florida, where my grandparents had retired. From an early age, when people I knew moved away, my parents would stand me in front of a large world map that hung in my father's study/library/guest room and point to the place they went and then spanned the difference with their fingers.

"See," they'd say, "not so far."

The trick had the opposite effect on me, magnifying the distance. Making our home and, consequently, me feel smaller than ever. A speck in the grand scheme of things. When I resurfaced from an intense re-read of *Salem's Lot*, the movers were gone. So were the boxes. In their stead was a tall skinny kid about my age with giant ears and a bad haircut, kicking a soccer ball around. That was the first time I saw Arms.

Our fence was short back then, more of a suggestion than a proper divider of land. Enough to stop a small dog, maybe, but that's about it. So, I could see the kid, and he could see me watching him.

He sauntered over and threw me a casual, "Hey."

Approaching the fence, I replied in kind.

"I'm Arms," he said. His smile was uneven, one corner of his mouth doing most of the lifting.

"What sort of name is that?" I asked, forgetting my manners.

"Short for Armstrong. A family name."

The kid's arms jutting out from his worn-to-see-through T-shirt were stick-like, making the name sound either mean or ironic or both.

"Riley."

"Nice to meet you, Riley." He shook my hand across the fence, wrapping his surprisingly strong, spiderlike fingers around mine. "So, what is there to do for fun around here?"

We got to talking and, it seemed, never stopped. It turned out that the most fun thing to do around here was hanging out with Arms. He was full of stories, he seemed to have lived all over. He was funny and outgoing in a way I wasn't, he invented games where all I saw were trees or rocks.

Arms was a strange-looking kid. I couldn't put a finger on it back then, but, if I had to describe him now, I'd say he looked like someone drew him, having never seen what a kid looks like. Describe a kid to an alien with limited artistic talent, and he'd put together someone like Arms: gangly, disproportionately limbed, his eyes too large, his nose and ears too pointy, his hair forever sticking up every which way, with broad shoulders and oddly small feet. He looked like a sprite, like a character out of *Peter Pan*. Had similar energy too. If our sleepy suburb was suddenly invaded by pirates, Arms would fight them.

He read too. Freakishly fast. I'd give him one of my beat-up King's paperbacks, and he'd return it in a day or two, finished. At first, I thought he was lying, but I'd test him, and he always proved well-versed on the various plot points.

We'd stay past curfew, debating the logistics of vampires and resurrected pets. The books provided a comfortable safe distance, I didn't tell my new friend about that. I wanted him to see me as an equal, as bold and brazen as him.

Arms' parents never seemed to be around.

"They're always working," he'd say, waving his hand dismissively.

They always left him money. Their kitchen was pristine, with blindingly white cabinetry and mirror-like stainless steel surfaces, with a collection of takeout menus prominently displayed.

The house was clean too, but in an unlived and unloved way I couldn't quite describe. Too quiet, too many empty walls.

My house had dust motes floating around, and pictures covering every wall, photos, framed posters, a large world map. But Arms' house had a giant TV, the latest game console, no parental supervision, and all the pizza we could eat. It wasn't even a competition.

I don't know if I genuinely appreciated it back then, the uniqueness of a connection we shared. When you're a kid, you think that sort of thing is easy enough to find.

As an adult, battered by a series of personal disappointments, you come to see it as rare. A flash in a pan sort of thing. A true meeting of minds and temperaments. Someone who really sees you, really gets you.

That was what I had that summer. That and so much fun.

It was as if I suddenly got promoted from being the quiet observer of my story to its proper protagonist. I loved it. The upgrade, the newfound agency. We were inseparable all summer, Arms and me.

Like most intense friendships—like most intense relationships of any sort—it felt like we had a world for just the two of us. Everyone else existed on the periphery.

In the books, specifically in King's books, friends usually came in larger groups, anywhere from four to seven seemed to be the magic number. Even back then, I didn't know how anyone managed to balance that out. Hanging out with Arms was taking up just about all of my free time, and I was glad of it. I think even back then, as a kid, I had a very strong sense of my emotional limitations. I tended to dedicate myself to manageable, smaller-scale pursuits, establishing and maintaining a limited set of connections.

I imagined myself pedalling down a small-town street in Maine, my friends in tow, shouting playfully at each other, racing downhill, but in reality, I knew, I'd probably always be something of a loner. One of those solitary characters who may or may not be a total weirdo, but no one knew for sure. In Arms, I had found someone who broke through my walls and made me feel less alone.

I didn't even register the missing pet posters at first. Not very observant by nature, I was also in the habit of getting lost in my thoughts, of looking down when I walked, establishing meaningful eye contact with the once-white rubber toes of my beat-up Converse shoes. It was only when my parents talked about it during the mandatory Sunday supper that I came to be aware of it.

There was indeed a surprisingly large number of pets, cats and dogs, and even a ferret, who went missing in our neighbourhood over the past months.

"Weird." I shrugged, picking at my meatloaf, wishing to douse it in ketchup but knowing full well that doing so would offend my mom. I couldn't wait to discuss the disappearances with Arms, see what his take on it might be.

Arms didn't shrug. Instead, he looked at me with a peculiar glint in his eyes and told me he might know a thing or two about it.

"Oh, yeah?" I challenged him, ready to call bullshit. "What do you know?

He wouldn't say. It was uncharacteristic of Arms, this reticence. I didn't like the idea of him keeping secrets from me, but I didn't push. Instead, I waited, comfortable in the knowledge that Arms wouldn't hold out for long.

When I was a kid, I thought secrets were like poison ivy. You couldn't keep it to yourself, the itchiness would drive you mad.

Later, I learned differently, coming to regard secrets as a bag of bricks you dragged around with you. You couldn't show anyone inside it, and you couldn't ask anyone to help you with the terrible weight of it. It was all yours and yours alone. Forever. Back then, we went on with our summer fun, business as usual. We were the heroes who rescued Mrs. Albertson's cat from the tree. We were the villains who let the air out of the bike tires of the bullies who hung outside of the arcade and pretended to enjoy smoking. We were the explorers who followed the local creek downstream the way you were supposed to and managed to get lost and come home late enough to warrant getting grounded.

The praise we shared; but the guilt Arms shouldered alone. He'd speak to my parents, as polite as a teacher's pet, taking all the blame, looking a perfect picture of remorse, his natural recalcitrance nowhere to be found. The kid could have been an actor.

I had all but forgotten about the missing pets and what my friend might have known about it, by the time he brought it up again. Guess the secret got too itchy for him, after all.

"Remember I told you I knew a thing or two about it?"

I nodded, eagerly, in anticipation of what Arms might come up with this time.

That's when he showed me the shack. Said he'd been waiting until I was ready, but waiting sucked so…

The shack sat at the very edge of his family property, abutting the local woods. It looked so ramshackle, I figured no one had any use for it. I was wrong.

Arms had definitely been putting it to some use.

There were no windows there, no overhead light, just candles. A small space, about the size of the eat-in kitchen in my house, it featured four dilapidated walls that were unenthusiastically holding up a patchy ceiling. The smell was like roadkill on a summer day. There was some random debris in the corners, but the main attraction was the sculpture.

That was how Arms described it then, and that was how I had thought of it ever since, though it was unlike any art project I had seen then or after.

Sometimes, a person is confronted with the things the mind doesn't readily provide a description for. Understanding and contextualizing it comes later. If ever.

Arms' sculpture was tall, stretching all the way to the ceiling, and hideous in a way that stopped your blood. Made entirely of bones, small and large, and tiny skulls, and decorated with bloody animal hides. The end result was an approximation of a human or humanoid figure, but Arms wasn't that much of an artist, and so it looked off. Really off. The way Arms himself looked like only an approximation of a boy.

Its head was too large, a conglomeration of animal skulls with luxurious white fur that I, horrified, recognized as Fuzzball, Mrs. Anderson's missing Persian kitty. The white fur was bloodstained. The sculpture's torso was hidden from view, clothed in a toga-like outfit of yet more fur. The arms and legs must have been easier to assemble, though they appeared to have too many joints. The fingers were long, too long.

I didn't scream. To my credit, I didn't scream. I shuddered and almost pissed my pants, but I stayed quiet. Deep down, I still cared about Arms' opinion of me, still hoped for a reasonable explanation.

"What do you think?" he asked proudly.

"What … what is it?" I stammered.

"It's what I've been working on. My parents gave me some instructions, but largely I've been improvising. See, I've always wanted a sibling. Being an only child sucks."

What about me? I thought stupidly, childishly. Aren't I enough? I had never really wanted siblings, but over the summer I'd come to think of Arms as a weird brother I never had.

I felt like the statue was breathing. Like it was sucking all the air out of the room. But no, surely, it was just my imagination. Just my fear. I hoped my voice wouldn't betray it.

"Is it … is it finished?"

"Almost. It just needs one more thing to bring it all together."

"And what's that?"

"Trade secret." He winked and playfully hit me on the shoulder. "You'll see."

More secrets? I almost shook my head, but I didn't care that much about it then. I only wanted to be away from that terrible sculpture, from that claustrophobic shack, and, for the first time, from my friend.

Arms was right. I did see. When, after about three days of hiding from him and pretending to be grounded for a made-up infraction, I heard that the Walkers' baby went missing.

The Walkers were a nice young couple at the end of our block. They held hands everywhere they went, an affectation I had never before associated with adults. Their baby was objectively cute in that Gerber-baby way, big blue eyes and pink cheeks.

Everyone was upset, terrified, outraged. Police came around and interviewed all the neighbours. Posters were made. A TV crew arrived to shoot an emotional plea from the parents.

In the midst of it all, I seemed to be the only one who knew what happened. At least, I had some idea of what happened, one I was nearly too scared to contemplate. Still, I had to know for sure what kind of monster my new best friend was, and so I worked up my courage and did the brave thing.

I went to see Arms.

He was kicking a ball in his yard and looked happy to see me.

"Done being grounded?" He greeted me.

I nodded.

"Just in time. Have I got something to show you."

He ushered me toward the shack excitedly.

On sneakered feet that suddenly weighed a ton each, I followed.

The shack was as awful as I remembered. If anything, the smell might have intensified.

There was an object inside, on a small wooden table surrounded by candles, and it took me a terrifying moment or two to recognize it. Human hearts, you see, in real life look nothing like they do in cartoons and greeting cards. In real life, human hearts look like messy bloody fists.

"I got the last ingredient." Arms beamed at me proudly. "All set now. Just waited for you, thought you'd want to be here."

I didn't. I wanted to be anywhere else but there. The last of my resolve, of my hopes had crumbled and I was left with nothing but the sheer terror of the monster before me.

The last drop of courage had evaporated from my fear-scorched heart, and I ran. I ran out of that shack like the devil himself was chasing me. But not before knocking over the lit candles.

The fire behind me blazed into life with a whoosh straight out of an action movie. Or, more appropriately, a horror movie.

And sure, knocking over the candles could technically be dismissed as a random act, but I did pause on my way out— while Arms was busy trying to save his precious sculpture— and latched the door from the outside. That was, by anyone's standards, a deliberate act. A murder, some might say.

There was an investigation afterward. The police came, asked me questions. Barely anything, really. Everyone was still too preoccupied with the missing baby, too ready to commit to the "terrible tragedy, no one's fault' narrative about the fire. I don't know if any of Arms' sculpture survived, or if anyone ever questioned all the bones found. Perhaps, they simply burned down in the fire. I didn't know; I wasn't told, and I didn't ask. It was the one time I was grateful for how overbearingly protective my parents were. I mostly stayed in my room until school started, reading. Never King again, no horror at all. I'd had enough to last me a lifetime.

By the time I emerged back into the world, Arms' parents were gone. Whoever they were. The house had a "For Sale' sign in the front yard once again. The people who bought it next had no kids. That was okay by me; I wasn't looking for more friends anyway. I was done with all that, done with summer friendships for good.

Madly In Love

Christabel Simpson

I wake to the drone of a vacuum cleaner – my landlady, Mrs. Farly, obsessing over the carpet on the landing outside my room. I don't bother grabbing my phone from my bedside ....e to look at the time. It's eight o'clock. I know, because she's been doing the exact same thing at the exact same time every morning since I moved in. She seems to think that because she gets up with the larks everyone else should too. Never mind that I've had to get a job as a barmaid to pay my way through uni and don't get home till after midnight most days.

It's so thoughtless. I had a bitch of a shift last night, so I could really do without this wakeup call. My boss was on my case, because my till was ten pounds down, and I had more than my fair share of creeps trying to get into my pants. For the record, I only like girls, but even if I was straight, I'm pretty sure cheesy chat-up lines and invasions of my personal space wouldn't do it for me.

Mrs. Farly's vacuuming the stairs now, working her way noisily downwards. I take deep breaths, count imaginary sheep, but there's no way I'm getting back to sleep. Hard to believe I'm paying eight hundred a month for this bedshit.

Finally, the vacuum stops, but I only get a few seconds respite before the fricking woman starts blasting out classical music from her radio – another daily occurrence as she sits down to her breakfast. She's on her way to total deafness, so I guess she doesn't realize how loud it is, but that doesn't make it any easier to stomach. Personally, I think she should change the first letter of her surname to 'E' as a warning to people – early by name, early by nature.

Talking of names, mine's Belle. It's French for beautiful, though I don't really live up to that. I have good hair I suppose – ash blonde and naturally glossy – and a nice complexion, but my nose is too pointy and I'm pale as hell.

I roll over, pulling a pillow over my head as the music goes on. The song that's playing is familiar, but I have no idea what it's called and couldn't care less. I just want to get back to sleep. It's not happening, though.

I get up and trudge across to the sink in the corner of the room. I feel dreadful, my head throbbing, my mood grim. It's a beautiful summer's day, the sun streaming through a gap in my curtains, the birds chittering away outside, but this doesn't help.

I brush my teeth with unnecessary vigour and stare at myself in the mirror. I look as bad as I feel – face puffy, hair messy, dark shadows beneath my eyes. Thank God for colour corrector and concealer. I put my bathrobe on over my nightie – a t-shirt with stars and moons on it – and head for the shower room.

***

"Emily's a pretty kick ass character, when you think about it," says Cathy, my girlfriend, as we sit by a window in Starbucks a few hours later. She's talking about *The Mysteries of Udolpho*, which was the subject of our Gothic Fiction lecture this morning. "I know she keeps swooning in that irritating nineteenth century way, but whenever she gets a chance to kick back against her problems, she never fails to grab it."

I nod absently, sipping on my drink. The scrummy whipped cream and cocoa combo has given me a much-needed sugar boost, making me feel almost human again. I wish I'd had a cup before the lecture. I'm into *The Mysteries of Udolpho* in a big way, but I was seriously struggling to stay awake.

Cathy reaches for my hand. "You're very quiet. Everything okay?"

I look down as she strokes my fingers. Her hands are so much nicer than mine – smooth and delicate with neatly filed nails. They're one of my favourite things about her, along with her high cheekbones, the cute little dimples she gets when she smiles, her thick blonde hair with its pink and turquoise highlights. Actually, there's not much I don't like about Cathy, and she looks especially lush today, dressed in tight black leggings, a Joan Jett t-shirt and red boots.

I meet her gaze across the table, squeezing her hand.

"I'm fine. I'm just tired."

She gives me a playful smile. "Farlyed again today, were you?"

It's the perfect opportunity to air my grievances about my landlady in the kind of colourful language that would make my mother and her Baptist church cronies want to wash my mouth out with soap, but I don't take it. It would only make me grumpy.

"I'm Farlyed every day. The bitch is driving me mad."

"Let's do something about it then," she says.

"I can't say I haven't thought about it," I reply, "but I don't want to do the time."

Her smile widens into a grin. "There's more than one way to solve the problem and they don't all involve breaking the law."

I lean forward. "If you've got something in mind, I'd definitely like to hear it."

She hesitates and then says quickly, "My tenancy agreement runs out at the end of the month and I'm guessing yours does too, so why don't we kick the bedsit life to the curb and get a place together."

There's nothing I'd like more than to move in with her, but I'm wary about jumping forward in relationships. It so often leads to heartbreak. My first love, for instance. We were friends when we were kids, but as we got older my feelings towards her changed, and one crazy night, we ended up kissing in my bedroom. I loved the taste of her, the velvety softness of her lips, decided we were meant to be together. Unfortunately, she didn't feel the same. For her, it was just a moment of madness, a dead-end detour on the road to a hetero marriage. She distanced herself from me afterwards, acted like I'd forced her to kiss me, which I totally hadn't. She made me feel rejected, ashamed.

My life with Cathy has been great so far, but I've taken it slowly every step of the way. We met at the Freshers' Fair on my first day of uni and I spent months admiring her in secret before I plucked up the courage to tell her how I felt. I was super excited when she said she was into me too and we started going out, but I didn't let my raging hormones carry me away and it was ages before we made love. Now here we are at another threshold. Part of me thinks sharing a home with Cathy will ruin our relationship, that if she's around me too much she'll see things she doesn't like and decide she wants to break up, but waking up next to her every morning would be so amazing. I take another drink, considering the pros and cons. Then I look into her eyes again and my mind is made up. I bend across the table, planting a sloppy kiss on her cheek.

"Okay, let's do it." She claps her hands.

"You don't know how happy you've just made me. We should go back to my place right now and start looking for somewhere."

"No can do," I say with a sigh. "I've got to work soon."

She shrugs.

"I'll find some places myself then, and tomorrow we'll go look at them."

"Sounds good." I hold up my drink. "To co-habiting."

"Co-habiting," she echoes, raising her cup to mine. It feels like a new beginning, and I can't wait to see where it takes us. Mrs. Farly won't get a chance to wake me up tomorrow morning, because I'm going to be too excited to sleep.

***

My mouth falls open as we pass through the gates in the imposing wall to visit the third apartment of the afternoon. The building in front of us – the Royal Leopold Building - is like a fairytale palace - towers at the corners, a larger tower rising from the centre. It has a steep slate roof and architectural flourishes everywhere – spires, gabled windows on the upper floor, gargoyles shaped like dogs. Above the entrance, there's a statue of a man in a suit, who I presume must be the eponymous Leopold. It's beautiful, majestic and surely way out of our price range. I tap Cathy on the shoulder.

"Are you sure this is the right place?"

She holds up her phone, pointing at a picture of the building in a property listing on the screen.

"I'm sure. See for yourself." She's dressed to impress today in a black dress, woollen tights and a fitted jacket of blue velvet, while I'm in my smartest pencil skirt and a white blouse. We want the estate agents to take us seriously, so it seemed like a good call.

"Well, the rent you mentioned must be wrong," I say.

"It's not wrong. I checked with the agent when I booked to see it."

She sounds excited and I can totally relate. Living somewhere like this would be fan-fricking-tastic. It's too good to be true, though.

"So, what's the catch?"

"I wondered that myself, so I did a little research, and it turns out the place used to be an asylum." She taps at her phone, opening a website about the building and reading out snippets of information. "It opened in 1859 and was in active use until 1995. It says here a lot of inhumane shit went on in the early days – lobotomies, electrotherapy. The living conditions were terrible, and the staff used to beat their patients, so not a nice history. Factor in that it's got a reputation as one of the most haunted buildings in the country and the low rent figure starts to make sense. People just don't want to live here. It creeps them out."

I gaze up at the place, my hands on my hips. It looks peaceful

and inviting. I can hardly believe anything bad happened here.

"And what are your thoughts on the subject?"

She answers without hesitation.

"I'm fine with it. I don't believe in ghosts. What about you?"

As if on cue, someone screams. I jump, my eyes moving back and forward along the building, checking the windows. Is it a ghost, a restless spirit racked with pain as it's forced to relive some barbaric medical procedure?

Cathy taps my arm. I turn to see her watching me with a grin. "Take a chill pill, babe. This isn't a close encounter of the

spooky kind. It's just some kid having a moment." She jerks her thumb in the direction of the gate.

I look across and see an auburn-haired woman in jogging bottoms and a stripy t-shirt arguing with a little girl about going to a playground across the street. The girl's hair is auburn as well, so she's probably the woman's daughter. She stamps her foot and screams, and sure enough, it's the same sound I heard before.

"See?" Cathy says. "So, what do you say – do you think you'd be happy living in a possibly haunted ex-asylum?"

I shudder. I've always been more open to the idea of the supernatural than Cathy. Loads of people claim to have experienced it and they can't all be wrong, can they? And even if the building isn't haunted, it doesn't change the horrible things that happened in it. It is lovely, though – the kind of place I've always dreamed of living in. It would be idiotic to let my imagination stand in my way.

"Absolutely," I tell her.

She nods and we move on. There's a parking area in front of the building, where the estate agent we've come to meet is waiting – a pretty young woman with braided afro hair, almond shaped eyes and the kind of curvy body I'd die for. She's dressed in a tailored navy skirt suit and leaning against a white BMW, her legs crossed at the ankles, a folder tucked under one arm. She walks forward as she notices us, her full lips curling upwards in a friendly smile.

"Hi there. Are you Belle and Cathy?"

"We are," Cathy replies. "You must be Sylvia."

She offers her hand. "I am. From Curtis and Oak. It's lovely to meet you." We take turns shaking the outstretched hand and she gestures at the building.

"So, this is it – the Royal Leopold Building. The apartment's on the first floor. Shall we take a look?"

Cathy glances at the entrance eagerly. "That would be great."

Sylvia nods and sets off across the car park. We follow her to the front door, and she taps a code into a keypad to unlock it. We go inside and find ourselves in a large entrance hall. I'm expecting it to be dark and gloomy like the asylums I've read about in gothic novels, but it isn't at all. The walls are painted white, and it's filled with light from a pair of huge, latticed windows. It has a vaulted ceiling supported by arching columns – some freestanding, others built into the walls – and a black and white checkerboard floor. There are doors to either side of us and a set of double doors ahead.

Sylvia leads the way through the door to the right and onwards up a winding staircase. The décor is white here as well with old black and white photographs of the building hung at intervals along the walls. I pause to look at one – women and men in posh Victorian clothes standing outside the front door between a pair of British flags. Printed at the bottom are the words 'GRAND OPENING 1859'. It's a single point in time, but I get a real sense of the people I'm looking at – the pomposity of one, the awkwardness of another. So relatable. It's weird to think not one of them's still alive.

I hurry onwards, joining the others on the landing above. Cathy slips her hand into mine. "Isn't it great?"

I nod as Sylvia leads us along a long corridor. It's light and airy, the wall on one side lined with windows looking down on a picturesque courtyard – rectangular with a grass border and a fountain at the centre. The other wall has numbered doors along it – apartments I suppose. We turn a corner, pass another stairwell. I'm going to need a map of this place if we do move in, or I'll end up getting lost. My sense of directions terrible. When I started uni I kept being late for lectures because I couldn't find the rooms. If it hadn't been for Cathy – wonderful, reliable Cathy – and her texted directions, I might not have got to them at all.

At last Sylvia stops at one of the doors – white wood with the number twenty-four on it in brass.

"This is it." She unlocks it with a key on a Curtis and Oak fob and we go inside. It's way nicer than the other two apartments we've seen today, like something out of *Good Housekeeping* magazine – exposed floorboards, magnolia walls. I give Cathy's hand an excited squeeze. I can so picture us living here.

"As you can see, you get a lot for your money. If I was looking for a place right now, I'd probably snap it up myself. Let me show you around." says Sylvia as she leads us along a hallway into an open plan room which is at least five times bigger than my bedsit at Mrs. Farly's. The right side is a living area with a plush beige corner sofa and a couple of armchairs arranged around a cast iron stove and wall-mounted TV. The rest is divided into a workspace with an antique leather top desk and two bookshelves, and a pine furnished dining area. There are three tall windows overlooking a park, and beyond the dining area, I can see part of a spacious kitchen through a serving hatch and door. Sylvia goes to one of the windows and gestures around her.

"As you can see, it's mainly open plan and has a stunning view. There's a homely feel, but it's also ideal for entertaining. The furnishings and fittings are top quality and the layout's very user friendly. In fact, I don't have a bad word to say about it."

Cathy grins. "I'll bet you say that about all your properties."

Sylvia holds up her hands. "Guilty as charged, but I actually mean it about this one. Take a look; see for yourselves how great it is."

We walk around, taking it all in. Cathy nudges me and points at the sofa.

"That sofa looks super comfy - perfect for snuggling up together on cold winter nights."

"Perfect," I agree. I take a minute to imagine it – the two of us wrapped in a warm blanket, Cathy's eyes sparkling in the firelight, our lips coming together for a kiss. It makes me feel warm and tingly inside. I turn away quickly as my imagination starts to build the kiss into something steamy, moving to the desk to distract myself. I can totally see myself writing gothic fiction essays there. An old desk in an ex-asylum – could there be a better environment?

Sylvia takes us back to the hallway where there's a second entrance to the kitchen and two other doors leading to the bedroom and bathroom. She shows us each room in turn, and the more I see, the more I want to make the place my home. It has a four-poster bed with gossamer drapes, a Smeg oven, a whirlpool bath – everything we need.

While we're looking at the bathroom, I suddenly feel the need to pee.

"Do you mind if I test the facilities?" I ask.

Sylvia looks confused, so I jerk my head in the direction of the toilet.

She chuckles. "Oh, I see. Be my guest. We'll wait for you in the main room." Cathy kisses me on the cheek, and they go out.

When I'm done peeing, I turn to the sink to wash my hands. I yelp as I look in the mirror, because there are two reflections looking back at me – my own and someone else's. She's about ten years older than me with deathly pale skin, sunken eyes and dull red hair hanging over her shoulder in a thick braid. She has no makeup on and is dressed in a coarse white slip with the words 'ROYAL LEOPOLD AYSLUM' embroidered across the front in bold black letters. Her outline flickers and I realize that I can see straight through her.

My head swivels around. There's no one in the room behind me, yet I see her still in the glass.

Ghost! My brain shrieks the word, and I start to freak out. I back away, shaking my head as the woman in the mirror steps to the side and our reflections merge. My temperature plummets like I've stepped out into a blizzard with no clothes on. She raises her arms, and they pass through the mirror, reaching towards me. Her hands lock around my neck. They might look insubstantial, but they don't feel it. They're bony, clammy and impossibly strong, dragging me towards her. I brace myself expecting my head to bump into the mirror, but the glass is like liquid, and it goes straight through.

I scream and struggle as she drags me further in, but she won't let go. Then it isn't just her I'm fighting, but the mirror itself. It's like some nightmarish version of Mrs. Farly's vacuum cleaner sucking me in. My feet lift off the floor and I plunge through the glass, unable to stop myself.

I'm in darkness now, plummeting downwards to God knows where. I feel the hands of the ghost still locked around me, but I can't see her. I'm dizzy, disoriented, no longer sure if I'm awake or dreaming.

Then there's a jolt and I find myself in the woman's body. I know I'm her, because I can see her plaited hair draped across my chest and I'm wearing that awful slip. I try to scream, but I can't. I'm seeing through her eyes, feeling what she feels, but I have no autonomy, no control.

As if that isn't bad enough, I'm in some kind of cell, presumably in the Royal Leopold Building in its asylum days – padded walls, a metal door with a grille in the middle. There are no windows, and the only piece of furniture is a cast iron bed, bolted to the floor. A light shines faintly through the grille in the door, but otherwise, the room is in darkness. It's cold too, so cold I can't stop shivering.

I hear footsteps outside and my body tenses. A key turns in the lock, bolts are drawn back, and the door flies open. Two women storm into the room – faces red with anger. They're nurses going by their clothes – black dresses, white aprons, white caps. One is elderly with a face like a prune and wiry grey hair wound into a bun. The other has brown hair and is built like a female wrestler – her body stout, her arms and legs at least three times wider than my own. Not the kind of person you want to mess with.

The older one is holding a lantern – brass with a circular lens protruding from one side and a swinging handle. She lifts it up, shining the beam in my face.

"What are you doing out of bed?"

I hear myself answer with a dignified defiance which is not my own. "I can't sleep. It's freezing in here."

The nurse looks irritated. "There's nothing we can do about that, I'm afraid. The heating system isn't working again."

"Can I at least have another blanket?" I ask.

"The one you have is perfectly adequate. Now get back in there." She points at the bed imperiously.

I fold my arms, locking eyes with her. "You can't treat me like this. I'm Lady—"

The stout woman's palm slams into my cheek, knocking me to the side. My face throbs. She shoves me toward the bed.

"Who you were before is irrelevant. In here, you're nobody, just another patient. Now do as you're told and get into bed."

Still, I stand motionless. The nurse raises her hand. "Do you want another one?"

She looks like she'll beat me to death if I go on resisting, so I'm forced to back down. I trudge across to the bed and lie down on it. It's deeply uncomfortable – the mattress lumpy, the frame sagging in the middle. I pull the blanket up. It's barely long enough to cover me and does little to shut out the cold. I try rolling onto my side and pulling my knees up to my chest, but it doesn't help much.

Nursezilla gives a satisfied nod. "That's more like it. We'll be back to check on you later, and I'll warn you now – if you give us any more trouble, it'll be the worst for you. Do you understand?"

I hide my head beneath the blanket, not answering.

"I asked you a question," she snaps, stomping across to the bed and grabbing my braid to force me to look at her.

I yelp, eyes watering. "I understand."

She gives a final yank on my hair and lets me go. "Good. Now go to sleep."

The two women leave the room. I shudder as the door shuts behind them. There's a finality to it, a sense that my liberty's been stolen away. My thoughts buzz, trying to make sense of what's happening. I'm sure it's a dream, but it doesn't feel like one. It feels like I'm wide awake and it's my life before that was the dream. Imagine if my lovely Cathy only existed in my mind. I couldn't bear it. I toss on the bed as the woman I've become tries to get comfortable. She can't get warm, but eventually, she starts to drift off to sleep, pulling me with her.

Then the nurses come back, stomping noisily up to the door and bursting into the room. The older one shines her lantern at the bed to make sure I'm where I'm supposed to be. I feel resentment burning in the ghost woman, but we don't speak.

The nurse with the lantern turns to Nursezilla. "It looks like she's finally settled. Let's move on." She doesn't bother to lower her voice, so if they hadn't woken me up before, they sure as hell would have now.

They leave again, closing the door with a bang. The ghost woman tries to get back to sleep, but it's useless. Every time we get close, something disturbs us – footsteps outside, nurses looking in on us, screaming and shouting from elsewhere in the building.

As for me, my mind's all over the place, trying to make sense of the situation. If it is just a dream, I wish to God it would end. I feel like the walls are closing in on me, like the terrible cold is sinking down into my bones and will never leave.

Suddenly there's a flash – a dazzling flare of light which seems to come from all around me. Then I'm my own person again, falling through darkness for what feels like hours, but is probably just a few seconds. I land back in the ghost woman's body, only it's somewhere else now – a tiled room with barred windows and five freestanding baths, where women are being washed by pairs of nurses. It's daytime, but the windows are covered in a layer of grime which keeps out most of the light.

It's as cold here as it was in my cell and the water in the baths must be cold too as the women in them look freezing – their teeth chattering, their bodies covered in goosebumps. The nurses are dressed like the ones I saw earlier with their sleeves rolled up to the elbows and are scrubbing at the patients roughly with bars of soap and grubby cloths. There's none of the compassion you'd expect to see in people in their profession. Most look bored, while a few actually seem to be taking pleasure in the distress they are causing – sadistic bitches.

More women are waiting to replace the ones in the baths in a long line which snakes backwards and forwards across the room, and I am among these. We are wearing nothing but asylum slips and my feet are numb from standing on the icy floor. The thought of getting into one of those baths – being stripped of my clothes and my dignity – makes me want to run away screaming, but there's no chance of that. Each patient in the line is manacled at the ankle to four others by a length of chain and there are nurses guarding us. The nurses stride up and down like patrolling soldiers, their mouths tight, their eyes watchful.

I scowl as I spot Nursezilla. As if this situation isn't bad enough without running into her again. She notices me looking at her and seems to take it as a challenge. Her eyes narrow and she comes towards me. Thankfully, a woman in the line ahead starts screaming and shaking her head.

"You're not putting me in one of those bloody baths! They've got vitriol in them. You want to burn us, hurt—"

Before she can finish, Nursezilla comes up behind her, thumping her on the back of the head.

"Stop shrieking. You know the rules – every patient has a morning bath. You might be dirty in mind, but you're damn well not going to be dirty in body."

The patient glares at her, fists clenched.

"Is there something else you'd like to say?" Nursezilla asks, arching an eyebrow.

The woman opens her mouth to speak and then thinks better of it. She shakes her head.

"I didn't think so," says Nursezilla, turning away.

The rest of us go very quiet, doing our best not to draw attention to ourselves in case we end up getting hit as well. For a moment, the only sound is the splashing of water. Then the nurses on washing duty decide their patients are sufficiently clean and order them out of the baths. I watch the nearest one as she stands before us naked and shivering, water dripping from her body onto the tiles around her. She looks vacant, broken – her eyes downcast, her shoulders hunched. She's in her thirties I'd say, but her blonde hair is lifeless and thinning, and her face is drawn. She's so thin, I can see every rib through her sallow skin, and her body is covered with angry sores.

She stares into space as the nurses dry her off with a threadbare towel. She allows them to raise her arms and tilt her head, but other than that she doesn't move. It's horrible to see – a pale reflection of a human being, a living mannequin. Do all the patients in this place end up like that? Will I? No, of course not, because I'm dreaming and any second I'm going to wake up. Except I don't.

The nurses finish drying the woman and lead her to a shelving unit piled high with neatly folded clothes, where two of their colleagues are waiting - a lanky woman with black hair flecked with grey and oval-lensed glasses balanced precariously on the end of a pointed nose, and a woman who looks like she should still be in school with plaited pigtails and pimples dotting her face. The first two nurses leave the patient with these others and return to the baths. The lanky nurse grabs a chemise of coarse dark cotton from one of the shelves and dresses the patient in it. She puts a white linen dress over the top of it and a pair of cotton booties on the woman's feet. None of it fits properly, but the woman doesn't complain.

The process is repeated for the patients from the other baths and the younger nurse chains them together at the ankles. Then she walks them to the door and knocks on it three times. Two more nurses enter. They lead the women out into the corridor and the door swings closed.

Meanwhile, the nurses at the baths are getting the next batch of patients ready for washing – unfastening manacles, pulling off slips. One of these women looks like she's going to kick off at any second, glaring at the pair of nurses who have taken charge of her. She's almost as big as Nursezilla with pale skin and freckles all over her body. She lets the nurses lead her to a bath, but as they order her to get in, her temper gets the better of her. She folds her arms.

"No, you're not doing it to me today."

I don't blame her. Not only is the water in her bath clearly cold, but it looks filthy from the women who have been in before. They should be changing it each time someone gets out.

One of the nurses – brown haired and brown eyed with chubby cheeks – points at the bath. "It's not open for debate. Get in."

The patient shakes her head. "I will not."

Nursezilla whirls around, locking eyes with the woman across the room.

"I'm going to count to five and if you're not in that bath by then, I'm coming over. One... Two..."

The woman holds out until four, before lowering her eyes and climbing gingerly into the water. She looks miserable, angry, but what choice does she have? The nurses begin to scour her with soap and a cloth, and Nursezilla resumes her patrolling.

There are two more groups of women ahead of me. I watch the nurses manhandle them into the baths with a hatred I haven't felt before. How can they treat us like this? We're human beings for fuck's sake. I'm hoping desperately to wake up before my turn comes, but it doesn't happen. The manacle is removed from my ankle and a pair of nurses pull me towards one of the baths – one auburn haired with close set eyes, high cheek bones and a wiry body; the other blonde and stout with a uniform which looks to be at least two sizes too small. I don't want to think about how many other patients have been in the water before me, the icky skin conditions they might have been suffering from. If it were up to me, I'd be screaming in protest, trying to scratch out the nurses' eyes, but the ghost woman does none of that. Sure, she's pissed off. I can feel her anger and indignation straining for release, but fear is holding them back – a burning dread, not just of being clouted by Nursezilla, but of the long-term consequences of disobedience.

We offer no resistance as the wiry nurse pulls off our slip, step obediently towards the bath, but then we stop, staring down into the murky water.

The nurse prods me in the ribs with a bony finger. "What are you waiting for?"

To my surprise, I don't move. Maybe the ghost hasn't lost her spirit after all. I look the nurse in the eye, speaking in a pleading voice, "Could you at least change the water?"

The nurse shakes her head. "As you well know, you're all treated the same. If the water was good enough for everyone else, it's good enough for you! Now move."

The stout one reaches for my arm, but I step into the bath of my own accord, grimacing as I do so, every muscle in my body clenching in disgust. It's totally gross – a sickly brown colour with hairs, fluff and I hate to think what else floating on the surface – and even colder than I was expecting – the kind of cold that takes your breath away, makes you forget what it feels like to be warm. My body quakes convulsively, my fingers and toes go numb.

The nurses bend over me, rubbing soap into my body. They're brisk and rough, but I let them get on with it. I guess the ghost woman is too browbeaten to fight them or just wants it over with as quickly as possible. They use the same soap to clean my hair, yanking painfully as they work it through the tangles. The next thing I know they're dunking my head to wash it off. It happens so fast, I don't manage to close my mouth and end up swallowing some of the awful water, which makes me want to puke my guts up. For one terrible instant, I think they're going to hold me under until I drown, but they don't. My head breaks the surface again and the larger nurse pulls me into a standing position, so she can look me over. With the water as it is, I'm sure I must be dirtier than I was before, but she seems satisfied.

"You'll do, I suppose. Out you get." She claps her hands, and I get out of the bath, almost slipping over on the wet tiles in my haste.

The nurses rub at me with a towel. It's soaked through from drying other women, but they somehow manage to make it feel abrasive on my skin. When they're done, they lead me to the shelves of clothes. Instinct makes me want to hunch over, hide my nakedness with my hands, but that isn't how the ghost woman rolls. She keeps us straight as we walk, staring straight ahead with proud defiance.

I'm given a set of clothes like the patient I was watching earlier. They're clean and neatly folded, but that's about all I can say for them. The material's thin and they stink of whatever chemicals were used to wash them.

The lanky nurse in the oval-lensed glasses gestures at the clothes. "Put them on... or do you need help?"

I eye her coldly, "Absolutely not. I'm perfectly capable of dressing myself." This show of backbone is gratifying to see and thankfully the nurse lets it slide. I give the clothes a final disparaging look and then put them on. The chemise is too small, the dress is too large, and they're both itchy as hell, but at least they help with the cold.

The women from the other baths are given clothes as well, and the nurse with the pigtails chains us together again. Then she escorts us to the door, where two nurses from outside take charge of us – one tall with narrow eyes and mousy hair in a tight bun: the other also tall, but older with deep set wrinkles around her eyes and a snub nose. They open the door and march us out. I stare at the corridor as we go. I'm sure it's one I walked along earlier with Cathy and the estate agent... no, it wasn't earlier, was it? Our visit hasn't happened yet. Will it ever? Was I really there in that distant future? I'm starting to doubt it. The memories are becoming more and more remote.

We stop at a door labelled seventeen – metal with a sturdy looking lock, bolts at the top and bottom and a grille in the middle. The snub-nosed nurse takes out a bunch of keys. She turns one of them in the lock and draws back the bolts, while the other nurse removes the manacle from the woman beside me. They shove her into the cell and the snub nosed one locks the door again. Then we move away, walking up a staircase and onwards to another door, this time with the number eighty-seven on it. As before the snub-nosed woman unlocks it.

The cell beyond is mine – I'm certain. I'll never forget those padded walls, that hard bed. The narrow-eyed nurse releases my ankle and pushes me forward. I cling to the doorframe, looking back at her.

"I don't want to be here."

The snub-nosed nurse smiles at me encouragingly – the first bit of kindness I've seen.

"You won't be here long. Doctor Elliot is making his rounds and once you've seen him, we'll take you to the common room."

I roll my eyes, "I'm not talking about the cell. I mean I don't want to be in this place."

The narrow-eyed nurse plants her hand in the small of my back and forces me the rest of the way into the cell.

"We'll have none of this nonsense. This is your home for as long as your madness lasts, so get used to it."

They lock the door, and I hear their footsteps retreat into the distance. I sit down on the bed. There's a wall light on now – gas I think – but it's still dim and nasty. I'm not mad yet, but if I stay in this place much longer, I damn soon will be. I think of Cathy – the day we met at the Freshers' Fair, studying together in Costa Coffee, our first kiss. God, I wish I was with her. I need to hold her, hear her tell me everything's going to be okay. I feel so alone.

The door opens. I look around to see a slender man in a grey three-piece suit enter the room – Doctor Elliot I presume. His hair is black, and he has a neatly trimmed beard and moustache. A gold watch chain dangles across the front of his waistcoat and he's wearing glasses of the half-moon type. He gives me a genial smile, and ridiculous as it is in the circumstances, I feel myself relax a little. He closes the door, and I hear it being locked by someone outside.

"Good morning. How are you feeling today?"

I wrap my arms around my knees, clutching them to my chest.

"Cold and depressed. The way you treat people here is an outrage. How are *you* feeling?"

"Capital," he replies.

"Of course you are," I say bitterly. "There's no reason why you shouldn't be, is there? You're not incarcerated like I am. When the day is done, the door will open, and you'll stride off home."

He nods. "Indeed, I will... because I'm sound of mind."

"So am I," I say firmly.

He places a hand on my forehead, checking my temperature. "That's not true, I'm afraid. Your husband caught you engaging in degeneracy with another woman. People of sound mind don't behave like that."

This statement makes me mad as hell, so I'm pleased when the ghost woman challenges him on it.

"How can an act of love between two consenting adults be degenerate?"

"It isn't an act of love when the two adults are female," he replies. "It's tribadism. Can I see your tongue please?"

Indignant as the ghost woman is, we poke our tongue out obediently. Doctor Elliot leans over to look at it, jotting something down in a pocketbook.

"You're what we term an introvert. We're still trying to ascertain how you became this way, but my preliminary opinion is that it was a combination of hysteria, menstrual issues and hypertrophy of the clitoris." He pauses to check my pulse, pressing his fingers against my wrist and making some more notes in his book.

I wish it was me calling the shots and not the ghost woman, because I want so much to give this idiot a piece of my mind. I know people in the past had some messed-up ideas about queerness, but to have them articulated like this is more than I can stand. Is that really why the ghost woman's here – for being attracted to her own sex?

"The good news is there's an excellent chance of recovery with the right treatment," Doctor Elliot goes on.

My lip twists disparagingly.

"Hydrotherapy, you mean? Smearing borax solution between my legs." I don't know what these things are myself, but I can tell by the way the ghost women says them, they aren't pleasant

"That's your program at present," he says, "but there are plenty of other things we can try. We're about to start trialling electrotherapy and you could be one of the first beneficiaries. It's a new treatment, which I have very high hopes for. Other options are a clitoridectomy to stop abnormal arousal of your pudendal nerve, and the removal of your ovaries, which will certainly produce results if your condition is related to menstruation as I suspect."

And he says lesbians are mad! How can he even contemplate such brutality? It's monstrous. The ghost woman thinks so too. I can feel the anger rising inside her. She doesn't let it show, though. She's too afraid of what will happen.

I stare at the floor, shaking my head. "I don't belong here."

"You most certainly do," he tells me. "This place was built for troubled souls like you. You're fortunate your husband brought you here. He must love you very much."

"You wouldn't think so if you knew how he treats me," I say.

The words trigger a memory which is not my own. I'm sitting on a window seat in a loose-fitting dress of peach silk, embroidering a band of leaves and flowers onto a man's hat – cylinder shaped and made of red velvet. The room I'm in has a stately home vibe to it. It's high ceilinged and filled with expensive looking furnishings – dark wood chairs with embroidered upholstery, Asian vases which are almost as tall as I am, a chaise lounge, a brass clock adorned with mythological figures. The walls are lined with portraits of people in old-fashioned clothes and there is a marble fireplace at one end with a log fire crackling on the hearth.

These details get steadily clearer until suddenly they aren't just in my mind anymore; I'm actually there, the wan light of a winter sun slanting across my face as it edges towards the horizon, my fingers working deftly at the needlework on my lap. The embroidery is way beyond what the real me would have been able to manage with the rudimentary sewing skills I learned from my mother, but here it's easy, every stitch landing in just the right place.

I reach the end of my thread and am just about to replace it with a new piece from a wooden sewing box on a table beside me, when I hear whinnying and the clatter of hooves from outside.

I raise my eyes to the window. There's a man riding along the driveway leading to the house on a glossy black horse. He's in his forties I'd say – shorter than average, but bulky with dark hair and sideburns speckled with grey. He's smartly dressed in a black woollen jacket, tan jodhpurs and a top hat, but his outfit's dishevelled and smeared with mud. He looks angry – his cheeks flushed, his back rigid. He steers his horse around a fountain – stone with a mermaid and other mythical sea creatures rising from the middle – and stops at the front door.

A boy with blond hair and buck teeth appears from a building to the side and jogs forward to meet him – presumably a groom or some such, dressed in a white shirt, black trousers and a flat cap. He takes hold of the horse's bridle.

The man dismounts, but his right foot gives way as it touches the floor and he stumbles to the side, grasping his saddle for support. He bends over and prods at his ankle, his face darkening. It's an expression I know well, the same one my mother had when I told her I was gay and she started screeching about sin and how I was a disgrace to our family - the look people get when they've lost control, when white hot rage has burnt away rational thought.

He raises his riding crop high in the air, his arm quivering.

"Blasted animal. Look what you've done." He looks pointedly at his ankle. "The damnable thing's probably broken. You could have easily cleared that hedge, but no! You had to show the white feather and throw me over your head. I'm going to be laid up for the Lord knows how long now, not to mention being the laughing stock of the county."

I know what's coming next and the thought of it makes me sick. He's going to hit it. I want to scream out the window at him, tell him to leave it alone, but just like in the asylum earlier, my body won't obey me.

The riding crop comes down on the horse's flank. It grunts in shock, pulling away from him. Its eyes are wide, and its nostrils are flaring. He continues to shout at it, punctuating each sentence with another lash.

"I can see them now, sniggering away as I hit the ground. I suppose you thought it was funny to hurt me. Well, let's see how you like it."

The horse shrieks and whinnies as he hits it again and again. It's horrible. It's also pointless. How's the horse going to know what it's being punished for so long after the event? It's not as if it can understand what he's saying.

As the man's wife I should be doing something about this and suddenly I am - ripping open the door and rushing out. I run along a corridor, holding up the hem of my dress to keep from tripping over. I emerge into an imposing hallway – wood panelled with a split staircase leading up to the next floor, paintings on the walls and a crystal chandelier hanging from the ceiling – and see the front door to my left. It seems to take forever, but eventually I reach it and hurry out to the drive. The assault on the horse is still going on. This woman I've become is afraid of the man before her – who I know somehow is her lawfully wedded husband – but she doesn't let it deter her and we run towards him, holding out a hand, "No, Archibald." I manage to get between my husband and the horse, but it doesn't stop him and it's me being whipped then. I scream in pain and outrage, the crop biting into my face and shoulder.

Then in a flash of light I'm somewhere else – seated at a dressing table – mahogany or something similar with tapering legs and brass handles - looking at the ghost woman's reflection in an oval mirror as a maid in a black dress and white apron brushes my hair. It's the same hair I've had throughout this bizarre experience, only now it's silky and thick, gleaming faintly in the light of two candles burning in a gilded wall sconce. I'm dressed in a nightgown with an embroidered bodice trimmed with ribbons and lace, and a pair of silk slippers. Again, the room I'm in is richly furnished – tapestries on the walls, a couple of chairs with velvet cushions by another marble fireplace, an elaborately carved closet with full-length mirrors on the doors. I can see a bedroom through a door, which probably makes this my dressing room.

The rhythmic movements of the brush through my hair are soothing, pleasurable. I feel almost relaxed, until suddenly, the door bursts open and Archibald the wife beater plunges in. He's wearing a dressing gown of crimson brocade and holding a bundle of papers. He grabs the maid by the shoulder and shoves her towards the door. "Out!"

She curtsies awkwardly and scurries away, closing the door behind her.

Archibald waves the papers in my face. "Look what came in today's post - invoices for dresses, jewellery, hats, shoes – a fortune's worth." He hauls me to my feet and shakes me furiously, his fingers digging into my arms. "What the devil were you thinking spending so much? I'm not made of money."

I start to feel dizzy, my teeth knocking together as he continues to manhandle me.

"Idiot woman!" he shouts. "Have you nothing to say for yourself?"

I never find out the answer to this, because the room disappears in another flash of light. I'm in a corridor now - panelled walls, doors to either side. There are candles burning in sconces at intervals, but they don't give much light. I'm dressed exactly as I was in the last place and am creeping towards one of the doors.

I stop in front of it, pressing my ear to the surface. I hear sex sounds from the other side – groaning, the creaking of wood. I open it a little and peer through the crack. Archibald is straddling a girl on a four-poster bed. She's a little younger than me by the looks of it and a hell of a lot younger than him – slim and delicate with wavy blonde hair. The real me has never seen her before, but the ghost woman knows her to be a scullery maid called Nancy.

Archibald means nothing to me, yet I feel jealous, betrayed, the ghost woman's emotions coursing through me. I lean against the wall, my breath coming in bursts, and there's another flash, another change of scene.

I'm in a horse-drawn carriage now, hurtling along a country lane. It's raining heavily, the water drumming on the roof, inky clouds scudding across the sky above. I'm travelling to or from an event by the looks of it, dressed in a low-cut gown of turquoise silk and a green cloak trimmed with floral lace, my hair pinned on top of my head in an elaborate style. The gown has a rigid skirt, so I'm having to perch on the edge of my seat, clinging to the armrest beside me to keep myself steady as we bounce repeatedly over bumps and potholes.

I have about thirty seconds to process all of this; then Archibald's hand hits my face. He's sitting opposite me in a black three-piece suit with tailcoat jacket, his face crimson with anger. He gestures down at himself, and I notice the front of his shirt has a red stain across it.

"Look at my shirt. It's ruined. Sometimes your clumsiness beggar's belief – spilling wine all over me like that, making a spectacle of us!"

He slaps me again. My skin burns painfully, and I feel a trickle of blood at the side of my mouth. I'm desperate to hit him back, but I pull away instead, cowering against the side of the carriage. Another blow connects, but this time there's a flare of light instead of pain.

Then I find myself in a conservatory – plate glass panels fitted into a cast iron frame with a sloping ceiling rising to a cupola at the centre. The room is crammed with exotic plants – pots of flowers and citrus trees, palms and ferns in beds, jasmine and honeysuckle climbing up wires and dangling from the rafters. It's daytime and the sun is shining fiercely through the glass.

I'm sitting on a wicker chair in a dress of navy silk with puffy sleeves. There's a table in front of me with tea-things on it – silver service, porcelain plates and cups decorated with birds and flowers, an assortment of cakes – and on the other side of this table is a woman.

The moment I see her, everything else fades into obscurity. She's the ghost woman's age and reminds me of Cathy – petite with a graceful neck, high cheekbones and eyes the colour of the ocean. She has wavy blonde hair heaped on top of her head in a braided bun and is wearing a dress like my own, only white with a repeating pattern of purple flowers. She likes purple flowers - I know this from the ghost woman – and they look great on her. Actually, everything about her looks great. I wish I had my phone, so I could take a picture of her.

She makes me feel breathless, hot. I know on some level these feelings aren't my own, but they're still overwhelming.

She's sitting down, studying me over the rim of a teacup. She seems concerned, eyes tight, brow creased.

"That cheek of yours looks frightful. Are you going to tell me what happened?"

I raise a hand to my face. It's swollen on one side, throbbing painfully beneath my fingers.

I have a flashback to the incident in the carriage and am immediately certain that this was the cause, but I don't tell her.

"I fell down the stairs. It was my own fault. One of my bootlaces was loose and I tripped over it."

It sounds plausible, but she doesn't believe it.

"It was that husband of yours, wasn't it? Infernal man! He ought to be hanged for the horrors he subjects you to."

"No," I say. "Archibald would never—"

She puts her cup down on its saucer with a bang and stands up, shaking her head.

"Don't waste your breath denying it. We've been friends since we were children. I know when you're lying." She turns away, staring into the distance. "It makes me apoplectic to think of you having to live with someone like that. You deserve someone who makes you happy, someone who respects you, loves you, someone like..."

She trails off, facing me again and tentatively touching my face. It's meant to be soothing, yet it awakens something in the ghost woman, something which has been dormant for years – desire. She tells herself it's wrong, tries to suppress it, but it won't be denied.

I take hold of the woman's hand, trembling, and press it to my lips. Her skin is soft and smells like lavender. I kiss it softly again and again.

She gasps, her cheeks flushing, but she doesn't stop me. Quite the opposite, in fact. She takes me by the arms, drawing me to my feet and pulling me close to her. Our eyes meet and suddenly we're kissing.

It's fumbling, awkward and totally wonderful. I want it to go on forever, but it ends abruptly, light exploding around me once again, and fading away to reveal a meadow – gently swaying grass dotted with daisies, poppies and other flowers. There's a stream trickling through a copse to one side, rolling hills and a distant village to the other. The sun's bright and the air is filled with birdsong and the chirrup of crickets.

I'm hand-in-hand with the woman from the conservatory, pushing through the long grass. We're wearing wide dresses – cream for me, pale pink for her – and straw bonnets. I don't know what she's just said, but it's made me laugh. I'm happy. I want to spend the rest of my life with this woman, love her with every fibre of her body and soul. She makes me feel special, adored.

Even as I'm thinking this, there are more flashes in quick succession, each one taking us to a new shared moment. Sometimes we're the age we are now, embroidering at home or going for walks; other times we're younger – playing hide and seek in the rambling house where I grew up, brushing each other's hair, climbing into bed together on a stormy night because I was too scared to be alone.

I see the first time we made love as well. We're in bed again, but this time we're adults, naked and quivering with desire. I'm nervous, telling myself over and over that we shouldn't be doing it, but how can it be wrong when she feels so divine? We're kissing, touching each other, and it's making me wild. I've felt this way myself with Cathy many times, but for the ghost woman it's a whole new experience. Her hateful husband has never given her pleasure like this or any pleasure at all, just brief trysts which were all about him and his gratification.

The scene disappears in another flash and for a few seconds we're walking along a beach. The flashes keep coming, but my view is changing now. In each new place I'm seeing her from further and further away as if something is separating us. The light of my life keeps retreating into the distance until she's just a speck. Then she's gone completely.

I close my eyes, wanting to scream and cry, because it feels like I've lost a part of myself and will never get it back. Finally, I look around and find I'm back on my bed in the asylum with Doctor Elliot standing over me. He's going on and on about how they're going to cure me, which makes me feel ever worse. I'll never see my lover again unless my feelings for her are driven out of me and life without those feelings wouldn't be worth living. It's not fair. We're not criminals or deviants. We're just two people who make each other happy.

The doctor leaves the room, and I feel the bleakness of the ghost woman's existence closing around me like an icy fist, making the room feel a million times colder than it did before. She sees only two futures – to live out the rest of her days in this terrible place or to be released into the care of a man she hates who will continue to knock her about until he inflicts an injury that she can't recover from – and she can't face either of them.

I lift up the hem of my dress and begin to tear strips of cotton from my chemise using the edge of the bed to help me. I tie the strips together to form a makeshift rope and tie a noose at one end of it. The other end I hang from a pipe above me – part of the heating system, I think. It might be broken, but it's not entirely useless it turns out. I step up onto the bed and put my head through the noose.

No, it's not me doing this; it's the ghost woman! I'm not really here. My life's in the future and any minute I'm going back to it. I have to be, but what if I don't? What if this body I'm in kills itself with me still inside and I die too?

I try to stop what's happening, to get back down from the bed, but I'm as powerless as ever, can only watch as I take a deep breath and launch myself into the air...

I'm expecting to feel the rope pull taut, to hear the crack of my neck breaking, but I don't. I fall for a moment and then land back in my own body in the bathroom of the apartment where this crazy experience started. I can't believe I was considering renting it. There's no way I can live here now. I'd like to pass off what I've just seen as nightmare or hallucination, but it's not happening. I was really there in the ghost woman's past. I know this without a doubt, because she's still with me, sharing my body the way I shared hers.

I'm kneeling limply on the floor, my shoulder pressed against the bowl of the toilet, my head lolling to the side. Although I've been aware the whole time, I guess in physical terms I must have passed out. I've got cramp in my legs, so I wriggle them around, grimacing at the prickling discomfort of the returning blood.

There's a knock at the door and I hear Cathy's voice.

"Belle, are you okay? You've been in there ages."

Simple words, but the sound of them fills me with a mad joy. I thought I was never going to see her again, but here she is. Things can go back to normal. I can't wait to hug her, kiss her, tell her how much I love her.

How lucky I am to have been born in this time, how utterly, unquestionably blessed. Things aren't perfect, but you can be with another person of the same gender and most people are fine with it. They don't see it as unnatural, something which needs to be cured with electricity, freezing water and Christ knows what else.

I let out a long breath, speaking to the presence inside my head. "You poor, poor woman," I mean it too. There's a bond between us, a kinship. If I'd been born in her time, I could easily have ended up in the asylum with her.

"Belle?" Cathy calls again. "Open the door." She sounds a little panicked.

I start to get to my feet, but halfway up, my body stops listening to me and the ghost woman takes control. It shouldn't be possible, not here, not now. I fight against her, but she holds me down. She's stronger than I am, hungrier for life, because she's been without it for so long.

Then suddenly, she isn't just subduing me, she's forcing me out, taking my place. It's like falling into a river on its final approach to a waterfall. Swimming against the current does nothing. I'm swept onwards, closer and closer to the edge.

No! I shriek the word in my head, but it doesn't help, and I'm flung upwards into the air. It's such a brutal sensation that I'm sure it's my body moving, but no. That's exactly where it was, standing by the door, and I'm floating above it – a ghost before my time.

Cathy knocks again. "Belle, I swear if you don't tell me you're okay in the next two seconds I'm going to kick the door down."

The ghost woman unlocks the door and pushes it open. "I'm okay."

Surely Cathy will know the person in front of her isn't me, but she gives no sign of it. She steps forward, kissing the ghost woman's cheek.

"Thank God for that. Why weren't you answering?"

The ghost woman shudders. "It's this place. I don't like it. Can we go?"

Cathy backs out into the hallway. "What's not to like? This apartment's amazing." She extends her arms, turning around on the spot. "Just look at it."

I drop downwards, hovering in front of her face, trying to talk to her. *That thing you're with isn't me. I've been replaced.*

She doesn't hear me, looks straight through me as the ghost woman speaks again.

"The furnishings are pleasant enough I daresay, but not the atmosphere. I can feel the echoes of the appalling things that happened here all around me."

How can Cathy think that's me? She doesn't talk like me, holds herself differently.

Cathy sighs. "It's your imagination, Belle. That stuff I said earlier is getting to you. Why don't we have another look around? I'm sure if you stay here a bit longer the feeling will pass."

"I've been here long enough already," the ghost woman says, "it feels like an eternity."

Cathy looks at her and then throws up her hands. "Fine. If you feel that strongly about it, I'm not going to argue, but I think it's the wrong decision. Think about Mrs. Farly and her vacuum. We move into this place and they're a thing of the past."

The ghost woman probably has no idea what a vacuum is and certainly doesn't know Mrs. Farly, but she covers it well.

"I'd rather endure a thousand nights with Mrs. Farly than spend a single night here."

Cathy nods. "Say no more." She turns to Sylvia, who is waiting a little way down the hall. "I think we'll have to pass on this one. Is there anything else you can show us?"

Sylvia sighs as if she's used to people turning the apartment down. "Of course. Let's go back to my car and I'll show you some of our other listings on my laptop."

The ghost woman squeezes Cathy's hand, "Thank you."

Cathy smiles and they leave the room. I follow them to the front door, trying to get Cathy to see or hear me, but she doesn't. They move out into the corridor, but I can go no further. I'm trapped in the apartment. The ghost woman walks away with my lovely Cathy to take over my life and there's nothing I can do to stop it.

Birth of a Serial Killer

L.N. Hunter

His eyes are the first thing you notice as he steps onto the bus. Flicking from side to side, resting just a bit longer on female faces, darting down if legs happen to be visible. He doesn't realize he's doing it; he's conscious only of the presence of pretty faces amongst the crowd while he searches for a free seat on his commute to work.

You don't have to try too hard to see his thoughts. Oh, he recognizes that sexual discrimination has no place in today's world—of course he does—and that men and women are equals. He tells himself he respects women… when it matters. A modern man, he considers himself a feminist, though he's not so pretentious as to actually proclaim it. He takes care not to tell off-colour jokes to those who wouldn't find them amusing. He'll hold a door open if the other person has their arms full, regardless of gender or inclination. He smiles politely at everyone.

But you observe that the smile is wider when the face is female and attractive.

It's different when he's sitting down on the bus, invariably somewhere near the front, when other passengers are facing the same direction and can't see his eyes. He places his backpack on the seat beside him, ensuring no one will sit there.

If you pay close attention, you can see the almost imperceptible dilation of his pupils and the micro-expressions that flit across his face. He doesn't notice you picking him apart. Nobody ever does, as you riffle through their lives. Not unless you want them to.

Just to show that you can, you send an icy chill down his spine, letting him know you're watching.

He peers round, a frown creasing his features, but sees nothing. He shrugs and forgets about you as the bus stops again. He evaluates each woman as she enters: this one carrying a bit too much weight, the next too skinny, then nice hair, large breasts, *no* tits, what on earth is she wearing, whoa that's ugly, she should smile more, fantastic legs.

As happens every day, he sits straighter when the bus approaches the end of Wardour Street, more alert, waiting. He leans forward as the door opens and people file in.

Suddenly, an intake of breath. *Oh my, it's her. What a vision! Won't you come sit beside me*, he silently pleads, moving his bag off the seat. Please sit here, he prays, so he can stare at those gorgeous nylon-covered legs while seeming to focus on his phone.

As she walks towards him, he drinks in her eyes, her hair, the contours of her legs beneath her skirt, her polished fingernails, the slightly parted lips—how he longs to feel her breath mixing with his—but she chooses a seat somewhere farther along the bus. You see him grit his teeth as she walks past the empty space beside him. He snaps his eyes shut, trying to imprint her appearance in his memory before it fades. High-heeled black courts, dark tights, black above-knee skirt. Lime-green blouse, matching this week's nail-polish and eyeshadow. Black jacket with a butterfly brooch on the lapel, a thin golden chain glinting through the unbuttoned top of the blouse. Her smooth-skinned neck.

He imagines how she's feeling from her expression, fantasizing about offering a sympathetic shoulder those times she looks unhappy. Sometimes she wears a smile; he smiles back, but he can see that she likes to tease as she walks on, pretending she doesn't notice him.

You scoff at his reaction when she appears one morning with a different hair colour. His face tenses briefly, eyebrows twitching in surprise, and he stares more intently. Does he approve of the change or not? Before you can decode his narrowed eyes and slightly pouting lips, his thoughts move on and his gaze skims downwards over the rest of her body.

He'd like to have a girlfriend, but he's so confused by women. He's scared to actually talk to one properly. Or—you know his mind better than he does—in case his suspicion is proven true, that he's not good enough. Not tall enough, not handsome enough, not clever enough, not witty enough. Not enough of a *man*.

On the bus today, you see him blink and tear his gaze away from a cluster of giggling schoolgirls. It takes him several seconds to remember he mustn't stare, lest he be accused of paedophilia. But later, at home, he browses schoolgirl porn, searching for videos where the fake school uniforms approach those of the girls he saw on the bus. Pornography doesn't matter, he firmly believes; it's innocent, he tells himself—everyone watches it. He can do whatever he wants in the privacy of his home. It doesn't hurt anyone, does it?

He peeks at his favourite dubious websites most lunchtimes at work too, after a morning of averting his gaze from his female co-workers' legs as they parade across the open doorway of his office. They're deliberately tormenting him, he knows—women do that, picking on him. A quick look at some "more accommodating' women for relief, that's all he needs. He does this via remote log-in to his boss's PC, using the browser's private mode, so his activities won't be as easily discovered.

He's all about not being detected—though he doesn't know about you.

He thinks he compartmentalizes his mind. He's convinced himself he can stay professional and polite in public, keeping his less seemly urges safely hidden at home.

He wants a woman. He *needs* a woman. He hungers for sex. More than the pleasure of his hand. He considers buying one of those realistic latex-skinned dolls—he can afford it. That'd be sufficient for his needs. Tidy. No complications; no arguments. No anxiety about being good enough. But he doesn't want the manufacturer or the delivery service to know something about him he's sure they would consider perverted. Better to find a real woman; perhaps that living doll from the bus.

He closes his eyes and pictures her, posing her like the women on the porn sites. *Oh yes.*

One evening, he gets off at the Wardour Street stop and follows her—at a discreet distance, of course. He's barely aware of anyone around him, his eyes glued to the swaying blonde ponytail and the curves of those glorious calves. He fancies he can hear her heels clacking on the pavement and the swish of nylon on nylon, though she's too far away for actual sound to reach him.

She lives in a tidy-looking townhouse that contains eight small flats. You see him stop by a payphone on the other side of the road, watching her enter the front door. Every night for a week, he watches, until he's certain which window is hers. Her apartment's on the upper floor, the one on the right. He paces the street a few times, trying to look like someone out for an evening stroll. He casts glances towards the front door and her window to see if she goes out or stays in, or if there are any visitors.

Only twice does he see something happen. A man, the same one both evenings, unlocks the door and enters. A few moments later, one of the ground-floor windows lights up—a resident of another flat.

One evening, he buys a kebab from a nearby van and spends an hour leaning against the phone box, not tasting the food as he mechanically chews and slowly swallows bite after bite. All the while, he stares at her window, imagining what's happening behind the curtains.

You make the phone ring. He almost drops his food. He looks around before scurrying away.

It's the end of summer, and he decides he'll aim for Halloween. It'll be dark when she gets to her flat, and there'll be trick-or-treating families creating bustle and hubbub in the street. He'll have enough preparation time to make sure there will be no mistakes.

He prepares well. He visits charity shops in parts of the city he seldom frequents and picks up clothes in styles and colours he wouldn't normally wear. He intends to buy some shoes a size too large or small, and to slice part of the heel off, to force his gait to be different—not identifiable in the footage from any CCTV camera that might happen to capture his travels. Spotting a pair of women's two-inch heels in a size that will fit, he decides they may work better. An ankle-length black skirt hangs from a rail just above the shoes and, on a whim, he adds it to his purchases.

He tries the shoes on at home to practice walking in them. It's only a tiny one-room apartment, all he's willing to pay for in the city, but sufficient for his needs. When he first moved in, he decorated the blank walls with soft-porn posters, then moved on to harder material printed out from the internet. He barely notices the pictures now. Currently, he's focused on the novel sensations of walking in heels.

You think his awkward prancing amusing, but he finds it stimulating, pleasurable even, to walk the few paces across the room, swaying his hips and adjusting his balance. He wears the shoes all the time at home now. The skirt too. Together, they make him feel more at one with his prey.

He bought these clothes second-hand because he hoped they would contain traces of their previous owners' life—DNA or stray hairs—to cover his tracks. He decides to shave all the hair from his body to further reduce the chance of leaving evidence behind. He applies depilatory cream to remove the last vestiges of stubble rather than risk nicking his skin. You can tell by his flushed cheeks when he strokes his legs in the evenings that he appreciates smooth skin. His erection lifts the front of his skirt as he wonders if her skin would feel like his.

He orders a lock-picking kit from an obscure online shop, figuring that no-one would be able to link the purchase to his planned deed. He spends several evenings training himself to use it, practicing with the help of YouTube videos and a selection of common door locks he bought in a DIY store near work. That's not all he learns from the internet: he manages to concoct some passable 'chloroform' from household bleach and vodka. He completes his internet shopping with a cheap digital camera, for pictures to keep as souvenirs. Although it has a perfectly good camera, his mobile phone could be tracked. Besides, leaving the phone behind to report its location will provide proof he'd been home all evening.

When the shops are full of Halloween paraphernalia, he buys a full-face skeleton mask and thin cotton gloves. He draws bone-like lines on the back of the gloves to make them look skeletal.

He skips work the day of Halloween to complete his preparations. Sleep eluded him the night before, but the adrenalin circulating in his system is more than enough to compensate. He waits until the sun has set before catching the bus. He's wearing his charity shop clothes, apart from the shoes and skirt. They're in a backpack along with his camera, lock picks, and chloroform.

He hops off the bus at the stop before hers and walks— almost bouncing along in excitement—to her building. Making a brief diversion into a narrow alley, he changes his shoes, taking care not to step on the broken glass littering the ground, then pulls the long skirt on over his trousers. He combs his hair, making sure he disposes of any loose strands—he contemplated shaving it all off beforehand, but decided that would attract too much attention. Pulling on his mask and gloves, he returns to the main thoroughfare.

Unhurried, he walks to her home, the strange-looking skeleton in the long black skirt, nodding and waving to the sporadic clusters of trick-or-treaters out with their parents.

He checks her window to make sure nobody's home.

Getting into her building is easy. Mash all the buttons in these places and someone will always buzz the front door open. The door to her flat holds no surprises, and his lock-picking skills have him inside in less than a minute.

It will be half an hour until she arrives, he estimates, so he has a quick look around, staying clear of the windows. There's an envelope on the kitchen counter and he squints to read it in the gloom—her name's Jane, simple and elegant. She looks like a Jane, he thinks. He whispers the name to himself: *Jane, Jane, Jane.* Her fridge is almost empty, a few pots of low-fat yoghurt, half a pint of milk and an opened packet of pre-chopped salad vegetables.

Her bathroom is windowless. He closes its door behind him and pulls the cord for the light. The sudden noise of the automatic ventilation fan makes his heart lurch. He lifts his mask and sniffs some of the lotions and creams in her medicine cabinet, not really knowing what they're all for.

Switching off the light and pulling his mask down, he exits the bathroom and explores her bedroom. He opens the wardrobe and drawers; he touches dresses of various textures, as well as soft jumpers and smooth blouses. It's too dark to tell what colour anything is, but he doesn't dare turn the light on. One of the drawers contains underwear, a mixture of silky smoothness and soft cottons that sends shivers from his gloved fingertips to his spine.

Tiring of this activity, he removes the light bulb in the main room before taking up a position by the front door, waiting for her arrival.

He keeps looking at his watch, but time itself has turned to treacle. What if she's working late or going out with colleagues—just because she hasn't done so before doesn't mean it could never happen. He dismisses those thoughts. Tonight, everything is going to be right—it has to be. Nothing will go wrong.

Even the coldness you blow on the back of his neck doesn't dent his confidence.

His penis swells as he thinks about what will happen later. His mouth is dry, and his face is clammy under his mask.

At last, a key rattles in the lock, jerking him to attention. He pours his homemade chloroform onto a cloth.

She steps through the door, groping for the light switch. She flicks it, freezing when the light doesn't come on. She tries the switch again.

He grabs her arm and yanks her fully inside, kicking the door shut. Before she has time to react, he punches her hard in the stomach. He knows chloroform doesn't act quickly, despite what happens in the movies. He needs to incapacitate her to keep her breathing the fumes for several minutes—the punch helps, by making her gasp and inhale deeply. She has no opportunity to scream, and her pained struggles weaken.

After she slumps into his arms, he holds the cloth to her face for an extra minute and then carries her to the bedroom, gently—reverentially—laying her down on the bed. He draws the curtains and turns on the light. Heart thudding, he stares at her—at Jane, his perfect Jane—for several seconds. He strokes her hair, pulling her ponytail loose. His hands tremble as he touches her.

Impatiently, he removes her clothes. He's panting hard now, his erection uncomfortably insistent. Yet, somehow, she doesn't look right naked. She doesn't look *real*. He wants her to look more like the images he masturbates to.

He opens her bedroom drawers and finds what he's searching for: a pair of sheer stockings and a suspender belt. He puts them on the unconscious woman, somewhat awkwardly thanks to his gloves. He adds a pair of black patent leather stilettos from the bottom of her wardrobe, and arranges her on the bed, legs parted and ready.

Despite all this, something still isn't working.

He's never heard her voice. She's never smiled just for him. Those pieces of the picture are missing. He tries to move her slack lips into the shape of a smile, but her mouth droops open again.

If he looks closely, he can see small wrinkles at the corners of those lips and blemishes on her skin; one nipple is asymmetric and fractionally larger than the other. She smells slightly sweaty from many hours in her workday clothes. Her breath is stale. Where is the perfection of his imagination?

He wants to touch her skin directly, but he dares not remove the gloves from his clenching and unclenching hands. His fingers cease their twitching, and he stands still for a moment, holding his breath before a long and slow exhalation.

You silently ask him if he *really* wants to do this.

Guilt starts to build inside him.

You snigger, and whisper that he's pathetic.

Perhaps, he wonders, he's not really the man he believed he was. Perhaps he really isn't good enough.

Tears come to his eyes, and he groans and punches the wall; the pain breaks the cycle of thoughts. He mutters, "Fuck it," and folds the duvet over the woman's nakedness.

You can't help but guffaw.

Head hung low, he eases his way out of her flat and walks slowly towards the bus stop, barely noticing his surroundings as he mulls over his failure.

A shriek of laughter halts him, and he looks up to see three young women—about seventeen or eighteen, he guesses—on the other side of the road, sharing some private joke. They're dressed for show rather than for warmth, wearing the standard uniform of skimpy cropped tops and slashed jeans, with pointy witch's hats as a concession to Halloween. Their slim figures and rosy-cheeked faces ignite something within him. Perhaps where he went wrong was choosing someone too old, too worn by life. A teenager would be better, he thinks. Just what he needs. Pure, smooth, innocent.

You scream at him, but he's oblivious.

He pulls out his camera. One of the girls scowls when he points it in their direction. He turns slightly and takes a photograph of the Halloween decorations in the window behind them as if that was what he intended to do all along, before continuing on his way.

He smiles as he lets his imagination scamper over the girls' bodies. You know he won't do anything to these three, at least not yet—he's not stupid. But he'll start making new plans as soon as he gets home.

The spring returns to his step as he walks on, Jane completely forgotten. Back at the alley, he stops to change his clothes. He holds up the skirt and sighs—should he keep it, or dump it here and start afresh?

You slip behind him and pick up a fragment of glass from the ground. He turns, and you drive the shard deep into his stomach.

He drops to the ground, making no more sound than a sigh.

Staring at the body, you smile. *One down.*

After a moment, you vanish back into the darkness, in search of another set of eyes to watch.

Drownin' Moon

Terry Campbell

Stuart Bosman didn't hear the oddly dressed stranger making his way down the length of the fishing pier at all; he supposed that's what made it so peculiar. He had been sitting in an old mildew-spotted lawn chair he had found leaning up against one of the huge bald cypress trees that hugged the shoreline of Caddo Lake in deep east Texas, lost in the sounds of nature: the chirping of the frogs, the screeching of the herons, the monotonous lapping of the gentle waves against the pier supports and cypress knees. And the smells—a distant whiff of pine needles, that underlying, but curiously pleasant, fishy smell, hickory chips burning inside one of the nearby lakeside restaurants. Maybe the fact was that he was so absorbed by this serene offering of nature's subtle wonders, in the overall peacefulness of his surroundings, that he simply hadn't heard the man approaching. But still, Stuart remembered the squeaking of the old weather-beaten boards when he had first walked onto this pier hours earlier, indeed how they had groaned every time he shifted in his chair, how they had squealed in protest every time he moved to check his bait, and he just couldn't believe he hadn't noticed the man's footsteps.

That, combined with the man's dress—some kind of dapper Civil War-era apparel, complete with a sharp, brown derby—and the way he just stood there staring out across the dark waters of the lake before even speaking, bothered Stuart. And something in the man's eyes, (what he could see of them anyway) something deep and troubling—*or sinister, was it sinister?*—disturbed him even more.

Stuart started to speak, found his voice rough with phlegm, and cleared his throat. "Doing some fishing?" he finally asked the stranger.

A furtive glance, and then that far-away look. "No sir. No fishing for me. Maybe later."

"Well," Stuart said, nervous at the lull, "I'm not having much luck myself."

"Yes, no luck." It was obvious the stranger wasn't really listening to him.

"I can't really say that, though. My luck was just getting away from the office, sitting out here in the peace and quiet with Mother Nature. To tell you the truth, I couldn't care less if I catch anything or not."

"This lake used to be filled with steamboat traffic. From far up the Mississippi all the way to New Orleans. You don't see it anymore."

Where did that come from? Stuart mused. "Is that a fact? Well, what do you know about that?" he continued. "Well, as I was saying, I'm not having much—"

"My good man," the stranger interrupted, turning to look directly into Stuart's eyes for the first time. "One hasn't properly fished Caddo Lake until one has fished it at night."

The conversation had distracted Stuart. How long had it gone on? Minutes? Hours? Surely not hours. He hadn't noticed the deep shadows of the Spanish moss and the cypress branches stretching farther into the water, hadn't noticed the sun dipping below the long line of cypresses behind him. Dusk had slipped up on him.

Stuart chuckled. "Maybe so. But I think I'll just head back to the bed and breakfast and leave the night fishing for those a little more dedicated to the sport than myself."

The stranger smiled, and the gesture forced Stuart to look away. He knew he was looking straight into the man's eyes, yet it felt blank, like there was no connection.

"As you wish. But things seem to bite better at night." He paused a moment, and his eyes returned to the lake. "Out here anyway."

"Yes, I'm sure they do," Stuart said, reeling in his line.

"Good night, kind stranger," the man said, and turned away.

"Good night," Stuart answered, not looking back. He pulled the end of his line from the water, the minnow, still energized and very much alive, dangling from the hook. Stuart imagined if it could, the tiny fish would give him the finger. Stuart smiled to himself and gripped the slippery fish, pulled it off the hook, and dropped it back into the water with a plop. "There," he said. "Go dance with the gators."

Stuart imagined a giant bass engulfing the minnow the moment it disappeared under the water. The thought made him laugh out loud. Then he thought of the stranger who had left his company only moments earlier. The frogs still chirped, now joined by more nocturnal varieties, the herons still screeched, the water still lapped.

But not one creak of a board.

Stuart turned and looked back across the parking lot of the secluded marina. There was no sign of the stranger. Stuart was about to decide he had imagined the entire conversation when, as he knelt to grab his gear, he noticed a dark silhouette standing on the adjacent pier, some fifty yards away, staring out into the ebony waters. Stuart shivered, though the evening air was still quite warm.

The temptation of landing even a world record largemouth couldn't convince him to stay on Caddo Lake one minute longer.

* * *

As fate would have it, Stuart would spend one minute longer, would spend many, many minutes longer on Caddo Lake, or at least on the long, dark road from there back to the town of Josephine. The battery in his car was dead. Hoping for a spark of life, he cranked the engine a few more times, but each time, the effort was weaker, the fading dashboard lights dimmer.

"Shit," Stuart mumbled. "Just terrific."

He sighed and looked back across the asphalt at the tiny dock from which he had fished. The water looked almost black now. Very little hint of the sun remained. It would be completely dark in a matter of minutes. And it was at least fifteen miles back to Josephine. His only hope was to start walking and look for a pay phone. He supposed he could call a wrecker to come and give his battery a jump. Or perhaps the innkeeper at the bed and breakfast where he was staying wouldn't mind coming out to pick him up. He could deal with his car problems in the morning.

But first things first; he had to find a telephone. Now how smart was it to leave the cell phone at home? But such was his desire to leave the real world behind, he had chosen not to bring it.

Stuart got out of his car, made sure it was secured, and headed back from whence he came.

* * *

He had to have walked at least five miles. His feet hurt. He had no idea where he was. He wasn't even sure he was on the right road anymore. It was so dark that he had probably missed any highway signs he might've run across, and if the road had veered away at a fork somewhere, he would've never noticed. It was a moonless night, and the dense foliage of the cypress trees and their decorative strands of Spanish moss blocked any futile light the stars might throw his way. Stuart breathed in. The night air had grown a little cool, but it carried with it a faint fishy smell, and Stuart was certain he was still not far from the shore of the lake. It was perhaps only a few dozen yards past the trees to his right. Somehow, that thought bothered him more than the darkness itself. Something about Caddo Lake made him uneasy, but what, he had no idea. Perhaps because the lake was natural and not man made, the only one of its kind in Texas. That natural state hinted of antiquity, of a feeling that there were things in its murky depths that had been there for years, even centuries. Things that *Belonged*, whereas he certainly did not.

Stuart shoved his hands in his jacket pockets. Many thoughts filled his head tonight, not the least of which was "why the hell don't I have a flashlight in the car?" But the uneasy feeling about the water that lay lurking near him, ebbing ever closer to his heart, wouldn't recede from the shores of his mind.

Some fishing show on ESPN had enlightened him as to what a beautiful body of water Caddo Lake was, how fantastic the fishing was, but it had neglected to inform him of how goddamned eerie a place it was, with the black limbs of the cypress trees like skeletal fingers clawing at the oily night for tasty morsels, the Spanish moss dripping from them like the severed heads of witches dangling upside down, the giant lily pads like the floating displaced scales of some ancient wyvern, the night frogs calling forlornly like unseen banshees, the gators—

"Oh shit, Bosman," he said aloud. "Did you have to mention alligators?"

But that was okay. The fishing show had admitted there were alligators in Caddo Lake, but they avoided people at all costs, and they only came out at night.

Well, hey folks, Stuart thought, is the sun shining right now, is it not darker than Hades out here, and take a look around would ya'? Do you see a frickin' soul out here?

Stuart stopped suddenly. He looked behind him, at what he wasn't sure. He had walked at least five miles; he was sure of it. His mind was set on finding a pay phone, not looking for cars on the highway, but he certainly would've seen one had it passed. But there hadn't been any. Not one car. Not one person.

Except for that guy who failed to creak the boards.

"Get hold of yourself, Stu. We don't need to start thinking about that. Not here in the dark."

And that man was probably still out here somewhere, wandering up and down this dark stretch of highway, going from dock to dock to stare out at the water like a ghostly sentinel.

Stuart started again. What the *hell* was he thinking coming out to this lake anyway? To any lake? He hadn't been fishing since he was a teenager. He had to go out and buy the stupid rod and reel just for this trip. That should've been his first clue that he was out of his element. If he wanted to get away, he should've just gone to Josephine, rested at the bed and breakfast, window shopped all the antique stores, hung out at Auntie Skinner's and caught some music.

But no, he had to be Jimmy fucking Houston.

"And now you're seeing things," he said suddenly, his mind not grasping the splash of colour his eyes were presenting him.

He stopped and peered through the trees and brush, toward where he thought the lake would be. It was difficult to see. There wasn't much of a breeze, but enough to keep the fine cypress leaves shifting and moving, preventing a clear gaze through them.

But he knew he could see lights. Bright red, yellow and blue lights. *The aliens have landed on Caddo Lake. They have heads like gators, and Spanish moss for hair, and they're going to abduct me and shove a big hook up my ass and hang me in outer space for some giant space fish to come along and eat me.*

Stuart moved into the ditch along the side of the road and pushed back some of the branches. The limbs creaked and sighed in the breeze.

It was a sign. A neon sign. A bright, glorious sign of rapture in the dark hell that had been Stuart's night to this point. A sign that beckoned 'OPEN'. At that moment, there was not a more lovely word in the English language.

Oblivious to the scraping of the branches, Stuart shoved his way through the trees toward the sign, toward the convenience store to which the sign was surely attached, toward the pay phone that was most certainly hanging on the wall below it. Stuart broke from the trees and stopped.

The steady *swish-swash* of the waves lapped against pier supports, the cool night breeze blew through his hair, bringing with it a strong smell of dead fish in the distance, and possibly a hint of rain from the west.

The neon colours of the 'OPEN' sign vomited swatches of colour that shimmied across the damp weathered boards of the building, across the wooden bridge that connected the structure to the blacktop parking lot. Stuart's ears registered another puzzling sign, a muffled *thump-thump*, (too many noises in the dark, too damned many noises) when he noticed the small aluminium fishing boat tied to the dock, bumping into the boards with every undulation of the water. A large halogen streetlight played host to every moth and night bug within a fifteen-mile radius, and its light spread across the roof of the building, illuminating a huge, papier-mâché depiction of a bass attached to the roof.

"A bait stand," Stuart surmised in mock wonder. "An all-night bait stand."

One hasn't properly fished Caddo Lake until one has fished it at night.

Stuart shuddered. He didn't care. If it sold minnows and worms, it probably had a phone.

That's when he heard the baby wail. The sound sent a shiver of gooseflesh up his spine. That's not a sound one should be able to hear in the middle of the night, in the middle of nowhere. Where had it come from? From the woods? On the road? It was hard to tell in the darkness. Stuart gulped. From the . . . *water?* Then he heard more voices. Then laughter. He looked beyond the bait stand and out toward the centre of the lake. Stuart released a sigh of relief and smiled; a bit embarrassed at himself.

There was a large steamboat out on the lake. The lull of the water and the floating breeze had combined to play a neat audio trick on Stuart's ears. The sounds had apparently drifted across the water.

Stuart paused a moment, studying the boat. It was obviously a reproduction. Not surprising, given the town of Josephine and its surrounding areas' penchant for playing up its history. It was more than likely a "dinner and a play" production on the water, similar to the Texas Queen steamboat on Lake Ray Hubbard near Dallas. Probably some piece of local legend was being reenacted even as he stood there. Whatever sounds of merriment flowed from the grand vessel. A good time was being had by all.

Too bad I'm here and not there, Stuart thought. He started across the bridge to the bait stand, trying to ignore the thought of the black water that slithered and rolled a few feet below him. Around the other side of the building, where the light from the streetlamp and the neon sign could not reach, it was much darker. But a faint glow emitted from somewhere inside the shop, perhaps the gentle light of a soda machine. The sign read 'OPEN'; someone had to be there.

Stuart gripped the knob and pushed, expecting to hear a clang from the omnipresent string of cowbells as the door swung open. But the door was locked. Perplexed and just a bit agitated, Stuart knocked on the door.

"Hello?" he called out.

Nothing.

"Hello? Are you open? I need to use the phone."

Stuart paused a moment. Still no response. He was about to knock again when he heard a shuffling noise on the other side of the door. Stuart waited. He heard the sound of a throat being cleared.

"What do you want?" a deep voice answered.

"I need to use your phone, please."

"We're closed."

Stuart tried to peer through the glass window set into the door. He couldn't see the source of the dim light; there must be a shade pulled over the window. He couldn't see anyone, but he could tell by the diction of the voice that the owner was a black man.

"But your sign," Stuart started. "You know, big neon sign."

"It's the drownin' moon. We ain't open. Only night of the year we ain't open." The voice chuckled. "Even open Christmas Eve, but not tonight." The chuckle quickly faded. "Not tonight."

"But your sign," Stuart argued.

"Don't pay no mind to that sign. Don't turn it off cause there ain't no one out tonight. It's the drownin' moon. Saw no reason to turn it off. Never anyone out on the drownin' moon."

"Look, I don't need to buy anything. Do you have a pay phone out here somewhere?"

"No, no pay phone. It's still early, mister. Take my word. You need to get on out of here. Go back from where you came."

"I'm trying to go back from where I came," Stuart pleaded. Leave it to him to find the only all-night bait stand that wasn't actually open all night. Just then, a thought occurred to Stuart. What did the man say about the moon? The drownin' moon? Stuart recalled his first thought as the sun sank earlier that evening when he had first walked away from his stricken car. There was no moon tonight.

"Wait a minute. What was that you said about the 'drownin' moon'?"

"Drownin' moon. The night of the drownin' moon."

"But there is no moon tonight. No moon at all."

There was a pause from the other side of the door. "That's right. There ain't. But it's the drownin' moon all the same. You get yourself back where you came from, ya hear? And watch who you talk to."

"Watch who I . . . What's that supposed to mean?" Stuart said, almost under his breath. He could hear the shuffling moving away from the entrance.

Stuart turned away from the bait stand and looked out across the lake. The steamboat was still there; the joyous noises still emanated from it. But now, looking at the grand vessel, a black lump against an even blacker backdrop, something struck him as odd, something he couldn't quite pinpoint. Then he noticed the water around the steamboat.

The night of the drownin' moon.

The black water around the steamboat, indeed across the entire horizon, sparkled in a bath of warm light. Shimmers of light danced and played across the gentle waters. The soft, lolling waves held brilliant splashes of light in the darkness, then lost them beneath the swells.

There were some lights shining from the deck of the boat, but not enough. Not enough to be doing this, Stuart thought. His eyes searched the skies, but only affirmed what he already knew.

It had to be some sort of optical illusion. He was no seafarer, had spent practically no time on the water as a child or as an adult, and certainly not at night. It *had* to be the lights from the boat. Maybe there were some powerful spotlights shining from the banks. Perhaps some lanterns that fishermen sat out earlier.

Ain't no one out tonight, because it's the—

Drownin' moon.

The light glistened across the water as if the fullest of moons shone down brilliantly, but it did not. There was no moon. There was no moon to illuminate the waters tonight.

Yet the lunar light skipped and bounced across Caddo Lake all the same.

"I have to get away from here," Stuart mumbled to himself. He supposed he would head back down the road. He couldn't be more than ten miles from Josephine now.

Stuart stopped in the gravel parking lot and looked back at the bait stand. The papier-mâché fish stared down at him with its big papier-mâché orbs, and Stuart took notice that the only light shining on the sculpture, unlike the waters beyond the pier, were the colours of the neon sign and the brilliance of the halogen streetlamp.

* * *

He hadn't gotten very far down the road when it happened. Stuart had been thinking about the drownin' moon, about the weird manner in which the lake seemed to be illuminated by some unseen light source and listening to the occasional shout or bout of laughter emanating from the steamboat settled on the lake in the distance.

It hadn't really hit him all at once; in fact, it sort of snuck up on him, like a black panther prowling the low brush in the swamp. He had noticed it, of that he was certain; it just hadn't registered in his brain, as lost in thought as he had been.

But the realization sank in at last. Something was happening on the steamboat. The voices were louder, more frantic. He could hear the hysterical cries of children, the high-pitched scream of women, the shouts of panic.

There was another break in the trees ahead, and a swinging, creaking sign signalled that another marina lay hidden just beyond the brush. Stuart ran toward it, gravel crunching under his feet. He turned the corner, spied the long wooden dock jutting out into the water. The sound of his hastened steps suddenly changed from the solid thunk of contacting hard asphalt to the muffled clomp of wood and Styrofoam. The boats thumped against the sides of the marina. Stuart reached the end of the dock and stopped.

The steamboat was still out there, now merely a dark silhouette almost hidden in the glow of the surrounding waters. The illumination was intense, approaching blinding in contrast to the total darkness everywhere else. It just couldn't be. There was no explanation for the light source. The reflections in the water directly surrounding the vessel seemed to take on a richer orange-yellow glow, and the waviness of the mirror image made the boat seem to shimmer, as if Stuart was witnessing a heat mirage. Maybe that's what it was, an intense vision brought on by exhaustion and frustration. Then the boat seemed to grow hazy, seemed to almost disappear in a cloud of smoke.

Only then did Stuart notice the flames erupting from the steamboat's roof.

"Oh my God," Stuart said aloud. "Oh my God. It's going down."

He placed his hands on the rails and watched. The screams were getting more frantic, the cries more panic-stricken. He could hear children crying, probably separated from their parents. A few audible words carried over the sounds of distress— "fire", "deck", and one that was obviously someone's name: "Stephens".

I have to get help. The feverish thought raced through Stuart's mind.

The bait stand. He couldn't have gotten very far down the road. If he ran very fast . . . The owner would let him in; he would simply have to.

Stuart started to turn away from the water when he heard the explosion. A great orange plume of fire and smoke and death climbed into the black night. Screams erupted and just as suddenly were stifled. Stuart could hear the splashes as many of the doomed people opted for the comparative safety of the water. The hull was now well illuminated by the raging fire, and Stuart could see that the boat was already at an unhealthy tilt. The initial explosion had dissipated into the sky, but the remaining flames stretched skywards, agile licks of fire reaching higher than the next as if in competition with one another. The flames reflected in the water, revealing tiny distant specks in the bright orange surface of the water, and Stuart realized these specks were souls attempting to stay afloat. Stuart strained his eyes in an attempt to see if the people were still alive, but the glare from the water was too great. It looked almost like orange-yellow daylight on the surface of the lake. And then Stuart saw that one part of the lake was even brighter. Bright and round and yellow.

That broke Stuart from his funk.

Bright and round and yellow. A vivid splash of light, brighter than the reflections of flame around it.

Drownin' moon.

It was a moonless night. But somehow, the moon's reflection was there in the water, lolling gently on the waves, its image broken only by occasional flashes of light from secondary explosions aboard the steamboat, oblivious to the tragedy unfolding around it.

* * *

Stuart raced past the papier-mâché fish, his feet pounding on the weathered boards, and turned the corner to the entrance to the bait stand. From here, he could still see the doomed steamboat amid the glow of the flames and the odd reflection of the ghost moon in the water. The stern of the boat was now pointing straight at the sky but flames still spewed from what remained above water. The cries had diminished, but he could still hear the occasional panicked shout or the muffled sob of a possible survivor. Stuart could hear movement in the water, different from the normal sounds of waves, and he wondered if it could be people attempting to swim to safety. The glow on the water did not reach the shore, and it was too dark to see what might be approaching in the black water.

Stuart pounded on the door. He could hear a faint tinkle from the cowbells hanging on the interior side of the door. "Open the door!" he shouted. "I know you're in there! There's been an accident out on the lake! Call an ambulance! Call the fire department, the police!"

There was no answer. "Goddammit, man! Open the door!" Stuart usually did not speak in such a manner, especially to strangers, and most especially to strangers whose faces he had never even seen. But these were dire circumstances. "Please, you have to listen! There was an explosion out on the lake. A boat is sinking."

Stuart tried to calm down long enough to hear if the owner was coming. He listened for any sounds of life from within the store.

The sound would come from outside the store.

At first, Stuart thought it was just the waves hitting against the fishing boat again. Then he heard a thump. He turned away from the door. A long pier led out away from the bait stand, parallel to the shoreline. The sounds were coming from the end of this pier. The light from the neon sign reached to the end of the pier, but just barely. Stuart listened. The water splashed. There was another thump. Then a moan.

Instinctively, he started in that direction. "Is someone there?"

There was a wet splash of water on wood. Stuart stopped. Another splash. The light was weak, but Stuart could see a dark shape rise above the wooden planks, and a rainbow of twinkling colours as the neon sign reflected off wet skin. There was another moan. "Are you all right?"

There was a squishy sound, as of soaked tennis shoes slopping on a floor, and another. Then a wet shuffling sound. The dark shape loomed before him, and Stuart stopped in horror at what he saw.

Just then the door swung open with a clang of copper cowbells, the doorknob striking Stuart's elbow. "Dammit, boy. You still out here?"

Still wincing from the pain in his elbow, Stuart felt a rough hand grab his other arm, and before he knew what was happening, he was yanked inside the dimly lit bait stand. The hand released him, and Stuart stumbled forward, a wire stand of Lay's potato chips the only thing keeping him from diving face first into the floor. Stuart straightened and turned to face the person who had jerked him around so roughly.

The only light illuminating the store were the various neon beer and sundries advertisements that graced the panelled walls, and the lights inside the soda coolers. The owner of the bait stand matched the previously unseen voice exactly as Stuart would've imagined. He was a large man and obviously quite solid, given the way he had yanked Stuart inside so easily. He was probably in his mid to late thirties, and his head was perfectly smooth. Stuart looked at the man standing there, his massive chest rising and falling, and for a moment, he forgot what had brought him back to the all-night bait stand. Then a low, muffled cry rose over the air outside, and that's all it took to snap Stuart back.

"Outside, out on the lake," Stuart started, his communication skills not quite at their normal levels. "An explosion."

The man did not react in the manner in which Stuart might have imagined; in fact, he barely responded at all. A muffled grunt, somehow perceived as an affirmative response, was all the owner gave.

"There's a fire," Stuart continued. "It's sinking."

"Drownin' moon," the bait stand owner said. "That's all it is, son. You just seen the drownin' moon. And there ain't nobody out on the drownin' moon."

"No, you don't understand," Stuart said. He couldn't believe the attitude this guy was taking. It's one thing to refuse use of a phone to someone experiencing car trouble; it's another thing entirely when an emergency is involved. "Listen to me."

"No, you listen to me," the black man said. "You take a deep breath, you relax, and you listen to me."

Stuart stopped trying to get through to the man. Instead, he listened to the sounds outside. He could still hear the slick, wet sounds of feet dragging across the drenched boards. And he could hear the voices. There were more now, and they sounded horrible. There were more footsteps as well, more splatters of water. Evidently, through some miracle he wasn't quite able to understand, many of the people on the boat had survived.

But judging by the sounds of their moans, they might not survive for long if nothing was done.

"I'm using your phone," Stuart said, and pushed his way past the cold-hearted owner.

"Go ahead. If that's what you have to do."

Stuart grabbed the phone lying on the counter and dialled 9-1-1. A man's voice answered on the first ring. Before Stuart could finish explaining about the sinking steamboat, the voice on the other end of the line asked a question that stunned Stuart more than any of the evening's events so far.

"Are you from out of town?" the operator asked.

Stuart couldn't find his voice. "W-w-w-what?" he stammered.

"Are you a tourist?"

"I don't see what that has—"

"Sir, you need to just go on back to bed and forget anything you saw."

The line went dead. Dumbfounded, Stuart's gaze wandered the room and finally met with that of the bait stand owner.

The man smiled and nodded once, as if he understood. "Now you ready to listen?"

Stuart laid the headset gently back in its cradle. "You're all crazy," he said, almost under his breath. He could still hear the cries of the people. They were right outside the door. From time to time, one would bump against the door, or scrape across one of the front windows. But mostly, they just shuffled up and down the length of the dock, moaning. That's when Stuart realized something; none of them were speaking. No one asked for help. No one mentioned the boat catching fire and sinking. No one asked to be let in.

Stuart watched their dull silhouettes as they passed before the door and windows. To and fro. To and fro. *Almost like zombies.*

The thought chilled Stuart.

He returned his attention to the black man and started to say something.

Instead, the owner extended his large hand to Stuart. "Reggie Finnel. I own this place."

Stuart introduced himself, but he heard his own voice as a faraway sound, not quite in the present.

"Have you ever heard of the `Mittie Stephens'?"

Stuart shook his head, then started. "Wait. I heard that name earlier. Stephens. Someone said it on . . . the . . ."

Reggie's gaze moved out toward the lake. "On the boat?" He chuckled. "Stu, you picked just about the worst night you could think of to come to Caddo Lake. What made you come out here at night anyway?"

"Well, actually, I was here in the day. Then my car broke down, I needed a phone and . . . well . . ."

Reggie pulled out a couple of bar stools from behind the counter and set them under the light of a Pepsi cooler. He reached into the cooler and brought out a couple of cold drinks, handing one to Stuart. The cool condensation was soothing to Stuart's hand. The blue and red of the sign gave ample light, and Stuart could see a strange kind of wisdom in the man's eyes.

"Have a seat, Stu. This is going to be a long night."

Stuart sat on the stool, and one of the legs skidded a bit on the hardwood floor. He couldn't help but notice that there was no response from the visitors just outside the door.

"First of all, let me calm your worries a bit. Those people outside. Don't worry about them. They can't be helped."

"But I saw the fire. There was an explosion—" Reggie held up a hand to shush Stuart.

"Listen to them out there, Stu. Just *listen* to them. And look at them."

Stuart looked toward the door and then back to Reggie. "Go on. Have a look."

Stuart got up and moved slowly over to the entrance door. With one finger, he moved the shade back enough to see out onto the dock. The bodies ambled slowly up and down the length of the pier, pausing momentarily in confusion when they reached the end before turning and continuing their macabre shuffle, like some sort of bizarre targets in an insane shooting gallery. He had seen the one that had climbed from the lake when he had first arrived back at the bait stand. He must've forgotten what he had seen, or perhaps he had *chosen* not to remember. But now, in the warm confines of the bait stand, when the fear and excitement had subsided a bit and reality had set in, Stuart could more clearly remember what he had seen.

The man's face, his entire body had been burned away, almost to the point of being skeletal. No one could survive injuries like that for more than a few minutes, much less swim the length of a lake and climb up onto a fishing pier. The muscles would've been burned away, rendered useless. All of them had similar injuries. Like the living dead. A pair of glazed eyes contained in charred, oozing flesh met Stuart's, but there was no intelligence in them, no pleas for help. It might as well have been the eyes of a cow watching a car drive by.

Stuart looked away from the door, a strange sadness in his eyes. "What did I see tonight?"

Reggie smiled, not a gesture of humour, but a grin of understanding. "Drownin' moon. You saw the drownin' moon."

"What is a drownin' moon?" Stuart asked.

"No one really knows what it is, or why it happens. That's just what us locals have grown to call it over the years. I asked you earlier if you'd heard of the `Mittie Stephens'. It was a famous steamboat that moved through the riverports from Josephine to New Orleans. Some people said it was more than just a transportation boat for goods. A lot of gamblin' went on in it, too. And with that came a lot of double crossin''.

"There was one man named Victor Jenkins, got into a little trouble with some of the other big-time players. To make a long story short, they took ol' Jenkins for everything he had. Everything but his pride, I s'pose. He had enough of that left to try to get his revenge."

"He set fire to the boat," Stuart said.

"Give the man a cigar, yep. One summer night in 1849. He thought he'd get those guys real good. But what he didn't know was that that weekend, the `Mittie Stephens' hadn't gone on its normal route, hadn't picked up its normal loads. Hadn't picked up the gamblers. Instead, it had picked up a whole mess of normal, everyday folks from New Orleans. Families, you might say. Husbands, wives, children. Whole lots of children. Was takin' em to Josephine for a stay at the Excelsior."

"Dear God."

"Yep. Jenkins set that fire and got clean away, never knowin' the boat was full of innocent folks enjoying a warm summer evening on the bayou. I guess he read about it a few days later. I can only imagine what might've been goin' through his head."

"So, what happened?" Stuart asked. "With the `Mittie Stephens', I mean."

Reggie shrugged. "It went down. It burned and went down. There's parts of Caddo Lake that's only three feet deep. But where she sank . . ." Reggie shook his head. ". . . it must be bottomless."

"Were there any survivors?"

"Nope, not a one. There was a team of scientists or something from Louisiana a few years back tried to find the remains of her, but they didn't have no luck. I think they never will." He paused a moment, listening to the slurping dragging sounds outside. "I think . . . she don't want to be found."

"That may be what happened two hundred and fifty years ago, but what happened tonight? What did I see tonight?"

Reggie shook his head again. "To be perfectly honest, Stu, I don't know what it is. It just replays every year on the anniversary of the sinking. I hear tell somewhere that when there is a powerful tragedy, a really terrible horrible thing, something like this can happen. The energy that gets released in that one place is so strong, that it crosses a barrier or something."

Stuart heard a soft wail, possibly from a child. It sounded like it was right outside the window across from where they were sitting. "And those . . . those people out there?"

"Spooks. Haints. Ghosts, you city boys would be more likely to call them."

"What do they want?"

"Same thing Jenkins wanted. Revenge."

"But how can they do that?" Stuart asked.

"Well, I can't say that this is the God's honest truth, but have you ever heard of the song of the siren?"

"Sure, something in Greek mythology, right?"

"Shit, I don't know about that. But I know that people around here say that on the drownin' moon, those people can lure poor innocent folk right into that lake. Make 'em walk right out into that black soup and never come up for air."

"You're joking, right?" Stuart laughed, nervously.

"Like I say, I don't know what's true and what ain't. But I do know that nobody around here goes anywhere on this night. Now you know why I told you to git when you first came along."

Stuart's mind drifted back to the blackened thing that had crawled from the water. He shuddered. "And why you pulled me inside the store before they could grab me."

Now it was Reggie's turn to laugh. "I don't think they can grab you, but they might just convince you to go swimmin'."

"How many people died?"

"Two hundred twenty-seven."

"But surely there aren't that many . . . ghosts outside your door."

"Not just out there. All over this lake. Everywhere. Like I said, ain't nobody on this lake on the drownin' moon."

"There was a full moon on the night of the sinking back in 1849, right?"

"That's what the legends say."

"I saw the moon tonight." Stuart caught Reggie's affirmative nod. "In the water. The full moon reflected in the water. I thought it was some kind of trick of the light. I guess that's why they call it the drownin' moon." Stuart paused to listen to the sounds on the dock. They seemed to be diminishing, lessening in their determination. Perhaps some of them had wandered off to other areas. "Has anyone ever, you know, drowned on this night?"

A glassy film seemed to pass over Reggie's eyes at that moment. "I've heard of people being found floating face down the next morning, but I've never seen it in the paper or nothin' like that. You know, nothing official. But I'll tell you things I do see, and that's what scares me the most." He leaned forward on the barstool, closer to Stuart. "You might even see it yourself in the morning. I had a dog "bout fifteen years ago, let him out that night without thinkin'. You know, just wasn't thinking about it being the drownin' moon. I found him floating on the waves up against the shore the next morning. To me, that speaks more truth than any rumours about people drowning. For all the legend, for all the lies people tell. That's the one thing that keeps me locked up all night on the drownin' moon."

"Whatever happened to Jenkins?"

Reggie paused to light a cigarette. Stuart noticed that his hands were shaking ever so slightly. "No one knows. But there's another local legend, claims that his spirit walks around the lake on the same night, but for a different reason all together."

"What's that?" Stuart asked.

"They say he tries to trick people into stayin' on the lake at night, so that the spooks go after them and not him. I guess people are saying that the dead don't care who they get to take down with them."

"He . . . tricks people?" Stuart said.

"That's what they say."

"How do you mean?"

"What I mean is, he goes night fishin'. He uses them for bait."

Stuart thought back to the man he had met on the fishing pier earlier that evening. Or was it yesterday?

One hasn't properly fished Caddo Lake until one has fished it at night.

Stuart shuddered. He suddenly felt very cold.

A warm glow was beginning to show through the closed shades on the windows. The voices and slopping sounds had completely dissipated.

Reggie glanced at the front door. "Dawn's breaking. Drownin' moon's done for another year. Thank God for that."

He stood and walked over to the door, holding the cowbells silent with one hand and peeking around the shade with another. Stuart stood and peered around the shade that covered one of the windows. The sinking steamboat was gone. Either it had completely sank, or the apparition had gone back to its spirit world. Either way, Stuart knew that what was left of the great boat and its occupants was down there somewhere in those black depths.

"It's six o'clock," Reggie said. "Johnny should be out and about by now. He's a local wrecker driver. Maybe you should give him a call."

Stuart moved back over to the counter and made the call. A man named Johnny agreed to meet Stuart at his stricken car by seven o'clock.

Reggie raised the blinds on the front window and door. The sun was beginning to grow in its intensity, but the morning air still held a cool, purple quality to it.

"I think you should be all right now," he said. "Grab yerself a soda water from the cooler. It's a long walk back to your car. Just be careful. Maybe it's over, and maybe it ain't."

"Just watch who you talk to, right?" Stuart said.

Reggie smiled. "Right. Well, Stu, take care of yourself. You come back any other time, and I'll take you out on the lake myself. I don't want you gettin' the wrong idea about my lake. Any other day of the year, it's a glory of nature and God."

"I'm sure it is," Stuart said. "I may just do that. Thank you very much for the interesting evening."

Stuart and Reggie exchanged goodbyes, and Stuart stepped out onto the dock. The morning sun felt good on his face. He had been cooped up too long. He heard the cowbells jingle behind him, and the door latch shut. He glanced at his watch. He had forty-five minutes to get back to his car and meet Johnny and his wrecker.

Stuart paused a moment and stared out across the water to where he had seen the blazing steamboat. In the early morning sun, the water looked a bright blue green, not black as it had the previous evening. It was hard to believe such a thing had happened. Hell, maybe it hadn't happened. Maybe he'd imagined the whole damned thing.

Whatever, it was over now. Stuart started across the dock and made it to the corner of the building when he stopped suddenly. Somewhere, a child was crying. Cold chills raced up his spine. Slowly, willing his legs to move, Stuart turned the corner.

The boy couldn't be more than five years old. He sat, cold and wet, his knickers dripping, huddled up against the side of Reggie's all-night bait stand. His head was buried in his hands, and he was sobbing gently, as if deeply saddened but almost out of tears. When he heard Stuart's footsteps, he looked up.

His face was not burned. It was dirty and wet, and smeared with something that could've been dirt (or smoke soot). He looked into Stuart's eyes. Stuart could see and feel an overwhelming sadness, an understanding of complete and total loss, and he wanted to go to the boy.

"Son, are you okay?" he said, kneeling before the boy.

The little boy sniffed. "I'm lost," he said. "I can't find my mommy and daddy."

"Where are your parents?"

The boy pointed. Toward the lake. "I have to go home now."

"Where do you live?" Stuart asked.

"Out there," he answered, again pointing to the deepest parts of Caddo Lake. "I don't want to go home, but I have to."

"You poor child," Stuart said, a tear forming in his eye. "You poor, poor little boy."

"Will you walk me home?" the little boy asked.

Stuart nodded.

"Will you come with me?"

Stuart rose and took the little boy's hand. It felt cold to the touch but was filled with a kind warmth he could not deny. He helped the little boy up, and together, they turned toward the lake.

"Stuart!" a voice called.

He had not heard the clang of the cowbells. He turned to see Reggie standing at the corner. "Shouldn't you be gettin' back to your car? Johnny will leave if you ain't there."

Stuart nodded. "Yes, you're right."

Reggie stood there for a moment before returning to his shop. Stuart turned his attention back to the little boy. He was at the far end of the dock, where Stuart had seen the first victim emerge from the water.

"I'm sorry, son. I can't help you," he said, fighting back tears. "Go home now. I'm sorry, but I can't go with you."

Stuart turned and started across the bridge. When he got to the asphalt parking lot, he stopped and glanced up at the giant fish. The sun shone brilliantly on its painted scales. Stuart looked back at the end of the dock. The boy was gone, if he had ever been there. Stuart stepped back to the middle of the bridge and peered into the lake. There was a diminishing ring of tiny ripples extending out from the pier, and a trail of air bubbles stretched toward the centre of the lake.

And somewhere in all of that, deep in the underlying blackness of the day-lit waters, Stuart thought he could see a faint, shimmering reflection of a moon long since drowned and forgotten.

The Monolith

Mike Schuhler

Her bloodshot eyes gaze upon the winding road ahead, twisting through the cavernous woods and rocky hillsides of the lonely pine-scented north. She has reached the last hour of the long drive with a painfully numb ass, accompanied with tingling legs and a full bladder that threatens to empty with even the slightest bump.

Come on, you're almost there.

Hot, sweaty palms refuse to lessen their grip on the wheel. Brief glimpses in the rearview mirror reassure her he isn't following her, yet the fresh cut on her forehead serves as a reminder why she cannot let her guard down.

He has no idea where the cottage is. He will never find you there. She smacks the steering wheel as she feels the tears threatening again. *I could have just stayed. Stayed and not argued...*

She takes a deep breath and wipes her cheek angrily. *No, I did the right thing.*

The radio fades in and out, filling the cabin with static and incoherent words of a distant Canadian voice. In the seat beside her lay her wallet and a half-eaten bag of potato chips that left her begging for something besides bland bottled water to drink.

A large wooden sign ahead catches her eye: Little Copper Valley.

Not much farther to go.

Sunlight falls behind her, painting the sky in gorgeous pink hues as she enters the rural valley town carved into the mountainous landscape. Outdated buildings skirt the main road of the aging town—relics that have stood the tests of time. Memories surface in her mind in short little clips that date back to her childhood. Brief, fragmented images of her and her sister running up the sidewalk with only a few dollars in hand. The old ice cream parlour, one of her favourites, still stood with its name painted along the top of the faded brick walls.

She misses those days. Days without bills, work, and a psychotic fiancé. Growing up and landing that perfect, high-paying job in the city does not seem as desirable as it once did. She would trade it all just to live here in peace. But that just isn't possible.

The cottage is situated in a remote area just beyond the town. Only a few families have property back there. Right off the main road is a narrow and unnamed gravel drive. Most people wouldn't even catch it. She can never forget it, though, not with the enormous black oak tree that stands near the entrance. It has to be the largest in the area. Both she and her sister used it as the single landmark that told them they were almost home.

The gravel makes the ever-familiar crunching noise under the tires of her luxury sedan as she approaches the family cottage.

With the car in park, she exhales. Her tight grip releases the faux leather wheel, finally allowing blood to circulate. Tingling shoots through her hand as she shakes it back to life. With sudden relief, she grabs her wallet as her license falls onto the floor.

"Come on, can't I get a break."

She retrieves it. Lisa Crawford of Grand Rapids. She realizes how close she was to taking his name. Chills run through her and she cringes before exiting the car.

The house has been empty since last October, and there is no sign of life inside. The patches of overgrowth in the lawn are proof the landscaper has not been out in a while. Notes of sweet field grass and honeysuckle fill the air as she makes her way to the front door.

From her pocket, she retrieves a single key she kept hidden in her nightstand back home. The key to her refuge—a symbol of her escape.

***

The dusty interior is just as she remembers. Two old couches form an L-shape around a small coffee table facing a large console television. A single bay window overlooks the front yard behind dingy white curtains. The stale air is laced with that unnameable scent: a perfect blend of dust, cheap air freshener and old carpet that calls back childhood one second and allergies in the next.

With the flick of a switch, a tall floor lamp illuminates the walls dressed in aging paint and wood panelling. The place is a time machine, complete with a look she was never fond of but also could never bring herself to change.

The floor creaks as she makes her way through the living room and into the kitchen. She stops at her old bedroom, the one she shared with her sister, Lauren.

The room has gotten smaller each time she visits. Gone now are the posters and black-lights, and only the two full-size beds, a single dresser and some stuffed animals remain. The cheap carnival toys she has treasured through most of her thirty-five years.

The cottage puts her at ease. Everything in order, with the exception of the empty fridge. For now, all she wants is a shower and rest.

He can't get you. Not here.

"Calm down. You'll be fine." Her own words do little to reassure herself.

The comforting silence of the cottage envelops her like a soothing blanket. Nothing bad can happen here. Not here— *except for...*

Her mind jogs away from a memory best left alone. Lisa retreats to the bathroom to distract herself, turning on the bathwater. The potent smell of the well water erupts from the faucet, fading as the water clears through the old pipes.

With a single hand, she tests the temperature. "The water heater is working, at least."

Hot water caresses over bruises of different shades, some old, some new. She tries not to look at them, those ugly, painful reminders of poor decisions. The crown of her head touches the low-hanging shower head. Bent at the knees, she runs a heavy amount of cheap shampoo through her hair, its lavender scent erupting from the suds as they travel down her skin before reaching the drain.

As she dries herself with one of the stiff towels from the hall closet, she recalls a memory of how her dad always used fabric softener on the towels, no matter how many times her mother reminded him not to. They were always like cardboard lined with sandpaper when they were line-dried in the sun.

A grin washes over her face as she recollects those times. Even in death, the memories of her parents' gentle teasing makes her smile.

A quick tour of the house, just to be sure, and she retires to her bed. The sheets are cheap, but also clean and more than inviting after the long drive. The mattress is smaller than what she is used to, but then again, it is also absent one asshole.

Not a terrible trade-off.

Although exhausted, she still takes the sleeping pill. Her mind is far too busy to do it alone. In the dark, she lies under an old down comforter. Its weight presses around her, embracing her in a peaceful grip. Within an arm's reach sits a kitchen knife—just in case.

***

Sunlight pierces the dirty glass of the small bedroom window, warming her face. Her eyes open, finding herself in the bed holding onto the large stuffed toy of a cartoon moose. She watches as dust dances in the rays of light until a passing cloud dims it just enough to make them disappear once more.

She sits up and stands with some difficulty. The bruises are sore and unforgiving still, yet she pushes through the pain and gets moving to distract herself from the life she escaped just twenty-four hours ago.

Paranoia. A bonus personality trait that she tries her best to hide. She moves into each room, checking for the slightest sign of disturbance before turning her back on any door.

The kitchen is her last stop, and the most disappointing. Her stomach growls at the thought of food, knowing the house has nothing of substance to offer.

Driving to town sparks a renewed sense of anxiety. *Calm down, please don't act weird.* Without further hesitation, she takes a deep breath and slowly exhales before leaving the safety of her car.

The old market smells strange, like vinegar and glass cleaner. It is almost as she remembers it, and she compares it against the large chain grocery stores back home. This place, with its few aisles and dirty floors, is in stark contrast to the stores she normally shops. Nothing fancy at all, just old signage and old employees. She may be the youngest person within a two-mile radius.

Her nerves still have the best of her, and she feels eyes on her no matter where she goes. Even if she were the only living soul in the aisle, he is always nearby. With little focus on actual shopping, her basket contains only frozen dinners, snack food and cheap soft drinks.

She approaches the aged clerk with a smile. A man well into his eighties reaches out and grabs her basket with trembling, liver-spotted hands. An odour of stale cigarettes surrounds him, the stench sticking to him as if to warn others of his impending death that should occur any day now.

"How ya, miss? Find everything okay?"

She nods. "Yes, thank you."

Avoiding any more questions, she refuses further eye contact and pays with the cash she had stashed away for months.

As she walks towards the door, she can feel his yellowing, cloudy eyes on her, peering from behind a pair of cheap bifocals. She doesn't have to look back to confirm it.

Maybe shorts were a bad idea.

Once outside, she shifts the flimsy paper bags, still feeling his gaze through his clouded, diseased eyes.

Get raped out here, and it's your fault for wearing the wrong clothes.

Back in the car, she locks the door and inspects the surrounding area. It finally dawns on her. Little Copper Valley is a broken version of its former self. From the outside looking in, it is the same as she remembers. But something is different now. It's a dying place with decaying businesses… and decaying people. The town she knew is now littered with elderly folks out for their morning walks and mid-day errands. On the surface, it's a charming, quiet town, hidden in the valley from the busy city life that now feels a world away. However, underneath the surface lies a decrepit and fading scar on a section of expensive countryside the world will easily forget.

What the hell happened here?

As saddened as she is, she still worries that he is around. That the next car she sees turn the corner onto the main drive will be his overpriced luxury car, standing out from the rusted pickups and beaters that litter the town. Its freshly waxed paint will sparkle in the sun as he searches every street and alley between here and Grand Rapids.

***

Hours go by slower out here. The morning drags into lunchtime as she sits on one of the dusty couches, reading without comprehending the story she holds. Instead, her mind returns to that dark place, tinged with fear and betrayal.

Stop it. Dammit!

Frustrated, she sets the book on the coffee table and cups her face in her hands, fighting back the emotions and worries she can't escape.

Should have gotten whiskey. That would do it.

"Well, can't go back to town now. Not today."

She gets to her feet and stretches as she looks through the window. The scene is calm as green leaves dance in the gentle breeze and shadows from the puffy clouds that pass in front of the sun.

Maybe some fresh air will do the trick?

The wood planks of the porch are splintered in parts, mostly near the steps where she sat. The sun-warmed wood feels good on her bare legs, but she remains careful not to risk a splinter.

Calm surrounds her, the only sounds the birds and the occasional chirp from a hidden cricket or the croaking of a frog. The sun glows against her lightly freckled cheeks, her eyes hidden behind a pair of expensive sunglasses. A sudden noise brings her to attention. Something not birds or chirping crickets. Alarmed, she straightens her back. Her breathing becomes quick and shallow.

"Help... help me... please." It is the distant voice of a child.

Lisa stands, brushing off her thighs as she descends the porch steps.

"Hello?" she calls out.

She surveys the yard and the trees beyond.

"Hello? Can you hear me?"

Only silence follows as she makes her way around the perimeter of the property.

"Please. I'm lost."

The voice of the little girl comes from just behind the brush, out of sight in the trees. Lisa sees an overgrown trail that she's never noticed before.

Shit, these shorts were definitely a bad idea.

Tall grass tickles the flesh of her thighs as she enters the path. "Can you hear me?"

"Come quick. Please." The voice sounds further away, but more urgent.

"I'm coming, hold on."

She ventures deeper into the woods, passing through thick brush while keeping an eye out for snakes and poison ivy.

"Can you hear me?" Lisa's voice carries far into the wilderness yet meets no response.

"Hello?"

Where the hell am I? I can't get lost out here.

As she goes deeper into the woods, she spots a clearing ahead. She moves through tangled vine and fallen timber to meet the rocky ground where nothing grows, opening the area to the face of a tall mountain that overlooks the entire valley.

Exhausted, she crouches to rest before standing once again.

"Can you hear me? Hello?" Her voice echoes off the rocky wall and still… nothing.

What if she's hurt? I can't just leave her out here, can I?

A sweet smell creeps into her nostrils. *Honeysuckle?*

The intoxicating aroma of the plant distracts her from the realization she now has to track her way back to the cottage.

No more chasing voices. You're letting your paranoia talk.

On her way back, she takes more time to avoid the sharp and itchy shrubbery that caught her legs on the way in.

What if he found me? What if he's waiting for me back at the cottage?

"Get a grip already. Come on."

***

There is something special about the countryside at night. With the cottage nestled away, carved into a section of northern woods, Lisa finds a certain tranquillity in watching the sun disappear slowly, leaving behind a sky full of fiery pinks and dark blues. But even the colourful sky cannot keep the girl's voice out of her head. Its desperation and helplessness.

Did I give up too easily?

"Shake it off."

It was probably a lost girl who finally found her parents. That's why she stopped calling out.

Random specks of dim, green lights illuminate and fade in the cool night air.

Lightning bugs.

She remembers how her aunt would always call them fireflies, but everyone else called them lightning bugs. They are a welcome surprise, something she forgot about back in the city. Then comes something more sinister. The kamikaze buzzing of a mosquito torments her ear, and she swats at the side of her head.

Frustrated, she retreats inside to escape the bloodsucking threat, closing the door behind her.

The comforting quiet of the night remains only skin deep as anxiety builds within her once again. Every window in the house is darkened, with curtains drawn to hide her from view of anyone who may be outside.

You're going to drive yourself crazy, old girl.

"Better safe than sorry."

She walks the small perimeter of the cottage interior not once, but twice. Nothing to worry about now. Door locked; windows locked.

No one can see me. They won't even know I'm here.

Now she can relax, nesting herself into the corner of the couch, submerged under an old turquoise quilt knitted by her great-grandmother decades ago. In her hands she holds a dated hardcover. Its binding remains intact, but its slipcover shows signs of wear. Her eyes travel along with the words, but she doesn't really read. Instead, her mind returns to the woods where she followed the voice with no success.

She thinks of Gary.

Stop it. Just stop.

Frustrated, she tries focusing on the novel. Pages turn and paragraphs flow by as she slowly absorbs herself in the story.

She takes in each sentence, forming the mental image in her head. She makes out the characters' features and the city landscape of an older time, a better time.

Her eyes grow heavy but remain focused on the pages. She refuses to let up, so much that she is no longer aware of anything outside of the current chapter. Not even the chiming of the grandfather clock on the opposite end of the room shakes her out.

***

Lisa awakens on the couch the next morning to the sunlight illuminating the aged fabric of the window curtains. Beside her on the floor lay her book, closed with no marker in place.

Within moments of her waking, her stomach growls.

I forgot to eat last night.

With creaking joints, she sits up, stretching her neck from side to side, triggering a satisfying series of cracks.

The kitchen floor, cold underfoot, creaks with each step. She remembers when she was a teenager, trying to sneak through the kitchen at night. The car keys were always in the same spot, but the floors were loudest at night. She only got out once without getting caught.

The party.

A grin washes over her face before fading, giving way as another memory creeps in. One much darker that she keeps buried.

That night so many years ago still fills her with guilt. She spots the phone on the wall, the dull, ruby-coloured handset that hasn't changed in the last two decades.

Lauren.

Her sister, although two years younger, always had her life figured out. Stability, independence—things Lisa always wanted but somehow threw away because her heart led her the wrong direction one too many times. She wants to call her.

She'll realize I'm a mess. Even more than she did before. And especially now.

Shaking away her inclination, she disappears into the bathroom. A quick shower to wake up and forget.

The bruising today is better, still noticeable but fading. *Never again.* She finds strength in those words. *Never again.* She turns off the steaming water and steps out, drying off before wiping the mirror of fog. Eyeing herself and her fading injuries, something inside her intensifies.

"Never fucking again," she repeats, this time out loud.

As soon as she says those words, a faint noise catches her ear from outside the bathroom. Her mind drifts into fear.

Did he find me?

Frozen, she stands bent at the waist, listening with short, shallow breaths. Again, the noise from outside. Lisa secures the towel around her body, and against better judgment, opens the bathroom door.

Nothing unusual, everything as it should be. She steps into the hallway, armed with nothing but the towel covering her body.

Once again, and with urgency, the scratching returns. Lisa jumps back into the bathroom before realizing it comes from the front door.

She looks through the small window in the wooden door but sees no silhouette.

An animal is all.

With slow and steady steps, she approaches the door. Her pulse quakes through her limbs as she grips the door handle and turns, opening the door just enough to see the empty porch.

Must have run away.

She steps outside to see the door bearing several light scratches, likely left by some mischievous forest creature. The sweet aroma of the morning breeze lures her further out to the porch as the rapid thud of a distant and unseen woodpecker throttles through the air. Over the noise, she hears something else. She cocks her head to focus on it as her eyes squint. Only seconds go by before she hears it once more.

"Help!"

The child's voice, just like yesterday. Lisa immediately backs into the cottage and rushes into the bedroom, wasting little time getting dressed in a faded pair of jeans and an old t-shirt. She slips on a pair of beat-up cross trainers and secures her hair in a ponytail before heading outside.

***

The voice of the little girl beckons her down the same worn trail as before. No matter how close it sounds, Lisa cannot reach it in time before it moves a little further away. The day is hotter than yesterday, and Lisa feels it wearing on her. Sweat trickles from her face and down her shirt, causing it to cling to her skin. She slows to a walk. No matter how frightened the voice becomes, Lisa has to conserve what energy she has left.

"Where are you? Stop moving away from me..." Her words fade with her quick breath and pounding heart.

Hearing no response, Lisa stops once again at the same rocky wall as before. The familiar scent of honeysuckle thickens the air. She takes deep breaths, letting the sweet smell fill her with a feeling of euphoria. Her extremities tingle and her head swims in a brief state of carelessness. Her muscles loosen, the pain in her back fades and disappears, and her stress is gone. Until the voice makes its presence known once more.

"Up here," the voice calls out.

Lisa's senses return to normal as she looks up to find the source of the voice. She sees nothing but a large plateau, thirty feet up and separate from the mountain itself, draped in thick vines covered in beautiful flowers.

That's the only place she could be.

She takes it all in, sizing it up.

How the hell do I get up there?

Better yet, how the hell did she get up there?

Lisa surveys the rock, looking for a way up. "Hey! Can you hear me?"

The voice does not respond, leaving Lisa to examine the rock from a different angle. There is a three-foot-wide gap between the body of the plateau and the steep mountain slope. In the cool darkness of the gap, she spots something. A gentle breeze greets her as she enters the narrow space.

"Are you there?" the voice calls out once more.

Lisa makes her way down towards the object. "Just hold on," she yells back.

Sharp edges of the blood-red rock scrape against her chest as she traverses through the uneven passage. She reaches out, and her palm fills with the rung of a tall, wooden ladder.

I hope this is sturdy enough.

She squeezes her body to position herself onto the ladder. She shouldn't have, but she does—looking up to see how high she must travel.

"Oh, you shouldn't have done that," she says to herself as she quickly looks back down.

Without further hesitation, she ascends. The narrow rungs press painfully against the soles of her shoes and creak under her weight. Lisa trembles with fear as each step takes her higher but she refuses to leave the girl stranded up there.

"I'm almost up."

Her fear of heights nips at her heels. She fights against it but knows better than to look down. Lisa has climbed nothing like this since... never. *Maybe the rope in gym class.*

Suddenly, a new voice makes itself known. "Hurry," it snaps in a guttural, inhuman rasp.

She stops, not replying to the hostile demand. Her breathing heavy and her mind confused, she backs down the ladder.

What was that?

"Please hurry," the familiar voice of the little girl returns.

Something isn't right. Just go home.

Her hands tingle with pins and needles. She can feel the empty space below her without having to look.

"No, keep going. You're almost there," she tells herself.

***

Finally, she stands on top, feet firmly planted on the rock, avoiding a wandering gaze that may reveal the distant ground below. She bends slightly at the knees amid a passing gust of wind and takes in the strange surroundings. The rocky surface is worn smooth, covered in thick tendrils of vines adorned with bright yellow and white flowers releasing thick notes of honeysuckle. Each vine traces to the centre of the plateau, leading to a large pillar: a monolith of black stone erected from the natural rock of the plateau.

What is that?

The monolith does not seem natural. Its base is secured into the ground, wrapped fully in the sprawling vines of the strange greenery. *Dare she approach?*

"Hello?" she calls out. Her voice echoes.

With no response, she feels duped. *What are you doing up here? Hearing things, that's all. Maybe there is no girl.*

Her legs respond with an instinct she cannot control, as if a foreign energy assists her towards the large monolith.

"Stop," she demands aloud, and her legs freeze in place.

With a deep breath and a rush of confidence, she takes control of her legs and walks closer to the odd structure, carefully navigating the vine-covered surface.

"Little girl? Where are you?"

An unexpected response cuts through the air, born from a voice not of a child. "I'm over here, on the other side."

As she walks the wide perimeter of the tall object, she notices the base of the monolith is heavily overgrown with the scented flowers. One side is thicker in the growth than the others, so much so that it has covered the stone underneath. And there is no sign of a little girl anywhere.

"Hello? Where are you?"

Frustrated even more now, she loses hope. Then she sees something in the tangle of the monolith.

Carefully she steps closer, her hopeful doubts fading as she nears the round, white object. Suddenly, she stops and leaps backwards. Her screams echo through the valley as she stares into the empty eye sockets of a child's skull. At the base of the monolith stand the thick entanglement of sun-bleached bone and ropy vines. The child's joints are still secured to the black stone in the deadly embrace of the plant.

Tears run down Lisa's flushed cheeks as she crawls away from the monolith.

"No... this can't be happening."

The voice never returns as she makes her escape, the dead sockets of the little girl still in sight. Her sobs fade as she focuses on climbing down the old wooden ladder.

Just get home. You can make it.

Her laboured breathing keeps her pace slower than she wants. Her clothes snag on hidden thorns and stray branches. She has the sensation of being watched but does not dare look back.

Something is back there. Move your ass.

Finally, she reaches the cottage and collapses on the steps, exhausted.

***

The call to her sister is long overdue and makes Laura feel small and helpless. In great detail, she explains everything about Gary. Lisa knows her sister would come. She always did.

She likes the drama. Stop telling her so much.

"Lauren. Please come up here. I can't be alone, and I had nowhere else to go."

But you know that, don't you?

"There is something else. I saw something... Listen, I just need you here, I'm kind of freaked out. I'm sorry."

"... Thank you."

The frustration in her sister's voice is enough to know that this trip won't be easy. *A sudden three-hour-drive into the night to meet your crazy sister who left her abusive fiancé.* Lisa couldn't help but feel like a train wreck. Her life again is in shambles because of some dumb decision.

"Don't sweat it, girl." That's what she'll say. When she means is, "Get your shit together for once. After so many years, you're still a mess."

But this time, it's not just her fault.

***

Lisa anxiously awaits her sister, rehearsing everything she wants to say. The recent discoveries, the terror of what she found on the mountainside. All things that have now brought her to tears.

What do I say? Do I tell her all of it? Will she deny it? Laugh it off and tell me I'm imagining things?

Buried in her thick comforter on the couch, she consoles herself with the rhythmic sound of the old grandfather clock. *Tick... tick... tick...*

Was there really a voice? Did I make it up?

She wants nothing more than to forget about it. Forget about the little girl whose rotted skeleton sits atop that plateau. Forget about the things she has seen that she never wanted to know.

Nerves. That's all it is, nerves.

She wraps herself tightly in the comforter, staring at the large console television but too tired to get up and turn it on. The aged VCR above it blinks 12:00 repeatedly, almost in sync with the tick of the clock.

Tick... tick... tick...

The air hangs still, overwhelming in the silence. She does not want to get up.

But maybe a show or two would help. By then, Lauren will be here.

Tick... tick... tick...

An unfamiliar noise sneaks in between the ticks of the clock and the flashing light of the VCR. A light knocking somewhere else in the house.

No, a scratch!

Like a scratching on glass, it comes from another room. She turns enough to see down the darkened hall. *Possibly just a branch scraping against the wall outside, or an animal scurrying about.*

It stops as quickly as it started.

Tick... tick... tick...

She pushes back the comforter as she stands, making her way to the TV.

The screen warms up, resolving into the staticky image of a news anchor. She doesn't care for the news, but any background noise will aid in her distraction.

Tick... tick... tick... tap... tap...

Her head snaps up. The noise came from a room down the hall.

A bird by a window, most likely.

Tap... tap... tap... tap

Taking a breath, she stands, tosses the comforter aside and walks down the hall. Forcing herself not to hesitate, she enters the dimly lit room and heads for the window. Her eyes dart back and forth, seeing nothing out of the ordinary. Not a bird, not even a squirrel. *Nothing.*

She turns away and sits on her bed, sighing and running a hand through her brown hair. "Got to relax. Stop getting so spooked."

The light from the outside dims, bathing the room in a melancholy shade of dark grey. The muffled jingle of a low-budget commercial plays from the living room.

Tap... tap... tap... tap

Her blood freezes. The culprit is back, tapping once more at the window. *Don't look, maybe it'll just go away.*

She resists fleeing the room. *What is there to be afraid of? Just a dumb animal.*

But it is obvious the tapping is intentional—*tap... tap... tap*—trying to get her attention. She hesitates, but ignoring her instincts, begins turning her eyes towards the window. They are met with a pair much like hers, only these are a sickly yellow. With a scream, she leaps to her feet and slams her body into the wall. By the time she looks back, the eyes have vanished.

Teary, puffy-eyed, she leaves the room. "What the hell is wrong with me?" she says aloud.

Stress, that's what it is. You're seeing and hearing things. That's all. Like the voice of the girl.

Tick... tick...

With the tapping ceased, she tries to collect herself. *Wild imagination you got there, girl.*

"Lauren, please hurry the hell up," she says, checking the time on the clock. She realizes that now she has another reason to look forward to her meeting with her sister.

Lisa paces around the living room, her efforts at staying calm failing. She stops at the front door and looks outside, checking the lock and resuming her aimless pacing.

Flowers? Her nostrils flare.

The familiar notes of honeysuckle have found their way into the cottage. *Maybe a breeze carried them from the mountainside… from the rock where…*

Lightheaded, she makes her way to the couch, falling upon it with dead weight. The air is thick with the strong floral aroma. The living room reeks of a flower shop, with wonderful scents that make her head swim and her limbs numb. With blurred vision, her eyes close as her body tingles with crawling ecstasy… then darkness.

***

Lisa stopped dreaming mostly into her adulthood. But there was always this one dream she would have. *The Dream*, as she would come to call it. It's been over ten years since it last showed itself. She always saw it coming, like the stillness in the air before a storm.

In the dream, she was seventeen years old and sneaking out of the cottage late that night for the first and last time ever. Only in the dream, the walk to the field was quick, almost instant. In the distance, she would spot the lights and the sounds of talking and laughing. She would hear the faint music that played from the cab of a pickup with its doors wide open.

Dreams typically played out in unusual rhythm, throwing strange details of little importance, and even the slightest thought could change the course of the entire thing. But not *The*

Dream. No, it's more like being caught in a movie that she knew the end to, but without any way to stop it.

Lisa remembered meeting him by his car, a dated muscle car like something she saw on TV, only this one was a little more beat up. He is older, a sophomore in college with shoulder-length dark hair. His face stubble scratched against her cheeks when she got close. In the dream, no one else talked, no one else mattered. Other people became mere far-off shadows in the background when they were together in the cramped front seat of the car.

She would look up and out the window while he was busy with her, and that's when she saw her. The little girl. Lost and scared, calling out for her mother. *What is she doing all the way out here at this time of night?* Her voice would be hardly audible through the foggy windows and the low volume of the radio.

She wouldn't stop, though, not until he had finished. And by then, the girl would have disappeared into the surrounding darkness.

Lisa hardly has time to put herself back together before he drives her half a mile up the dark road and drops her off by the enormous tree. In the dream, his face hides behind shadows as if light avoids it. His last words to her are "Thanks," then she closes the door. Gravel kicks up, pelting against her legs as the car speeds off. The glow of the taillight's shines in the glassy reflection of her eyes before disappearing.

The last moment was by far the worst. Lisa's walk down that gravel road begins with the tears of guilt and shame. *You ignored the helpless little girl for a man who used you and threw you away like trash.*

That's when she hears it. The little girl's scream of pain filling the night air from deep within the surrounding woods. In the dream, Lisa would never reach the house. Something was following her, something hidden. Each time she would get a little closer to the house before it comes up from behind and grabs her, pain shooting through her sides as it pulls her slowly into the brush.

***

She awakens with a gasp. Teary-eyed, she finds herself in the dark, sunken into the mattress of her bed.

How the hell did I get here?

She looks around, confused. Not a single light in sight, except for the bluish hue of the moon washing in through the window near the foot of her bed.

The box spring creaks loudly as she sits. Her mouth is dry as cotton balls.

He found you, dummy. You slipped up, and he found you.

She swings her legs from the bed. The painful tingling of rushing blood follows. Limping across the room, she pauses at the open door to the hall until she regains the full function of her legs. Faint remnants of honeysuckle cling in the air like old grease in a dirty kitchen. She has no recollection of even falling asleep, and here she is standing in the hallway of her darkened cottage.

Tick… tick… tick…

Something is not right. She can sense it. The apprehension of being watched and being helpless… vulnerable.

Tick… tick… tick…

Anxiety builds deep inside her. Something is waiting for her. *In the other room?*

Don't go in there. Not the other bedroom. The back bedroom where they let it happen.

Tick… tick… tick…

Its presence is heavy, like a celestial body of such enormous mass that it pulls at her, wanting her to come into the room.

Tick… tick… tick…

Lisa fights the ever-increasing urge, instead navigating the black silhouettes of the bulky living room furniture. Her hands guide her, fingers tracing the wall, fishing for the door. As she moves closer, a calm breeze brushes the skin of her neck. *It's open? But how?*

Her mind jumps to a million possibilities of why the door would now be open, but only one sticks. *He found you.*

Tick… tick… tick…

"Lauren?" she calls out gently. *It has to be her sister. Lisa knows her sister has been here recently, so she would know the house well.*

The door creaks loudly as she pulls it open. In the darkness outside, she sees an SUV with its driver side door open and the interior lights glowing.

"Lauren? Where are you?" She steps into the drive slowly, the jagged rocks crunching underfoot as she makes her way to the abandoned vehicle. She spots her sister's leather purse in the passenger's seat. The same purse he bought Lisa for her birthday last year. *Definitely Lauren's SUV.*

"Lauren?" She looks around, frustrated. *Was she in the house already? In the back bedroom?*

She looks back to the house. Nothing—no sign of anyone or anything.

By the time she hears the running footsteps approach her from behind, it's too late. A blinding, heavy blow to the back of her skull sends her crashing to the ground.

***

Tick… tick… tick…

Lisa hears the clock once more, her head throbbing with each tick. She whimpers as the muscles in her face send a sharp pain through the flesh of her forehead.

"Hey there, beautiful, welcome back."

It was him. He found you! Now what?

Her eyes struggle to open through the dried blood.

"Don't move too much. I wouldn't want you to hurt yourself more," Gary says.

Her head hurts and her body feels scraped and sore. *He dragged you through the gravel. What a piece of shit.*

Lisa moves her mouth. It is dry and swollen. "Fu… fuck yo—"

The slap comes before she can finish her sentence. Her face stings and she cannot hold back a whimper. Tears cascade down her cheeks, salting her sore, cut lip. The slap is harder than the ones she remembers.

Guess his gym membership is really paying off now.

"That's no way to talk to the guy who just travelled many hours to come see you now, is it?"

Lisa works her eyes open. Through blurred vision, she can see him crouched in front of her. The living room is still dark. Her back rests against the smaller couch, and as her vision clears, she gets a good look at his face.

It's him, alright. How did he know where to find her? Did she call him? Certainly not.

"Where's my sister?"

His only answer is a few chuckles. His dark eyes are flanked by crow's feet and his breath reeks of bourbon.

Typical.

"Lauren is fine, babe, don't worry. She won't wake up for a while, though, so I hope you didn't have any plans."

So, her too. I'd wondered when it would start.

His body straddles her, keeping her pinned in position against the couch.

Tick… tick… tick…

"What do you want from me?"

"Nothing, not anymore," he says as his face moves closer to hers. "I'm just here to teach you a lesson. No one leaves me without my permission. Not you, not her. All you had to do was ask."

Sure. Like she asked—begged—the night before she left.

Suddenly, something to Gary's back catches her eye. Something in the dark space of the hall. The door to the back bedroom slowly opens.

Is something really in there? Maybe it's Lauren.

Something leaves the bedroom, but its shape is hidden in the dark. The asshole was blocking most of her view down the hall.

"Are you even fucking listening to me?"

Her eyes snap back to meet his, filled with such hatred. "Gary, let me go." She no longer fears him as much as what is hiding in the dark behind him. It must be crawling, since she can't see it, only the top of the open doorway it left behind.

Lauren?

"Sure, once you tell me how sorry you are for running away like that. And then, you can ask me nicely for permission."

He doesn't hear it coming over his own voice. Lisa watches silently as it stalks towards him on all four limbs. It definitely isn't her sister. When she sees the pale, sunken face hidden beneath strands of matted, dirty hair, Lisa screams. Gary jerks away from her in surprise, inadvertently planting his head directly into the sickly, scarred flesh of its chest.

Its head tilts up just high enough for her to see its dead expression as its clay-coloured lips curl back. She stares at the maw of jagged teeth before they disappear into Gary's head, scraping strips of flesh from his scalp.

Lisa watches, unable to move, as large talons wrap around his face like a vice. His screams grow more desperate as the creature drags him off of her. Gary pisses himself, crying both tears of fear and pain. His arms and legs flail helplessly as it pulls him into the abyss of the back bedroom.

Their bedroom.

She muffles her own screams as she makes her way to the door, trying to not bring attention to herself for fear that it may come for her. The minute that follows lasts an eternity as it toys with its prey. Finally, his screams stop, to be replaced by the sound of limbs cracking and the wet splatter of something being tossed against the wood floor. Guttural growls and grunts echo down the dark hall of the cottage, then pause.

Lisa swings open the front door, the sound filling the room. She stumbles into the cool dark of the night and then falls to her knees on the damp ground. Lightheaded and terrified, she gets to her feet and makes her journey down the porch steps, limping across the jagged gravel of the drive to her car. She reaches with a shaking hand and grabs the handle, pulling it.

Locked. You locked it and left the keys inside.

She continues to jerk the handle until she hears the thing inside pound against the floor relentlessly as if angered by her panic. Her legs buckle and her palm slams against her mouth to choke back the scream.

Lauren's SUV...

"Please be in there," she says as she limps to her sister's abandoned vehicle. Even with her back to the house, she can feel its hungry glare. She refuses to look back and jumps into the seat, fumbling in the dim light by the steering wheel.

The keys!

Without further hesitation, she turns the ignition and closes the door, locking it.

Lisa backs out of the drive and turns down the narrow road. Parked by the large black oak tree sits one of Gary's overpriced luxury cars.

The son of a bitch followed her. He followed her.
I never should have asked her to come.

Her tears stretch for miles along the long and lonely highway as she heads south in the pre-dawn morning. Low-lying fog swirls around her tires.

Where was she? What did he do to her?

"That son of a bitch."

Her palm strikes the wheel as she navigates the vehicle through the desolate countryside. As the miles pass behind her, she thinks of her sister, stranded out there alone.

Should I go back? Maybe she's alive and needs me. We are still sisters, even so.

"I'm sorry, Lauren," she cries as she passes yet another exit.

Gaylord, Exit 282. Still so far to go.

Little slices of civilization, the truck stops and desolate strip clubs and sex shops, are the only beacons of life outside of the four-wheeled, overpriced fortress. Not a single vehicle appears along the isolated stretch of highway cutting through the thick woods of the cold and lifeless northern landscape.

What was it? An animal? No, couldn't have been.

She exhales slowly. "Calm down, bitch." His words, said so often, ringing in her ears.

Whatever it was, it killed that asshole.

"He's gone! That motherfucker is gone!" She laughs with tears in her eyes as she slams her palm against the wheel. Then her laughs become sobs. Her mind replays the chicken wing sound of limbs being twisted from their sockets and the screams that followed.

Her palms sweat against the leather wheel. Gary always was partial to leather, she remembers, tamping down a rising anger that almost overshadows her terror. He probably even bought this car for her.

The night sky gives way to the dawn, revealing a landscape of both forest and large, open fields. Her nostrils tingle. Something sweet in the air… something familiar.

She inhales the aroma of honeysuckle.

"What?"

Her skin tingles and her senses cloud with fuzzy ripples of euphoria throughout her body.

With a deep breath, she tries to compose herself.

Look, you're almost to Grayling now. Just keep it together.

She rolls down the window, blasting her face with cold air, but the scent remains and grows stronger.

Her grip on the wheel loosens and her eyes tire, straying off the road in front of her to the rearview mirror, where she catches something unusual.

The shadows are broken, but she can see the outline of the backseat—and something else. Her fingers feel numb, and the steering wheel slides through her palms like silk as she struggles to make out the strange figure within the limited frame of the rearview mirror.

Two sickly yellow orbs form in the darkness. Eyes born from diseased, blackened sockets stare back at her from a pale face. The eyes burn like wildfire, full of a hatred that goes back to the beginning of time.

It lunges from the darkness, and her palms release the wheel, falling to her side as it grips her head. Useless breaths of air leave her body as the vehicle turns violently to the shoulder, running off the road. Its tires squeal and skid as her feet scramble for the brakes.

***

"No!" she yells, sitting up and finding herself in the twisted sheets of her own bed. She reaches to her chest, feeling her pounding heart.

Beside her is the empty side of the bed. His side. It's been almost a week since she witnessed Gary's death. Processing what she saw was no simple task, and neither was reporting him missing… him and her sister.

Her guilt of leaving weighs heavy in the form of nightmares. Dreams of that thing killing her sister… poor Lauren probably never knew what was coming.

She remembers the story she told the police.

I let Lauren borrow the car to go up north. Cheaper on gas than her SUV. That thing is a beast and not cheap to drive all that way. There is no way they can blame me. And if anyone did know about the affair, and them meeting up together at the cottage, then that explains why Gary was there.

Memories of Lauren collect in her mind. Tears stream down her cheeks as she breathes the stale air of the bedroom.

Is she even dead? Should she have gone back?

Lisa fills the bathtub with steaming, scorching water. If anything will relax her, it'll be the bath—and maybe a glass of wine. Gary always bought the good stuff.

Good riddance.

The Chardonnay he bought last year. *Excellent choice.*

Her bare skin tints pink under the warm soapy water and she closes her eyes, sipping straight from the bottle. "Good fucking riddance."

Half a bottle down and still the water remains hot. Lisa wants to sleep, a drunken sleep where time fast forwards into the headache of the next morning. A place where nightmares cannot reach.

Tick… tick… tick…

She sits up, exposing her chest to the cooler air. "No."

She hastily dries off, wrapping the towel around her body, and walks to her bedroom.

Tick… tick… tick…

She cannot pinpoint the source of the noise in the darkened room. Suddenly, the phone rings, causing her to jump. "Shit!"

Who calls this late?

She picks up the phone from the nightstand. The number of the caller ID matches that of the phone at the cabin. "Hello?"

"Lisa." Her sister's voice.

She breaks down into tears. "Lauren, oh my god... where are you? What happened?"

"Lisa... it... it has me. It found me." Lauren's voice is laboured. "It wants to kill me like it killed Gary."

Lisa's sobs intensify as she struggles to hold the phone to her ear. "What?"

Then, the voice changes. A guttural, inhuman voice speaks back to her. One she has heard before. "You forgot your sister, Lisa... Come back."

The phone disconnects.

Tick... tick... tick...

The Muse

Callum Gracey

Dad strikes another match and lights another fancy candle, so that the living room smells like a potent mix of vanilla chucked on an autumn bonfire.

More matches lives are spent on the lighting of four pumpkins. One for him, one for Mum, and one for each of the twins. Dads carved them all of course, Hallowe'en is his night, but he's carved his own pumpkin the best and set it on the coffee table, its eyes watching the gathered family closely.

"There we go," he says, "that's set the mood. Let me get the light."

The room is plunged into a darkness that's undercut by a dancing orange light that casts spectral shapes on the wall. "Everyone comfy?" he asks, taking their silence as an excited 'yes.'

Outside it's pouring down and blowing a gale. Dad watches through the window as the streetlamps and the moonlight catch illuminated speckles of rainfall that seem to fall one way, only to be caught by a violent gust of wind and sent spiralling another. Dad tests the atmosphere in the room with the curtains open and then closed. Open. Then closed. Closed, definitely closed.

"All we need now is thunder and lightning," he says cheerfully as he sits himself down in the spot, his spot, where he does all his writing now. Where the cushion is bowed and buckled and depressed to the shape of his arse.

"Let's just get sorted," he says, pulling out four labelled envelopes. He checks the titles handwritten on each envelope and lays them out on the table, the edge of each envelope perfectly flush with the edge of the coffee table.

"Okay. Thanks everyone, you know how much this night means to me. Thanks to our lovely Mum for getting the night off work so she didn't miss our yearly tradition, yes? And well-done boys for writing your own stories this year! Not bad for eight years old, perhaps one of you will be a writer, like me."

He winces at his own words and hopes no one, especially Mum, says anything. 'Some writer you are' they might say, 'never sold a single story.' No. The boys wouldn't say that. Unless they'd heard it from Mum. They might do then. He looks at Mum and tries to read her eyes in the candlelight, but nothing's given away. Maybe I'm overthinking it, Dad says to himself, give your head a wobble and enjoy your night! Don't ruin the tradition!

He picks up an envelope and smiles at the tremor in his own hand. Yes, he's excited too.

Every year since Dad met Mum it's been the same, every year for twelve years. Of course, it was just the two of them in the early days. They'd each write a ghost story to be read on Hallowe'en, they'd read each other's story out loud and they'd each enjoy drawing gasps and laughs and shivers of discomfort from the other. It seemed a lifetime ago now, so much had changed. Dad doubted the twins' stories would be up to much, probably lacked any kind of cohesive narrative and characterisation, relying entirely on grossness and shock, but still, everyone starts somewhere.

"Let's see whose we should read first," Dad says, unable to keep the gothic giddiness out of his voice now. He piles the envelopes together, shuffles them about a few times and then fans them out like a deck of cards in front of Mum to pick one. She doesn't make a move, doesn't pick one. No surprise, tonight's too important for her to choose. He thanks her under his breath and chooses the envelope himself.

"Well, look at that, I chose my own. You boys don't mind, do you?"

The twins' heads shake back and forth in the dancing vapours of candlelight. That'll do. They're too sweet to say otherwise, even they know that it's better to let Dad go first, and anyway their envelopes feel very light, they can't be more than a couple of pages each. He rolls his eyes and smiles to himself, *watch how it's done, my boys. Watch how it's done.*

"Welcome, one and all," he says playfully, full of overegged grandeur, "to the annual family ghost story read-a-thon! Prepare to be scared out of your wits, frightened out of your very skin, terrified to the deepest parts of your soul. Ooooooooo. Tonight, we take you on a ghostly ride through four terrible tales written by four horror masters," but I'm the master of masters, he thinks, "and then, when the reading's done a challenge remains … will you ever be able to sleep again? Will you be able to walk down a dark corridor alone again? Will you scream at the unseen things that go bump in the night? Only time will tell."

"First up on this stormy night we have the tale of a writer who sells his soul for a shot at fame and fortune. The story of a man who is finally given the answer to everything he ever wanted, only to find the cost is too great, too horrifying to have even considered. Tonight's first tale is called 'The Muse', written by … me."

He pauses for dramatic effect and is pleased when the wind suddenly rises and buffets the windowpanes violently. Did they? A trick of the light? Or did they jump, just a little? Mum jumped more than the twins; he thinks.

"Let's start … no, no. Something's not right. What is it?"

He holds a hand up for silence, trying to work it out for himself. He wants it to be special. He clicks his fingers,

"The hot chocolate! Leave it with me."

Dad whips into the kitchen to prepare the hot chocolate in each of their mugs. Mum always has hers plain, nothing fancy, no frilly stuff, but an extra scoop of powder. The twins have less scoops, but their cups are crowned with cream and speckled with tiny marshmallows. In years gone by they would giggle uncontrollably at each other as they realised their faces were tagged with white cream moustaches, 'just like daddy,' and then they would inevitably get cream and hot chocolate on their freshly bought pyjamas. This year's jammies are cute and match their bedding; green and blue and purple dinosaurs smiling sweetly, and certainly not thinking about the meteor that's about to make them all extinct.

In the living room they leave their cups to cool, and the steam and the smell of cocoa mingles with the smell of Hallowe'en. Dad settles himself back in and takes up his manuscript.

"'The Muse'…" he says again. Takes a breath. Begins his tale.

"… Mr Harry Townsend awoke with a start and a snort, disturbing the pile of crumbs that had settled in the crease of his gut. The boys were still asleep, so it wasn't them who had disturbed him. He was bathed in the blue light from the TV and all other lights were gone, extinguished. It was the early hours of the morning, and Mrs Harry Townsend still hadn't returned home. Harry shifted, groaned, cracked another beer and switched the channel.

Static. A fuzz and a bang and a crackle. The TV went black and then it shifted back into view, the standby light flashing red like a blinking, all-seeing, malevolent eye.

Harry frowned, smacked the remote hard on his lap and punched it towards the flickering TV, but it just went on a-flickering. Mrs Harry Townsend must have been mucking about with it. He slapped the remote again. Still nothing, the TV went on debating with itself whether to turn on or turn off.

It came to Harry in a flash, his wife, Mrs Harry Townsend, had done something to the batteries to force him out of his spot in front of the TV. Yes, that was it. It was all some clever ruse of hers to get him to stand up and leave the living room, and that dopey cow thought that would somehow shake him out of his rut? That something so simple would dissolve his writers block? This from the woman who had told him to 'snap out of it' and 'just write something, anything!' This from the woman who had placated him with the kind of supermarket seasonal aisle philosophy that drove him crazy. 'You miss one hundred per cent of the shots you don't take' she would say. 'The only way to fail in this life is to give up' and the ever popular 'You only know your strength, when you're at your weakest.' That kind of thing. If Harry closed his eyes, he could see those platitudes printed in distracting fonts on cheap paper, with scenic landscapes behind the words, framed and hung in his very own bathroom, right next to the toilet…

… For Gods sake!"

There's a knocking at the door and there shouldn't be. Everyone on their street knows not to knock on for trick-or-treat until Dad puts the pumpkins outside, when the stories have been read and the scaring's done. He huffs and puffs and tells Mum and the twins that he'll get it, they should just stay put, stay in the moment, remember the story, he won't be long.

"Trick-or-treat!"

A snotty boy dressed as a witch stands on the front porch holding his bucket. The poor lad's drenched and he has pulled his witches cloak up tight around his neck, though he seems happy enough with his haul so far, but it's enough to melt Dad's anger at being disturbed. Dad recognises the boys' chaperone, who isn't dressed for Hallowe'en. His name's Ben, he's a personal trainer and the witch-boys' uncle or cousin or something. Ben is all muscle on muscle and symmetrical dimples either side of a winning smile that Dad would really like to ruin.

"Well, don't you look scary! And, of course, the young man looks scary dressed like a witch! I'm joking, here you are let me get you some sweets."

"Thank you," the boy says. Ben wipes rain from his head and shifts to peer past Dad into the corridor, saying,

"Thank you. What a night for it, eh?"

"Quite the night."

"Quite the night. How are the boys? How's the wife?"

"All good, you know what we're like with Hallowe'en, we love it. We're just settling in for our stories actually."

"Very good, very good. And the wife? She's okay? Only, I've not seen her for a bit, she's not been coming to our training sessions. I didn't know if she was ill?"

"No, no not ill. Just busy, you know how it is running round after twin boys and she's working late quite a bit. But she's okay."

"Good, and the boys? Maybe I could pop in and say hello?"

Dad glances behind him, rubs his jaw irritably, turns back and opens his mouth to speak.

"Uncle Beeeeeeeeeeeennnnn," whines the witch-boy, "there are so many more houses to go to and sweeties to get. That'll be boring and you'll talk about old people stuff and it's raining."

Dad and Ben both laugh at the unfiltered honesty that must abandon all children sooner or later. They leave, Witch-Boy is happy with his haul. Ben gives a backward glance and frowns but doesn't hover for too long.

Dad settles back into his seat and claps his hands before Mum can ask who was at the door.

"Now where were we? Oh, yes. 'The Muse'…"

"… Mr Harry Townsend was too clever to fall for his wife's games. She could run off all she liked with her personal trainer, with his designer arse cheeks and symmetrical dimples and his winning smile and try to manipulate him from afar. And she could judge him, because she didn't know what it was like to pour your soul into something. She'd given birth, sure, but what did she know of creation...?

…What are you laughing at?"

Dad's eying Mum and his nostrils are flared. He's sure he heard something and sure he caught the ghost of a smirk on her face. Perhaps she didn't, Dad thinks, perhaps the screaming wind laughed for a moment instead, and perhaps the wobbly candlelight cast a smile that was never there.

There's a lot Dad could say right now, but he doesn't, not in front of the boys.

Dad carries on.

"… Mr Harry Townsend stood shakily and lost his footing in the room. He smacked his chops and made a move, but not to get batteries for the remote, no. He'd get a beer. That'd show her. He looked down at the weight in his hand and was surprised to find himself still holding the remote. He glanced at the blinking standby light. On. Off. On. Off. He didn't like it, didn't like to feel its eye on him. He chucked the remote deep into the couch and made a move.

'You look like a man in need of a cure,' said the man who had suddenly appeared on the TV. Mr Harry Townsend frowned and sat back down, transfixed. The TV had changed, come to life in between one of those menacing blinks. The quality of the image staring back at him was like watching a gameshow from the 1980s, all fuzzy edges and beige colours and hosted by a man with a dodgy pencil moustache perched above a mouth with not enough teeth who seemed to be looking right through the screen, right through time, right at him. 'Oh yes, a lost soul in need of direction,' the man continued, though there was no one in the studio with him.

Bleary-eyed, confused, curious, Mr Harry Townsend waited.

'What would you say if I could give you that direction? Hmm?

Hey! I'm talking to you. Yes. You. Hello? You! Mr Harry Townsend. That's right. Yeah, that's it, sit up and take notice. No. No sense looking around the room, the room hasn't got anything to do with it, pal. It's all me. Now tell me, what ails you? … look, if you're not going to answer then you may as well switch over. In fact, no, you stay right there, and I'll go. That red eye will be back any second. Standing by in three … two …'

'Wait!' Mr Harry Townsend cried, sitting forward and hoping he hadn't disturbed his sons, then he reasoned that he must be dreaming so why should he worry about that? His heart was pounding hard in his ears as he said 'I … my wife's having an affair.'

'Oh, that's true enough. Goddam whore, right? But that isn't what ails you. Now c'mon, don't hold back,' the TV host sat back on a couch that had clearly seen some scandal over the years and lit a cigarette. 'Why is she having an affair? The answer to that, is what ails you.'

'I'm … I'm a loser. No, I'm lost. I'm so lost. No! Wait, don't go. I feel like that because … because … I'm stuck. I can't write. It – it's been my dream for as long as I can remember, but I don't think I have it in me.'

TV host blew a cloud of smoke so strong it fogged the screen over and gave the appearance smoke from a fire was creeping towards him, 'Oh dear oh dear. Mrs Harry Townsend has realised she's backed the wrong horse. So, what would you do to fix it?'

'Anything.'

'Anything?'

'Anything. Just tell me.'

The TV host clicked his fingers and jumped up, 'you need a muse! That's all. A muse. Inspiration.'

'So, you're going to be my muse?'

The TV host laughed, 'No. I'm a man who knows what other men need and can usually find said thing for said aforementioned man. You in?'

Mr Harry Townsend nodded and crossed the room and sat cross-legged right in front of the TV, the way he did when he was a boy and all those stories and characters would rush at him at a hundred miles an hour and he would sit, transfixed and inspired.

'Good.'

The TV host crossed the studio cockily, walking with a confident flick to his steps. Draped on the wall was a maybe-white dustsheet that hung down to the floor, the profile of some ornate picture frame visible along the top edge and at the corners. The TV host caressed the outline of the frame and then gripped the sheet, as though about to rip it from the wall in some grand reveal. Harry's heart was ready to burst out of his chest as he waited to see what lay beneath.

And then the TV host dropped his hand to his side and shook his head,

'Na, you're not ready. Not *committed.*'

'No!' He sobbed, gripping the TV with trembling hands, 'no! Show me! Please! I can feel it! Please!'

The TV host barked a laugh that sent another mushroom of green-blue smoke out into the black space of the studio.

'Show me? Play it again, Sam! Play "As time goes by!"' The TV host slapped the wall by the frame and Harry winced, as though hurt by the smack.

'You want it? Yeah, I can see you want it. Well, you can have it. All you need to do is pick up the phone, yes, that one right there by your hand, pick up the phone and dial the number flashing up on screen now. You see it? Good. Yes, that's it. But! Before you commit to buying, make sure you read the terms and conditions that will be appearing on screen right about … now. What do you mean that was too quick? Don't worry about it, it's simple, all you need to do is receive your one-of-a-kind, just-for-you, bona fide, genuine muse painting and let it inspire you. And then you can write, write until your hearts content. And, Harry, write something great. Something that will change the world. Oh boy, you're going to get some ideas, all sorts of ideas! Not just writing ideas, because you're more than a writer, aren't you? That's right, you're a complicated man. So, you just make sure you listen to your lovely muse in all things, and it won't steer you wrong. You hear that? The audience wants you to do it! They're applauding you, Harry. You in? I said … are you in?'

Mr Harry Townsends face was scarred with tears. He had shifted from a sitting position to his knees with his arms outstretched, praying at the altar of real truth and illuminated by a halo of crackling television light. He nodded. The TV host smiled and cocked his head and the tilt of his head said 'you can't say I didn't warn you!' and then he ripped the dustsheet from the wall and revealed…

"…For shit's sake who is it now? Sorry, boys, sorry, that word is bad. Don't look at me like that. One minute, one minute."

Dad's breathing is laboured and strained, he had been reading with real passion, feeling every word as if reading it for the very first time. He steadies himself, wipes some sweat from his sallow face and, heavy handed, rips the front door open. He doesn't care who is standing there dressed as a ghost or a vampire or Boris Johnson. The pumpkins aren't out, so *no* trick-or-treat.

"Listen, if there's no …"

He stops. Stood on the porch, half set in the white glow from the streetlamp, is a police officer. He's young, still has acne in some places, his cheeks are red from the icy cold and the mists of his breath curl up in front of him. He has to squint through the pearls of rainwater that drip steadily from the shiny peak of his cap.

"Good evening and sorry to disturb you, sir," the young officer says, "I'm looking for … this address."

He hands over a note and Dad reads it.

"You're here, this is my house. What's the problem?"

"Oh, how's that for luck? I'm sorry to disturb you, sir, it's just that I've been sent to do a welfare check."

"A welfare check?"

"Yes. We've had reports of concern for your wife."

"From who?" Dad knows who, or thinks he does. His hands clench tightly around the note with his address on it.

"I can't go into that. Is your wife in? Could you go and get her for me?"

Dad scratches at the back of his head irritably, "No. No I can't go and get her, we're set for the night. We've got a yearly tradition see, campfire ghost stories kind of thing, and we're all set, and I don't want to break the atmosphere. But you can come in and speak to her."

Dads' confidence throws the young officer, who loses some of the colour from his cheeks. He checks up and down the street and then says, "well, if you don't mind, it shouldn't take very long."

"Not at all," Dad says, stepping aside to allow the officer past. Dad guides him through, stands at the door to the living room and beckons him in, "now mind your shoes though, please. It's carpet in there and you're sopping wet through."

"Oh, course. Sorry, I'll just stay here on the flooring. Hmm, that's a funny smell, what is that?"

"Candles, pumpkins, perfume, take your pick."

"Right," the officer pops his head further around the doorframe and squints through the murk. He sees Mum and the twins sat with their backs to him, waiting patiently for the horror to resume. "Evening folks, everything okay in here?"

Before they can answer the light shifts by some unseen manipulation, pulling away from the gathered family and casting a menacing glow onto the wall, and the large painting which hangs there.

"Well, that is some painting, isn't it? Oil?"

"Yes, I believe it is."

The candles bluster again, and the officer tries to fight off a shudder. He fails. "Sorry, quite a creepy looking thing if you don't mind me saying. What's it called?"

"You know, I was never told the name. I call it 'The Muse.'" Dad can't keep the tenderness from his voice.

"'The Muse?' Fancy that. Mind if I take a look?"

"Well, now I did say about the carpet, didn't I?"

"Oh, of course. You're right. Well, I'm sorry to have bothered you. Them kids are well trained, aren't they?"

"Oh, they're the best. Wish I could train the wife the same way. You married?"

"No. No. But maybe one day. Anyway, sorry, I'll leave you to it."

"Sure I can't tempt you into having a cup of coffee?" Dad hasn't offered him a coffee to be rejected in the first place, but the officer doesn't notice as at that moment there's a crackle and a muffled, disinterested call from the radio fixed to the left breast of his stab vest.

"No, no thank you, I'd better get going, plenty more calls on Hallowe'en night. Some folk just can't behave themselves, they get up to all sorts."

"Well, I do appreciate you coming and checking in on us," Dad says, gripping the officers' hand and guiding him out in a fluid motion. He doesn't mind the *drip drip drip* of water leaving a trail behind them. Outside the officer nods and tips his cap, "well, you have a good night," he says before mumbling something into his radio and walking away from the house.

Dad watches him leave, fists still clenched, and clenching still tighter, when he sees the officer stop and look back at the house with a look of confusion on his face, as though he's just woken up but doesn't ever remember falling asleep. He's stopped, frozen in a moment and teetering between coming back and getting in his car. The paper in Dad's hand is crushed to pulp now. He waits.

A crackle from the radio shakes the officer out of it, he seems to chuckle to himself as he gets in the car and drives off, blues-and-reds flashing but no siren wailing.

Dad sighs, loosens his grip, shakes out his shoulders and returns to his family. Before sitting back down to resume the story he pauses at the painting to inhale his muse. He strokes the intricate inlay and carving of the frame. His eyes watch as the yellow-orange flame catches in the sheen of the black paint and the tormented figures within seem to twist and morph and turn, wrought into cackling devils filled with beautiful, wonderful, terror-filled knowledge.

Dad turns to look at his family and smiles, a tear touching the corner of his eye.

Mum and the twins stare back, eyes glazed and fixed, rictus smiles stitched into their ashen faces. Dad pats Mums arm, almost lovingly. Her head lolls over and she sags like a puppet with its strings cut. Dad curses himself and hurriedly fixes her back in place.

"Sorry about that, my love," he says, "I'll be more careful. And boys, you haven't *touched* your hot chocolates, they're going cold."

Dad turns to the boys, who have sunk down in their seats, their pyjama tops bunching up awkwardly so that the little dinosaurs are all squished and their distended bellies are exposed. He contends with moving them, with fixing them, but the thought of touching them again makes his stomach feel like jelly and he turns away from their hollow eyes.

Dad settles into his seat to finish his story, The Muse hanging by his side, uninterrupted. He'll never be interrupted again, and they'll listen, they have to listen now, for as long as he can write them, they'll listen.

"Now, where was I?"

Colonel Malcontent

M. Legree

He chose the apartment for its view overlooking the boulevard. He chose the girl for her eyes—a distinct pale blue that seemed to beckon him out of the crowd on the street corner. She had auburn hair and freckles, the high colouring of a woman whose passion would flush her whole-body pink, and he found himself wondering what it would be like to lean hard into her and feel her thighs against his. The blue serge dress she wore was surprisingly modest, with a high collar and long sleeves down to her wrists.

The girl had seen him. She waited, standing tall and smiling while he negotiated the crowd. Moran touched the brim of his top hat, glad of the inches it added to his apparent height. Now that they stood facing each other, he thought that she might have the advantage of him.

"Lost?" said the girl. "Can I aid you in your search, sir?"

He leaned in close so that he could speak against her ear over the din of the street: "Can you cook, my dear?"

"Oh, it"s *cooking* you"ll be wanting, then?"

"You"ll do," said Moran. "I have a room nearby." He took her by the arm, affecting not to notice the knife she had up her sleeve. *That* was the reason for the dress, then.

"A girl"s got to look after herself, you know."

Moran nodded. "These are troubled times," he allowed.

She smiled again. Moran began to conceive that her clear-eyed gaze, if turned on him in his moment of weakness, might see through him all too easily. He wondered if she might be a honeypot set to entrap him. No matter: he would keep his enemies even closer than his friends.

Moran was uneasily aware that people on the street were beginning to stare, and he quickened his pace. No doubt they made a striking couple, but it was no part of his plan to draw attention to himself. He feared no man, but the Big Smoke had changed much during the four years he'd languished in gaol. In the London of 1898, there were worse things lurking down drainpipes than tigers, and man was no longer the most dangerous game.

***

"Have you seen them?" asked the girl. "Are they as terrible as they say?"

Moran considered for a moment. She had told him to call her Tryst, and he wondered idly if that were her real name; it sounded like something an actress might assume for a performance.

Just now she was standing in the view that he had worked out so carefully. Whilst appearing to watch the crowded street below (costermongers rubbing shoulders with teamsters and clerks slumming from the West End; beggars;

whores; a gang of navvies looking for a drink), she had framed herself most prettily against the afternoon light. Clever girl!

"They hardly ever come out of their tunnels, do they?" The girl was watching him again with the blue eyes that so captivated his attention, and Moran came back to himself with a start.

"Bloody insects!" he grumbled. "Bloody insects walking about like men. However, our new landlords may find John Bull an unruly tenant." He smiled his quick, vicious smile.

"I don't have many fine gentleman callers," said the girl with a sigh.

Moran shook his head. "I'm no gentleman. Did my turn in gaol." He spoke with some bitterness; he could no longer profit by playing the part of the swell. "Now, if you will do me the favour…" He held out his hand.

Tryst moved slowly away from the window, looking back once over her shoulder, and took the proffered hand.

***

Later, much later, the fare slept supine with his mouth slack and open—an odd contrast to his waking face, which was shrewd and dangerous.

"You're a rare one, all right," he'd told her earlier. "A real beauty."

The compliment had pleased her all the more because she knew without conceit that it was true. Even as a child, strangers had approached her parents to remark on her good looks. She had grown into a tall, long-legged young woman with strong hips and heavy, pointed breasts. If she had the body of a voluptuary, her strong-boned face pretended to refinement, even elegance. She had good teeth and great guileless eyes of cornflower blue. A portraitist would have made much, too, of her smooth skin and lustrous auburn locks.

Her family—poor labourers from Edinburgh—had bequeathed to her health, beauty, and the prospect of their own impoverished existence. Tryst had left home at fourteen, determined to make her own way in the big city. And she had, after a fashion...

She waited until the fare began to snore softly and then slipped naked out of the bed, toes curling against the ridgy old floorboards. Once, a loose plank creaked under her heel and she froze like a startled rabbit, but the rhythm of the fare's breathing continued uninterrupted. After a moment she went on.

She could tell that he had only just moved into the flat. He dressed like a toff, but aside from his clothes and his fine blackthorn walking stick, she had marked no possessions of especial value—except, perhaps, the sea chest in the second room. She noticed how he slipped the key into an inside pocket—out of her sight, as he thought. She smiled to herself as she knelt beside the chest. The lock mechanism clicked faintly, and the chest opened easily on oiled hinges. She was disappointed, at first, to discover more clothes inside.

She found it at the bottom of the chest, swaddled in an old blanket. She turned the double-barrelled rifle over carefully in her hands, startled by its cold weight, all steel and close-grained English walnut. Then her fingers found the long, double row of notches carved into the gunstock—dozens of them. She shivered and glanced back over a bare shoulder. The fare had not moved. Tryst wrapped the rifle again in its blanket and laid it back in the bottom of the chest.

She lay still beside the man for a long time afterwards, listening to him breathe.

In the morning, Moran dismissed the girl with an extra guinea in her pocket. She curtsied prettily, looking at the floor, as if suddenly attacked by modesty. He went out onto the landing with her, frowned when he saw another figure already coming up the stairs: a vulpine, a little fox-faced hybrid that bowed as she squeezed hurriedly past. Then she was gone, and the vulpine looked up at Moran and grinned at him with its pink mouth hanging open like a dog's, full of sharp little teeth.

"Sacrebleu!" said the vulpine. "Who is this ginger? She has enough legs to go around you twice, yes?"

Moran did not answer at once. He moved forward another step on the landing and looked down his nose at the figure on the stairwell.

"You"re Mycroft's creature, aren't you?" said the Colonel. He twisted his face into a disdainful sneer and held out his hand. "You must have something for me."

The vulpine stared back at him, no longer grinning. The thing had great yellow eyes without whites, observed Moran. They must shine in the dark like a beast's, making fine points at which to aim. The index finger of his right hand crooked as if squeezing an invisible trigger.

Then the grin returned, and the vulpine made a little bow and touched its forehead with a short-fingered black paw. It reached inside its waistcoat and withdrew a cigar box, held it out to Moran. The box was heavier than it should have been. Moran bounced it once on his palm, letting a smile play about his mouth as he listened to the metallic chink from within. Then he turned his back on the little vulpine and slammed the door shut behind him.

***

Moran thumbed open the cigar box to admire its contents: a double handful of bright brass shells—they were each nearly the size of cigars, at that. He selected two of them and dropped them into his pocket. Then he went to the sea chest. He found the gun just as he'd left it, hefted it and broke it open, loaded both barrels with the shells from his pocket. He snapped the breech shut and looked at the timepiece on the wall: it had just marked ten o'clock. As if to emphasize the point, Big Ben began to toll the hour in the distance.

Moran went to the window overlooking the street and threw open the shutters. Below, the hellish parade had already begun; the slaves of the Lords Insectile were nothing if not punctual. An open-topped carriage—one of those newfangled petrol-burning machines—had just turned the corner, carrying three soldiers in the livery of the Domestic Mandate.

The drawn shutters shivered and rattled. Something huge and black hove into view behind the carriage, flanked by an escort of pale, grey-furred little figures wearing tinted spectacles and carrying long-handled goads. The great black beast seemed to swim laboriously forward, its forepaws gouging cobblestones out of the road's surface every time they touched. Rocky fragments bounced and spun off to either side, causing the spectators lining the street to curse and hop awkwardly out of the way.

One of them—a street urchin of ten or twelve—picked up a stray cobble and pitched it back, scoring a hit on the beast's hindquarters. The boy ducked into an alleyway a moment later.

"Good show, lad!" said Moran. (He wondered if the boy were one of the Irregulars; they weren't far from the intersection of Marylebone and Baker Street, after all.) "But

I've got something here a bit more lethal than brickbats." He bared his teeth, patted the stock of the big rifle.

The previous occupant of the room had been a book dealer and had left crates of remaindered stock everywhere. Moran dragged one of them in front of the window and laid the double barrels of the rifle across it, snugged the gunstock into his shoulder and took careful aim.

In the street below, the great mole paused, lifting its snout. The pink tentacles wreathing its face squirmed as if testing the air. The beast's handlers milled about, fingering their goads.

Moran squeezed the trigger. Behind the roar of the muzzle blast, he heard the bullet strike home with the sound of a meataxe thudding into a side of beef. The mole slumped forward, spraying blood from its nose and mouth. The shutters rattled again as it struck the pavement; the whole town home shivered on its foundations, sifting dust down from the ceiling.

Moran saw several of the little grey figures go spinning away like ninepins. He smiled at that. He had an inclination to clear the street, to spend the rest of the half-dozen or so shells out of the cigar box, but there was no time. On this occasion his only object was misdirection. He had been assured that the real blow was being struck in another quarter...

He drew a bead on the shroud covering the carriage's bulky engine and fired the second barrel. Sheet metal buckled with a crash. The machine spewed gouts of black smoke and began to burn fiercely. The three soldiers scattered, ducking for cover.

Moran nodded to himself, pleased with his aim. The beast had to weigh as much as an elephant; its massive carcase— along with the wreckage of the soldiers" transport—made a roadblock of five tonnes or more, besides drawing the attention of every policeman in the area.

He retreated from the window, found the loose floorboard and prised it up. There was a hollow space beneath, just long and wide enough to conceal the rifle. He laid the weapon into the hidey-hole and tamped the floorboard back into place with his shoe. Moving quickly now, he snatched up his walking stick and made for the front door. There were a few clothes left in the apartment, and his spare bullets, but the police would make nothing of those. With luck, he could return in a few days' time to retrieve the rifle.

He was out on the landing when he saw the policeman climbing the stairs to meet him. Moran could not imagine how he had been discovered so quickly. The man already had a whistle raised halfway to his lips.

"He went that way!" shouted Moran, pointing. As the bobby turned to look, Moran's thumb found the catch concealed in the head of his walking stick. He drew forth the hidden blade and ran the man through, just under the left shoulder. The silver whistle rattled on the steps.

Moran put his heel into the policeman's back; the sword stick's Toledo steel creaked as it flexed. Then the blade popped free, and the body tumbled away down the stairs. The policeman came to rest crumpled up on his side in the foyer. A casual observer might think him a vagrant sleeping off a drunk.

Moran cut the air twice with the sullied blade, leaving bloody spray on the walls of the stairwell, and sheathed it. Then he went to the front door and stepped out into the crowd on the pavement.

Moran paused a moment on the street in front of the club. The building's stone façade was draped with triple banners, the Union Jack flanked by the silver-and-black pennon of the Lords Insectile and the gilt-edged, sea-green banner of the Deep Ones. He did not look too closely at the heraldry embroidered into the alien flags, preferring to hurry up the marble steps to the great bronze double doors at the entry.

The doorman, a dignified old silver-backed simian attired in the livery of the club, did not want to let him pass. He stood blocking the entry, not quite meeting Moran's eye and apologetically telling him over and over that it was impossible.

"Tell the fat man that the Colonel is here to see him," snapped Moran.

The doorman went away. The Colonel smoked a cigarette on the steps while he waited, frowning out at a skyline smudged by the brume of a thousand chimneys, dark as his mood. Not for nothing did they call his city the Big Smoke: London wore its sooty pall like a soiled old garment.

The apologetic doorman returned, apologized once more, ushered him into the quiet confines of the club. The fat man was waiting for him in the Stranger's Room. The interior of the chamber was a high and windowless space with dark wood panelling from floor to ceiling, hazed blue and redolent with cigar smoke. A dismembered newspaper lay open on the tabletop, next to a piece of silver plate piled with well-chewed cigar butts, empty cups and saucers, and the debris of a meal recently past: crusts of bread, and the wax rind of a gourmet cheese.

Mycroft looked up as Moran entered, his ravaged face broad and deeply lined under a shock of white hair. Moran stared at him for a moment. The man looked weary and unshaven, and it occurred to Moran that he had been up all night, awaiting the results of his machinations. How like him, thought Moran, to send better men off to die doing his bloody business!

"Good morning, Colonel," said Mycroft.

"Colonel no more," said Moran. "The Army has disowned me, along with most of polite society."

Mycroft withdrew something from his coat pocket and laid it on the table between them, keeping his hand on top of it. "Is the deed done?"

"The Beast is dead," said the Colonel. "But there were... unforeseen expenses."

Mycroft slid the cheque across the table to him. "This is the amount we agreed upon. I assume Coutt's is acceptable."

"As I said, there were expenses—"

"Perhaps I should call on Lord Roxton the next time I require a rifle."

"That popinjay!"

"Meanwhile, Lieutenant Hawes played his part admirably—"

"Fucking American!" snapped Moran.

Mycroft went on as if he had not heard, but over his shoulder the portrait of the club's founder in its gilt frame seemed to stare down at Moran with disapproval.

"—The cannisters of chlorine gas were delivered and dispensed as scheduled. In a few hours" time, we shall know the result of our plans."

"I have legitimate costs," said the Colonel. "There's not a gentleman's club in the city will welcome me within its walls—your dear brother saw to that. Damned hard to make a living at cards, cheating shopkeepers and students out of a few quid here and there."

"Perhaps you should write another book," said Mycroft. "Copies of *Heavy Game of the Western Himalayas* are selling for ten pounds on the second-hand market. Your recent notoriety has only increased its value."

The Colonel sneered and made a show of looking about the richly appointed room. "Ha! You'd like that, wouldn't you? Slaving away like a common scribbler while you live like a posh toff." Mycroft had scattered sterling silver utensils over the tabletop, and Moran wondered briefly if he might secret a couple spoons in his jacket but gave up the idea as impractical. He shrugged, and went on in a more thoughtful tone: "I expect your famous consulting detective has acquired more than a few enemies, in his line of work…"

"I need not remind you," said Mycroft heavily, "if there were any hint of foul play—"

"I merely make an observation."

Mycroft stared at him with something like hatred in his gaze, and Moran felt the full weight of the man's attention as if he had just opened a furnace door and were standing too close.

"You presume too much, Moran. Someday soon, perhaps, your presumption will be your undoing."

"Until that day, then," said Moran savagely, snatching the cheque off the tabletop. He stood, touching his hat with a sneer, and turned on his heel.

To Prey or Pray

Khala Grace

An orange haze hangs over a holding facility. Prison guards dressed in black tactical gear and smoke masks charge after their target. Bullets hiss through thick smog. Despite their training, the guards fail to land a hit. Heartbeats pound frantically during the plight. A middle-aged man with chestnut hair and charcoal eyes stares ahead in anticipation. The prisoner pulls a little girl closer to his chest. Her fingers cling onto his shirt.

"Where mommy?" She wails.

"Mommy's okay, Ava," he lies. The man peers behind. "Mommy can't be with us now."

"Why?" Ava screeches.

"Well." The man chokes on the fumes. "We can't talk now, sweety."

Ava rubs her snotty nose on his shirt. Another bullet blazes towards the prisoner's head. With a stroke of luck, he stumbles on the cracked ground. The guards curse as their prey successfully avoids capture.

"Come on, Garrett!" An unnamed guard complains. "The hare is in range!"

"Then you shoot him!" Garrett retorts.

The other clicks his tongue and remains silent. As they continue their chase, a loud explosion erupts from within the building. Garrett fumbles with his radio before finding the emergency station.

"Recovery Team cease all action!" A female's voice flickers through the static. "There's been a break in the gas line!"

"Shit!" Garrett swears. He attempts a final shot at their target. "Slimy bastard! Whatever, we have more important matters to manage."

The prisoner reaches the barbed wire fence. He laughs while watching their retreat. In the distance, black smoke pillows into the sky. *Thank you.* He smiles. The man returns to Ava.

"Time for piggy-back," he insists.

Ava nods her dirty face. She repositions herself like a bear cub on their mother's back. He ascends. The fence rungs have bits of metal sticking upwards. Each pull bloodies the prisoner's hands. In spite of the pain, he continues their escape. Once at the top, he carefully swings his legs over the barbed wire. Scratches decorate his thighs.

"Keep going, Lance," he whispers. "There's no turning back."

After what feels like hours, Lance lands on the ground. He turns towards his daughter. *Asleep?* His thoughts ring with a chuckle. He casts a sad glance at the prison. Lance shakes his head and places a foot forward. *We can't stay.* He concludes. The sun burns hot beneath the smog. Two escapees begin their quest. A man and his young daughter must fend off the unknown.

***

A barren wasteland provides no relief. Smoke fills the lungs of travellers. Lance coughs up black soot. *This can't be good for Ava.* He thinks. The concerned father turns to his daughter.

"Are you okay, sweety?" He asks.

"Mmmm...." Ava mumbles. After a few coughs, her brows wrinkle. "Can't... breathe."

Lance stops the hell march. He searches for a solution. Previously, he ripped his sleeves to bandage his hands. Now, Lance peers at the bottom of his shirt. Ava watches her father tear apart his clothing. He gently wraps the torn fabric around her face like a mask. Lance carefully ties a knot beneath her ears.

"It's not much," he smiles. "Though this should help."

Ava nods. She raises her arms to be held. Lance picks her up and returns to their task. She sniffles while the fabric periodically clogs her nostrils. Ava stares in the distance. Not a single soul is seen. She buries her head in Lance's chest- quietly whimpering from the stress.

Hours turn as the sun threatens to set. *If only a town was nearby.* Lance thinks. His legs throb with each step. *Keep going.* He demands. Suddenly, a thunderous roar shakes the dirt. Lance peers towards the sound. His heart races as he locates a gang approaching on ATVs.

"Shit." Lance mumbles.

Lance tightens his hold on Ava. Feet run in an attempt to escape.

Eeeerrrr! An air horn screams. The gang of six reverberate their engines. They weave around their targets in sport. Lance notices carts attached to two of the vehicles. *Cages?* He observes. *For people!* The assumption is proven accurate.

"Woot!" A bandit is eager to taunt their prey. His mangled grin reveals several missing teeth. "He's carryin' somethin' useful!"

Lance uses an arm to avoid being sprayed with dust. Unfortunately, he is no match for the engines. The drivers circle around the man and his daughter like vultures to carrion.

"Come on!" The initial bandit shouts above the noise. He points at the little girl. "Give 'er to us and we'll let ya go!"

The desperate man stares at the lot. *Six men.* He notes. *All seem to be around my age. Yet, they're in better shape.* His lip twitches from frustration.

"I'd get out of here if I were you!" Lance yells as best as his parched throat allows. "Nightfall's coming!"

"Aw, are we scared of the dark?" The bandit cackles. He stops his ride and draws out a gun. "Give 'er up!"

The lackeys follow suit. The little girl stares at the dangerous men. Ava is too frightened to scream. Lance grits his teeth. *I must act...* His thoughts trail off. Another bandit goes to knock his skull with the butt of a gun. With Ava in one hand, her father pushes the weapon away with the other. Bullets fly beside his feet. Before the gang leader can complain about the sad shot, a sharp screech resounds.

"Ah, hell nah." The cretin's eyes bulge from inside his goggles. "They're here, boys!"

Lance watches as the team of bandits withdraw their guns. He stares at them with a mixture of concern and confusion. Each of the six accelerate their vehicles. The riders leave their targets in a cloud of dust. In the haze, Lance watches as strange silhouettes surface. His ears ring while heinous cries cut through the air like a knife. *Oh no!* His heart sinks. Ava leans towards the commotion but is stopped.

"Keep your eyes closed, sweety!" Lance insists.

The little girl wants to ask why. However, she refrains and follows the advice. Still, in the darkness of her mind, an image of smoke appears. She hears the screams of the *bad men* as something attacks them. The screeches of unknown creatures pain her eardrums. Ava uses her hands to dampen the frightening noise. Though, what's that new sound? *Shirt.* Ava concludes when remembering the noise of her father ripping fabric.

Lance's legs grow heavier. He hears wailing from behind. Without turning his head, the man knows that time is limited. *If six don't satisfy, then we're fucked!* Lance's charcoal eyes flicker uncontrollably as anxiety piques. The doting father fights through the pain to better their odds of survival.

Minutes pass as the screams halt. The silence is disturbing. Lance casts a wary peek over his shoulder. A heap of ATVs and... bodies litter the barren ground. Lance's heartbeat falters. *Please don't notice us.* He begs. The man whips his head forward.

"We have to hurry," Lance whispers.

"What wrong, daddy?" Ava's voice cracks.

"Don't worry, sweety." Lance hugs her. "We're going to be fine. Daddy just has to run a bit farther."

Ava nudges him. She doesn't understand that her father has his doubts. The little girl turns towards the sky. The setting sun glows like an amber jewel. On the left, a silver moon becomes barely visible. Ava shivers as another screech crosses the wind.

"They come?" She cries.

"I'm sorry, Ava," he coughs. Lance clears his throat before admitting the truth. "They're like doggies. Except, they... eat all that moves."

"They... eat me?" Ava asks.

She looks up at her father with a new terror in her eyes. Lance shakes his head.

"I won't let them." he smiles.

Lance continues to cough. *I'm talking too much.* He concludes. A different wail pierces above the cracked earth.

Evidently, six sizable meatheads aren't enough to quench the pack's hunger. Lance's blood pounds through his veins. He feels faint. *Don't stop!* Lance commands his body.

The night sky drops within moments. The creatures in pursuit come into view. Lance cannot resist another glance. The *doggies* are more reptilian in design. They have black scales decorating their hides. Needles, similar to those of a porcupine, stand along their spines. The lead creature runs on all fours with their long claws digging into the dirt. Abruptly, the creature's jaw opens wide and releases a fierce battle cry.

"Scared!" Ava whimpers.

The little girl clutches tightly onto her father's shirt. Ava's tears soak through the fabric. Her father's determination heightens. Despite the agony of his muscles, Lance does not give up. Suddenly, the tired prey falls. According to the pack's perception, their target simply disappears. Disappointed shrieks echo through the chilled air. Irritated with their loss, the creatures snap at one another. They then run deeper into the wasteland in search of something to kill.

***

In the dark, an acrid smell wafts. Two bodies lay flat on the concrete floor. Groggy, Lance hears his daughter coughing. He leans forward and pats her back. *What can I do?* He frowns. Lance waits for her coughs to subside. Teary eyes stare back at him.

"Want Mommy," Ava whispers.

Lance wraps his arms around her.

"It's going to be alright, Ava." Her father lies while rocking her back and forth. "We'll see mommy again. It's just... going to take time."

"When?" She demands with a puckered expression.

"When we can," Lance replies.

Without words for her discontent, Ava resorts to a scowl. She babbles to relay her frustration and fright. Although caught in her own thoughts, Ava's father listens. Lance continues to console her the best that he can.

"Hungry," Ava frowns.

"I'm sorry." He remarks with a pinched brow.

"Too dark," she complains. "Where here?"

Lance sighs. He cradles Ava and rises to his feet. *I forgot.* The realization surfaces. *She doesn't see like I can.* Despite her father having better vision than most, Ava wasn't gifted with the same perception. Lance treads through the darkness.

"Seems we've fallen into a tunnel," he answers.

"What that?" Ava asks.

No matter her frightful hunger, the little girl cannot resist curiosity. *Daddy knows.* Ava guesses. *Right?* She thinks again while waiting for a reply.

"I'm sorry, sweety," Lance apologizes. He releases a long yawn. "Daddy's tired and I bet you are too. But we have to keep moving."

"But what tunnel?" Ava inquires again.

"Oh, it's a pathway beneath the ground," he explains. Lance takes a right turn. "Though, this tunnel seems to have more than one way to go."

Ava slumps her head onto his shoulder. The little girl nods as though she accepts his response. *Path.* Ava records the new word to memory. Without food to quell her stomach, she falls to slumber.

During the next few hours, Lance navigates through the series of tunnels. *Oh, another dead end.* He scoffs. The wandering man has one arm supporting his daughter and the other extended towards stone. He requires touch to decipher the mysterious channels. Lance shakes his head and returns to the main corridor.

He rounds the next corner. To his surprise, something shines dimly in the distance. *A... flashlight?* He wonders. Lance readjusts his hold of his daughter. Ava mumbles in her sleep as she shifts to the opposite shoulder. The curious man tilts his head. *Could be risky running into someone here.* He evaluates.

"There's no turning back," Lance asserts.

Cautiously, he approaches the mysterious glow. Curiosity twists upon Lance's face. In front of him stands a young man in a tattered suit. Two black curls frame his jawline. *Who...* Before Lance can finish his thought, the other's mouth drops.

"Oh, *what* have we here?" The stranger muses. He shines his light onto Lance's face. "Another survivor in these trying times?"

Ava grunts in her sleep. The father raises a hand to keep the unexpected glow from waking his little girl.

"Please, she's resting," he demands. Lance's throat cracks from dehydration. "Would you mind?"

"My apologies." He lowers his flashlight. The young man takes a step closer with an inquisitive glance. "Didn't expect to see anyone walking down here. Where did you come from?"

"Good question," Lance replies. He pauses and lets out a cough. "Though, you first. It's rude not to introduce yourself, right?"

The stranger gives a light chuckle. He watches as Lance falls into a coughing fit.

"Here, let me help," he insists. The young man throws down a heavy backpack and removes a canteen. "You must have travelled a long way."

Lance nods. He shifts Ava to allow a better grip onto the canteen. After a long gulp, he returns the flask.

"Thank you..." Lance pauses while seeking a name.

"Tovi," he answers. The young man returns the canteen onto his person. "You're welcome. Who might you two be?"

"Lance and Ava," he replies.

The father studies the other. *We don't know much about him, but...* Lance's mind reels. *An ally is critical.* He offers a hand.

"Great to have someone else along for the ride." Lance smiles.

"Likewise," Tovi beams. He shakes his hand. "So, where did you two come from?"

The small trio continue to meander through the tunnels as they look for an exit.

"We came from a prison camp due... west." Lance explains. "What about yourself?"

"Similar situation," Tovi nods. He stares at the path ahead. "I was held in a facility towards the north. I've been in flight for the past week."

For an entire week? Lance muses to himself. Regardless of a mark in fortune or skill, the young man survived. Lance takes a moment to reflect. *How long will we have before finding sanctuary?* His thoughts frown. A sudden stop brings Lance to a halt. Ava murmurs awake from the motion.

"Daddy?" She yawns.

"It's okay, sweety." he smiles. Lance hoists her up on his arm. "We've met a friend... Tovi, what's wrong?"

The improper introduction warrants a scoff. Tovi turns around. He goes to greet the little girl, but her father's eyes demand otherwise.

"Okay, I've forgotten!" Tovi sighs. He observes the father's raised brow in the dim light. "Don't worry. I've been down this channel before. Though, I can't remember if I came from that way... or there..."

Tovi shines the flashlight down each respective corner. The older man shakes his head. *He should've made a trailblazer to figure out which path he already covered.* Lance exhales his disappointment. He carefully slides to the floor. His new friend watches him with concern.

"Are you alright?" Tovi asks while bending down onto one knee.

"I'm... tired," Lance replies. He cradles his daughter and closes both eyes. "You can wake me up when you've decided where we should go."

"Sounds good... I guess," he replies. Tovi stands at the fork. "I think I've come from there. No, that cannot be right..."

A couple of hours pass. Tovi continues to murmur to himself while searching for a clue. *Goodness why didn't I...* A loud shrill breaks Tovi's concentration. He turns towards the back of the corridor. Another sharp screech pierces Tovi's ears and paints his face white. He crouches down towards the sleeping father and his daughter.

"Wake up, Lance!" He screams in a hush. Tovi shakes the man's shoulders. "We've got bad news!"

"Shit!" Lance curses while hearing the eerie symphony. He rises to his feet. "I didn't think that *they'd* follow us down here!"

"You knew about those monsters!?" Tovi drops his jaw. "Why didn't you say anything?"

In the distance, they can hear a flood of claws scraping against the slab. Lance pulls his frightened daughter closer. *Damn, we've got no other choice.* He grits his teeth.

"Which way do we go?" Lance demands. Without a reply, he takes initiative. "Come on, Tovi. We've run out of options!"

The young man nods. He jogs beside Lance. *Shield and shelter us beneath the shadow of Your wings.* Tovi prays. The two run down the corridor. The unnatural howls of their predators send shivers down the youth's spine. *What are they?* Tovi wonders while his heart pounds at a deadly rate.

The corridor appears longer as danger looms close behind. Sweat beads down Lance's cheek. His sights follow the beam of a shaking flashlight. As the clock ticks, so does doubt spins through the father's thoughts. Suddenly, Lance notices something ahead.

"A ladder!" He shouts.

"Great!" Tovi laughs.

The men force themselves forward. The sinister screams drawing near prevent them from stopping. Lance repositions Ava onto his back as he climbs.

"Shit!" He curses while his hands sear with pain.

"Go, go, go!" Tovi pushes him.

The young man places the flashlight in his mouth. Through gritted teeth, he continues to cheer the other on. Tovi's eyes squint as sunlight shines down. His heart rejoices when Lance opens the trapdoor.

Snapping maws are heard from below. The sound of scraping claws triggers another adrenaline surge through Tovi's veins. He reaches the final rung of the ladder. However, an impulse catches the young man, and he peeks behind. A reptilian beast relishes the opportunity. A hundred of needle-like teeth dig into Tovi's leg. His blood curdling scream echoes above the gnashing beasts. The flashlight falls to the hoard below. Tovi's hands struggle to hold onto the metal bar. He frantically kicks down on the beast's snoot.

"A little help here!" Tovi cries towards the opening. "Lance, are you still there?"

The thought of being abandoned crosses the young man's mind. A bead of sweat forms along his brow. Tovi's heart races while hearing the beast growl and rip at his pants. No, more than just fabric is torn to ribbons. The pain continues to sear as the beast threatens to sever the young man's leg. Tovi releases a wail. Yet, another horrifying scream rings louder.

"What's... going on?" Tovi stammers.

Suddenly, the beasts below have a change of prerogative. The violent creature opens its bloody maw and recoils. The pack of monsters scamper further down the dark tunnels with urgency. Tovi glances above to see an open palm.

"Take my hand!" Lance insists.

An injured leg makes climbing difficult. Tovi grits his teeth and winces with each consecutive step. *I'm alive at the very least!* His optimism emerges. Once on solid ground, Tovi falls to the side. Little Ava stares at him with big eyes.

"Hurt!" She cries out.

"I'll be fine!" Tovi smiles.

"Not yet." Lance remarks with a heavy heart. "I'm sorry, I wish we were out of there before they came."

Lance closes the hatch. He removes his shirt. *We need a tourniquet.* His thoughts ring. Lance proceeds to rip the shirt in half to provide enough wrap for the wound. He shakes his head.

"We need supplies," Lance asserts. He pats the other's shoulder. "Too bad you didn't run into a med kit."

"No, but I do know," Tovi replies. His voice shakes from the adrenaline rushing through his blood. "We're close to town."

"What do you mean?" He inquires.

Ava stumbles over to investigate further. The sight of Tovi's wrapped leg gives her more reassurance. She watches with a curious gaze as the young man removes a parchment from his tattered coat.

"Map!" Ava cheers. "Map! Map!"

"Yes, this is a map, Ava!" He chuckles. Tovi unravels the roll. "See, there's a town marked due east from where we stand. I guess whoever made this map didn't know about the tunnels below."

"Now, that's interesting," Lance muses. He studies the map further. "Looks as though the town is gated. But hopefully we'll be able to manoeuvre around the walls."

"We won't know until we try." Tovi replies. He offers the map to Lance. "Though, if I end up slowing you two down..."

"Nonsense!" Lance declines the parchment. He goes to lift the other onto his feet. "I'm not going to forsake someone in need. Besides, Ava's taken a liking to you, and I trust her judgment."

The young man smiles. *It's been a while since I've seen anyone as kind as you have been.* A memory surfaces within Tovi's mind. He balances himself with Lance's arm.

"Time for up." The man addresses his babe. Ava yawns and grabs hold of her father's neck. "So, east, huh?"

"Yes." Tovi nods.

The party of three begin their trek for sanctuary. As the moon exchanges places with the sun, they come across a scarce forest. Lance insists on resting despite his new companion's rebuttal. *We have to keep a close eye on the leg.* The man's thoughts demand. Lance regards his daughter with a frown. *She must be starving.* He observes while kissing her on the head.

"Hey, I have some MREs remaining!" Tovi beams. He pulls at a bag hoisted on his waist. "Here, you two should eat some."

"What about yourself?" Lance lifts a brow.

"I'm fine." Tovi coughs. He takes a short sip from the canteen. "I ate in the chambers before I met you two."

Lance smiles. He breaks open the packages. Already he can tell that Ava wouldn't find them at all appetizing. She puckers her face at the smell of what is *supposed* to be called *food.*

"Yuck!" She retorts.

"This is all we've got." Lance chides.

Reluctantly, Ava listens. *Daddy knows.* She thinks. As she chews the crumbling bits begin to form a paste like peanut butter. *Blegh!* Ava smacks her lips and deems to spit out the mixture.

"Ava!" Her father scolds. He smacks his own tongue. "Trust me, I don't like this much either!"

The little one ignores her distaste. As children often get distracted by unexpected remarks, Ava turns towards laughter. Her father joins in and pats her on the head.

"That's better." He smiles. Lance turns towards the young man. "Thank you..."

Tovi has fallen asleep against the tree trunk. His leg is outstretched and poised on a rock. Lance notices the blood pulling around the wrap. *The town better have a medical kit.* He hopes. The two finish their impromptu meal. Lance nudges his company awake.

"Come on," Lance says. He goes to stand with Ava clamouring on his back. "We have to get moving before those wretched things find us."

"Okay," Tovi answers. He readies himself with Lance's aid. "I appreciate your help."

The older man nods in response. *Leave no comrade behind.* The phrase echoes from somewhere deep within Lance's mind. He watches as the sun blazes the soil. *No matter what, we're making it to that town today!* His determination burns. The weary group trail further through the growing heat. Sweat trickles down each of their necks. Tovi's face flushes from exhaustion mingling with infection. Lance pushes them onward like a fierce captain.

***

A wall stretches skywards beyond fields of sand. The stone is worn and fractured in many places. As Lance brings his party forward, he observes several scratches along the rock. *So, they've been here too?* He glowers at the thought. Carefully, he walks through the tattered gate. With everything in shambles, it's evident that they're the only people present.

"Could be worse, huh?" Tovi stifles a cough. His arid throat makes talking difficult. "The beasts could have nested in these rundown buildings."

"True," Lance replies. He regards his startled babe with encouragement. "Don't worry, Ava. Daddy won't let them get you."

She buries her head underneath his chin. Lance peers around for any indication of useful items. *There must be a medical ward somewhere in this town.* He muses. Tovi's weight shifts along his shoulder.

"Are you alright?" Lance asks.

"I think I need to lay down," Tovi replies. He places a hand on his head. "I don't feel well."

"Okay." Lance glances around until finding a suitable location. "Here, the house up ahead looks stable. You can rest inside while I look for some medical supplies."

The other agrees with a quiet grin. The three wander through an open door. Immediately, a wave of coughing ensues from the dust and debris. Despite the house's poor repair, there's some old furniture suitable for seating. Tovi falls onto an old sofa. Lance finds a chair for him to use.

"Keep your leg elevated." Lance instructs. "Can't have the swelling worsen."

"Aye, aye." Tovi salutes him in jest.

Lance rolls his eyes and takes his leave. He turns towards his daughter to ask should she stay. However, two arms lift up in his direction. Lance brings her to his chest. *I didn't expect to leave you behind anyways.* He thinks with a warm sentiment.

The sky overhead hangs at noon. Lance and Ava wander through the town with haste. The little one takes in the sights with excitement. She hasn't seen so many new things before! Sure, the houses are broken, and the cobblestone cracked. However, the little one is eager to observe. She watches earnestly as her father's head moves on a swivel. *Help friend.* Her mind musters. Ava peers around a corner and notices a strange sign.

"What's that?" She inquires.

Lance looks towards the direction of a tiny finger. His eyes widen with fervour.

"The hospital!" He chimes.

"Hospi... Tal." She repeats.

The man hurries towards their new destination. He walks beneath the sign decorated with the twisted serpents of old. *Caduceus.* Lance recalls. He enters the lobby. The marble is cold against his feet. Lance fights the urge to pee and manoeuvres through each corridor. His quest at first seems at a loss. Several of the rooms have caved in on themselves.

"I wonder if there was an earthquake," he contemplates.

Ava joins in on the search. Yet, her understanding of what's needed is close to nil. She snorts in frustration. Lance gingerly pats her back.

"Ava helped a lot," he cheers.

The compliment makes her chuckle. Before Lance admits defeat, he locates a storage room. The door is locked. Lance peeks around for anything of use. A broken wheelchair catches his eye. He places Ava a few feet away. Lance then raises the chair with the metal legs facing a glass panel. Within several strikes, the window breaks. Shards of glass fall to the floor.

"Wait here for Daddy, alright?" Lance insists.

He waits for Ava's confirmation— a small thumbs up. Lance reaches through the pane to unlock the door. Fortunately, the room contains a myriad of supplies. On one side, there's a medicine cabinet that includes pain killers. Towards the other, Lance locates a wound care kit with fresh bandages, antibiotic ointment, and peroxide. *May be old, but this is better than nothing.* Lance observes. He even finds a scalpel that gets placed in the box. Lance walks carefully over the glass shards towards his little one. He holds up the box with a smile.

"Yay!" The little girl claps as she is lifted in her father's arm.

Swiftly, they navigate back to Tovi. The young man's cheeks are covered in sweat. He looks onto Lance with a sad smile.

"Ava, don't look." Her father asserts.

Ava regards him with confusion. Still, she sits down on the floor. Lance turns towards the wounded leg while dreading what's beneath the shirt. Gingerly, he undoes the tourniquet. Tovi winces as the air touches his wound. Dried blood cakes over pus filled gashes. The beast's teeth marks reveal necrotic damage.

"That's... Not normal." Tovi grimaces.

"No, but…" Lance struggles for words. "Perhaps the ointment will help. I've also found peroxide to flush out the bite."

"Go ahead," Tovi replies.

The young man closes his eyes while Lance begins his work. He cuts through the remaining fabric with the scalpel. Once the wound is fully visible, Lance pours the peroxide. Tovi's screams shake the room. The man peeks behind to check on his daughter. Ava has her ears covered and huddles into a ball. *I'm sorry.* He apologizes internally. Lance glances at the bubbling wound. He removes the pus with a clean rag. Once the leg is ready, Lance applies the ointment and fresh bandages.

"Thank you," Tovi squeaks. His head hangs back on the couch cushion. "I didn't know how bad those monsters were. Heh, I thought they were just like wild dogs. Yet, they're more than that aren't they?"

"Seems accurate." Lance flatly replies. He rises to his feet. "I'm going to check the pantry. If we're lucky, then there may be something useful to eat."

Lance heads towards the kitchen. His daughter isn't too far behind. She watches him with big eyes.

"Ava help!" She announces while flipping through the bottom cupboards.

"Alright, sweety." he beams.

The top doors reveal nothing but dust and cobwebs. The kitchen counter is cracked in some locations. *A fight must have occurred in here.* Lance concludes. While glancing around the back door, he observes a break in the window.

"Don't come over here, Ava," he instructs. "Broken glass."

Ava grunts with a determined nod. As she turns to a cabinet behind her, an open door catches her attention. She investigates further and comes across a metal circle tin.

"Cookies!" She cries out in triumph. Ava dances over to her father holding the treasure high. "Cookies! Cookies!"

"Hold on, let's check." He laughs. Lance removes the lid and lifts a brow. "Not cookies. Though, there's enough sewing thread and needles here to be used."

"So, Ava found good?" The little girl asks.

"Yes!" Lance replies. He pats her on the head. "Ava does good."

The little girl cheers. She begins to dance in the centre of the kitchen. Suddenly, an unsteady foot causes her to stumble. Lance is quick to react. The man lowers the sewing tin onto the counter. He then grabs her with his arm before Ava can fall.

"Careful, dear." He chides.

"Sorry..." Ava bows her head. With her sights on the floor, she notices something wrong. "Broke too."

"Broke?" Lance repeats.

He gingerly moves Ava to the side. Lance kneels to the floor with a curious gleam. One of the planks twists above the rest. Lance tugs at the warped board and unveils a secret latch. *Could this be?* He wonders with an excited heartbeat. Diligently, he begins plucking up the other floorboards. The metal handle stares at him and dares him to release the lock. Lance pulls the latch open and immediately picks up his daughter in victory.

"You found food, Ava!" He laughs. Lance swings her into a circle. "Great job! These poor people didn't have a chance to finish their wares!"

"*Wears*? Like clothes?" Ava inquires with a confused puckered lip.

"No, *wares* like food!" He corrects her.

"Yay!" Ava claps upon being returned to her feet. She scuttles out of the kitchen. "Tovi! Food, food!"

Lance hears a laboured laugh echo from the living room. He descends down a set of wooden steps. The secret room has shelves lined with pickled and canned goods. Although some have technically expired, they still provide some nourishment in the meantime. Towards the floor are metal containers of water. *What a lucky break!* Lance cheers. A tear crosses his cheek.

"Let's see what we can make," he mumbles.

Lance procures an armful of fruit and canned chicken. He creaks upstairs. The man lays the cans atop the counter. He then peruses through the drawers for utensils. On his left, are rusted silverware and a can-opener. *At least some aren't corroded where the mouth goes.* He muses at the forks and spoons. He turns behind to look at the cabinet filled with bowls and plates. Several have chips along the rim. Yet, he is careful with which to select for use. *Can't allow Ava to get cut.* Lance thinks. He prepares a salad with chicken, pears and peaches. The man offers them to his party.

"Here you go." Lance smiles.

"Thank you," Tovi replies. "Seems as though there's someone watching out for us after all."

"Perhaps." Lance remarks dryly. The man turns to his little one. "Have some food, Ava."

"Yay!" She cheers.

Lance sits on the floor and eats his portion. As they finish their meal, the man cleans up the dishes. *How unfortunate.* He sighs. *There's no running water.* Lance shrugs. He proceeds to maintain the house. He dusts the furniture and manages to find bedding for the couch. The other rooms of the house are in disrepair— broken floorboards and a cracked bathtub.

"Well, at least we have a toilet..." He lifts his brow. "One that doesn't flush."

Ava approaches him with a curious glance.

"Tovi red." She frowns. "Tovi sick."

"*Red?*" Lance reiterates with concern.

He hurries back to the living room. Tovi lays on his back now while pouring with sweat.

"I'm sorry, but you needed to keep that leg elevated!" Lance scolds.

"I'm sorry." Tovi coughs. "I thought that I could get some rest."

Lance shakes his head. He retrieves water from the cellar. Lance returns to pour water into the young man's flask.

"Stay hydrated," Lance orders. He notices Ava in the corner. "Keep watching him. Daddy needs to get more supplies from the hospital."

"Kay!" Ava nods.

The man grabs an empty sack and storms out of the house. He winds through the streets with a frantic energy. *I don't know...* He goes to think. *Being negative will only make matters worse.* Lance confers. As he steps into the hospital for a second time, something unnerves him.

"Shit, they were here." Lance infers from the claw marks along the floor.

He navigates towards the storage room with caution.

Once inside, he fumbles through the provisions grabbing acetaminophen, epinephrine, and a few vials of antivenom. *Can't believe that I forgot to take these.* Lance grits his teeth. He locates a few syringes and stuffs them into his bag. Lance hurries back into the halls.

Outside, the sun dips behind the ruined houses. The man jolts through the streets. An eerie howl in the distance causes the hairs on his neck to stand. *They've caught our scent.* His thoughts burn into his stomach. *We have enough issues at hand.* Lance shakes his head. To alert the others would create a state of panic. Instead, Lance insists on taking one matter at a time.

"I'm back," he calls out. Lance sprints towards the young man's side. "I have medicine."

Tovi's eyes are wet and distant. His face is pallid. The expression of fear sets in Ava's gaze. She turns to her father with tears.

"Tovi... Sick..." She squeaks.

"Daddy knows," Lance replies. He readies a syringe. "This will help him."

The sight of the needle stabbing into flesh makes Ava squeamish. *Ouch!* She thinks while casting her sights elsewhere. The sound of gasping catches her attention. Tovi coughs up foam from his mouth. Ava watches as he vomits onto the floor.

"He needs water." Lance addresses.

The man fetches a flask. He assists the other to drink. *Please.* Lance begs any who can hear him. Another round of coughs persists until Tovi's symptoms lessen. The antivenom relieves the young man of his suffering. Lance embraces him with joy.

"It's working!" He cries out. Lance lays the young man gently onto the couch. "All you need is rest now."

Still weak from his ordeal, Tovi replies with a grin. He falls asleep with a steady heartbeat. The man faces his daughter as a new urgency arrives.

"Daddy has to go out for a while," he explains. Lance presses a finger against his lips. "Stay here while he's asleep. When I come home, we can eat dinner. Okay, Ava?"

The little girl stands with her jaw dropped. *Why?* She thinks to herself. Doubt and fear surfaces Ava's mind. Yet, she affirms her stance with a thumb's up.

"Good." Lance smiles. He pats her on the head. "There's water in the bag if you need a drink. Don't worry dear, Daddy won't be long."

Indeed, with haste Lance carries out his agenda. He storms into the darkening streets. Ears pique to study the surrounding sounds. As Lance walks through the town, he approaches a large building.

"A... Sanctuary?" He muses. Lance gawks at the large building made from marble. "This may come in handy."

The man records the location to memory. Lance draws towards the nearby houses. To his surprise, their doors are bolted shut. *A final stand.* He shakes his head. Lance peers into a broken window. Inside the dark room lies broken furniture and bones. Bodies of those who could not escape those reptilian creatures. *Such a pity.* Lance sighs. He recoils from the wreckage. As the clouds block the moonlight, Lance retreats to the house.

Upon his return, Tovi and Ava are fast asleep. The man smiles and covers his daughter with a blanket. He sits with his back against the couch. A passing glance at the stars fills his heart with a sad pang. In the still of the night, Lance mourns the probable and questions the uncertainties plaguing his thoughts. *How?* The answer does not surface. A yawn provokes him to join in the slumber.

***

For the next few weeks, the trio reside at the house. Tovi's leg is healed, although nerve damage persists after the necrotic venom. He stands in the kitchen preparing dinner. Lance's absence troubles him. *But I can't let Ava see that I'm concerned!* The young man sighs. He glances into the living room. Ava sits on the floor playing with a ragdoll.

Tovi opens up a tin of shredded chicken and empties the container into the pot. An additional pot rests underneath the first— lined with stones and a flame. Since the stove isn't working, Tovi must improvise with what they have available. He stirs the broth layered with thyme, sage, canned carrots and pickled onions. The soup wafts through the kitchen. Tovi samples a spoon and puckers his lips.

"Probably should have done without the onions!" He frowns.

Despite the slight setback, a ready customer gives him a laugh. Ava approaches him with her nose sniffing the air.

"Food!" She claps. Ava looks with an eager expression. "What food?"

"Chicken soup!" Tovi announces with a smile.

He removes the main pot and pours water on the flame. The fire sizzles out with a hiss. *Alright, where's the bowls again?* Tovi muses. He hums while gathering the dishes. The front door opens and his heart trills.

"You're just in time!" Tovi calls into the other room.

"Tovi make soup!" Ava runs up to her father with excitement. "Soup! Soup!"

"That's great!" Lance replies. He gives her a kiss on the cheek and approaches the kitchen. "Smells delicious."

"Oh, I don't know." Tovi blushes. He pours a few portions. "I would've loved to have made a fresh pot. But as you know there's no chance of that."

"No worries." Lance shakes his head. "We're lucky to have the food we've got."

"True, true." Tovi smiles. He places two bowls on the table. "Well, enjoy!"

In spite of the vinegar aftertaste, the chicken soup is a success! The three enjoy small talk. For a moment, life seems *normal.* Yet, a lingering suspicion hangs on the back of Tovi's mind.

"What have you been working on?" He asks Lance abruptly.

"Nothing much really." He shrugs. Lance observes the look on the other's face. "Don't believe me, huh?"

"Uh, no." Tovi replies. He taps on the table in a rhythmic pattern. "I'm nervous, that's all. I don't understand why you don't want me around..."

"That's definitely not it, Tovi." The man wrinkles his brows. "I need you here with Ava. She would only get scared heading out late."

"No scared." Ava pouts. The little girl slams her spoon on the table. "Ava brave!"

"I know," Lance laughs. He pats her head. "Daddy means that he needs to..."

A sharp shriek interrupts the conversation. Lance removes himself from the table. He walks over to the back door. To his dismay, a couple of creatures stalk the distance. *Not now!* He grimaces. Lance turns to the others with a finger poised to his lips.

"Be quiet." He instructs.

What's out there? Tovi mouths the words.

They're here, Lance replies.

Ava covers her mouth. Her eyes grow wide with fright. *No brave!* The little girl criticizes herself. She quietly walks over to her father. He picks her up and proceeds to ready their bags.

"What are you doing?" Tovi whispers.

"Preparing for the worst." Lance remarks with a sombre expression. He hands Tovi a bag. "You carry the food, and I'll have the medical supplies."

A sudden scream chills their bones. The beasts have caught their location. From the living room, Lance peers into the kitchen. *Another one!* His mind races. Three beasts can be seen prowling the backyard through the broken windowpane.

"We must leave." Lance insists. He goes to exit. "Come, I found a safer place to stay in town."

"Ah!" Tovi exclaims. He shuffles beside him. "So, that's why you've been sneaking out?"

The man nods in response. Tovi sighs and returns the gesture. The trio venture outside with wary steps. Tovi turns to close the door. He follows the other's lead. *May it be Your will, God, our God and the God of our fathers, that You should lead us in peace and direct our steps in peace.* Tovi begins to pray. A crash from inside the house causes alarm. *Guide us in peace, and support us in peace, and cause us to reach our destination in life, joy, and peace.* He continues. The young man looks to Lance with concern.

"We have to keep pushing forward," Lance relays. He points towards the next direction. "Beyond that street is a straight run for our mark."

"Understood." Tovi gulps.

The three weave along the town in haste. In the distance, Lance can hear the grunts of the predacious beasts. *We're almost there.* His thoughts cheer. A smile crosses his lips. However, joy is short lived as a deafening screech carries above the rooftops. *Shit!* Lance curses. He glances towards the creature. Beady eyes lock onto his own with a feverish glow.

"Lance..." The young man grabs Lance's shoulder. Tovi's words fall quickly. "We better not have far to go now."

"We don't," Lance replies. He feels Ava's heartbeat palpitating. "Don't worry sweety, we have one more block."

Tovi sighs with relief. He wants to speak but refrains. Sweat beads down his cheek. *Grant me grace, kindness, and mercy in Your eyes and in the eyes of all who see us.* Tovi's mind races. *Bestow upon us abundant kindness and hearken to the voice of our prayer, for You hear the prayers of all. Blessed are You God, who hearkens to prayer...* The young man loses focus. His leg starts to shake from the exertion.

"Don't fall back!" Lance urges.

The sound of thunder catches the trio off guard. However, a peek skyward suggests the sound is not coming from the clouds. Lance swivels his head to observe their surroundings. A swarm of beasts are on their tail! *The creature dancing on top of the roofs must be their leader!* Lance grits his teeth. He doesn't want to run. Only, there's no longer an option.

"Daddy," Ava squeaks. She points down an alleyway. "Bad doggy!"

"How many are there?" Tovi asks in a panic.

"Too many to handle!" Lance answers. "We're going to have to run for it!"

"Won't that..." Tovi's words are cut short.

A series of howls from the main creature prompt the others to give chase. Claws dig into the ground for additional traction. The beasts are yards away and eager for their prey. The men break out into a sprint. In spite of his discomfort, Tovi makes his best attempt at distancing himself from the pack.

Ava buries her head into her father's chest. *No good!* She cries. The screeching beasts draw tears to her face. Ava listens to the sound of stamping feet. *Stairs.* She observes Lance lifting his knees. A fierce howl forces her gaze to pass behind. The beasts are gaining on their quarry!

"Hurry!" Lance shouts. He opens the chapel door. "Come on Tovi!"

He places Ava down. She doesn't need direction to take cover in the corner. Lance exchanges his bag for a standing candelabra. *I can't let them take him!* The man's eyes gleam with tenacity. He sees Tovi struggling to reach the entrance. An opportunistic attack takes the poor man by his leg.

"Lance!" He cries while falling to the ground.

"No!" The man storms to his aid.

Lance swings the iron staff at the beast's maw. The creature twists its massive head without letting go of his prey. Tovi attempts to poke at the creature's beady eyes. Yet, another two beasts arrive with snapping jaws and razor-sharp teeth. Lance receives a heavy scratch on his right arm.

"Shit!" He yowls.

Lance readjusts his stance. He takes the sharp end of the staff and pierce through the snoot of the beast on his right. The creature recoils and threatens to remove his weapon with a flick of his head. The man stomps the creature's head to retract the iron prongs out of its flesh. Dark blood litters the cold marble.

The young man continues fighting with his adversary. The reptile's jaw doesn't appear to let go, regardless of how many times Tovi kicks its face. *Time for plan c.* Tovi's mind churns. He leans over and bites the beast. Despite his efforts, Tovi's teeth are no match for the tough hide. He leans back and returns to deliver a series of punches.

Suddenly, several projectiles come flying through the air. Lance watches as religious texts fall to the ground. He peers behind his shoulder to see little Ava causing a commotion. The two beasts peer towards the new sound. Their noses sniff at the air. *If they pick up on her scent...* Lance's thoughts halt. A loud scream in front of him sends chills down his spine. Tovi's leg is sawed off!

"Damn it!" Lance curses.

He beats the other beasts. Fortunately, the presence of fresh meat entices the creatures to fight like a pack of hyenas. Lance grabs the ailing man by the arm and hoists him onto his back. Frantic feet cross towards the church door. Tovi's blood leaves a trail that attracts more of the creatures. Tovi screams in pain as he is placed onto the church floor. He watches the foul beasts in his peripheral vision approach the door. Lance slams the entrance shut. However, a few snoots dig in the crack. *I can't.* Tovi wavers. He collapses.

"Back!" Ava demands. She takes a book and starts slamming against the fierce creatures. "Bad doggy!"

The snarling hoard recoils. An explosion outside of the town excites them more than their difficult prey. The reptilian predators leave while anticipating a more advantageous meal. *Good.* Lance heaves the door shut. He turns the lock and looks at the wounded.

"He's losing too much blood!" He remarks with a cool tone.

Lance grabs the medical bag. *I have to stop the bleeding.* His thoughts race. The man soaks up the wound with gauze. He bandages what's left of Tovi's kneecap. *Where's that syringe?* Lance's hand navigates through the supplies with a fury. He locates the needle and draws out a vial of the antivenom.

"Tovi..." The little girl whimpers. Tears stream down Ava's face. "Be, okay?"

"I believe so," Lance replies. He tosses the used syringe into a corner. "He needs rest."

Ava snuggles up to her father with concern. *Scary.* Images of the beasts flood her mind. The sound of Tovi screaming as his bone snaps apart echoes within her skull. She buries her head into Lance's chest. Within moments, the scared child falls asleep.

***

The sun dances within the church. Lance's eyes readjust to the surroundings. He hears a shuffle as his friend wakes.

"I'm sorry," Lance apologizes.

"Don't be," Tovi replies. His eyes are bloodshot. "You've done your best."

Ava stirs with a hungry belly. Her father gives a warm smile. He goes to gather a jar of peaches for them to share.

"We'll have to be careful," he advised. Lance portions the peaches into three tin mugs. "Otherwise, we'll run out of food before we can develop an escape."

"Escape?" Tovi coughs. He slurps a peach. "I'm not sure how we can do it now... I'll just be a burden."

"Nonsense!" Lance furrows his brows. He places a hand on the other's shoulder. "We've made it this far. We're not going to just leave you to get eaten."

Tovi studies the man's expression. *He's honest.* The young man stifles a blush. He averts his gaze— glancing around the chamber. Towards the altar hangs a stone sculpture of a triangle within a circle.

"The Triad," Tovi mumbles.

"Excuse me?" Lance's ears perk.

"The Triad," he repeats. Tovi points towards the altar. "Back in the day they sought to merge the three western religions. Yet, in the end, people still found a way to bring more harm than good."

"Such a pity." The man shakes his head. Lance peers into his cup with a sombre tone. "Seems as though humans were always aiming to take advantage of one another. I mean, why else would they think of imprisoning those that didn't agree with them?"

"That's true." Tovi shakes his head. "That's why Rhaniya and I were taken in. We kept to our own traditions rather than adhere to The Triad."

Lance clicks his tongue. Then he realizes.

"Who's she?" He asks.

"My cellmate." The young man replies. "She came to aid my escape. I promised to come back for her when I could. Though, I'm not sure if that's even possible now."

A sad remorse hangs over Tovi. He looks at the blood seeping through his bandages. *I hope this heals soon.* His thoughts run unrealistically. Yet, Tovi cannot forgive himself should his wound lead to another's harm. *He's been so attentive.* Tovi muses. He finishes his breakfast in a rush.

"Thank you!" He smiles. Tovi hands the other his cup. "Now, what's our prerogative?"

"Doing our best to stay alive." Lance remarks with a sigh.

The three continue to meander through the church. Tovi manoeuvres to a pew with the man's assistance. Once his leg receives fresh bandages, Tovi can't help but to fall asleep. Ava sits next to him while playing with her ragdoll. The toy provides some comfort while seeking refuge. Lance peruses through various bookshelves lined with artifacts and religious relics.

"What's in here?" He wonders as a red door catches his attention. Lance turns the knob. "I can't believe this!"

He stands with shock. Decaying bodies litter the floor. A glance at the backside of the door reveals several scratch marks and dried patches of blood. Lance picks up a lone dagger. *Should come in handy.* He confers. Lance leaves without wanting to disturb the dead any further. He studies the new weapon. *Still sharp.* He concludes with a finger prick.

The man walks up to the platform. The altar is covered in a red tapestry. An old rug covers the flooring behind the rectangular frame. Lance doesn't notice anything interesting about the setup. Several goblets are overturned, but the location has not seen any combat. He returns to his supplies. Lance puts the dagger into his bag. *Now what to do?* He sighs. Lance sits on the floor and falls asleep.

***

Time in the chapel ticks like a broken clock. The party becomes anxious without direction. Still, the trio pass the moments away with stories of their days before being clasped behind bars. As Lance uses up more of his medical supplies, he braves the streets to restock. *We haven't heard from them in weeks.* Lance muses about the creatures.

"Just be careful," Tovi urges.

"Don't worry about me." Lance smiles. He pats his daughter on the head. "Keep him company, okay?"

"Kay!" Ava nods.

The little girl watches her father exit. *Why he leave?* Ava wonders. She doesn't understand what her father means to keep her alone. Though, she turns to Tovi with a grin. *No lonely.* Her thoughts beam. She enjoys his company. Especially since Tovi has his own ragdoll too!

In the still of the afternoon outside, Lance staggers through the hospital. He ventures back into the storage room and refills his bag. *Tovi has to keep that leg clean.* The man thinks. He grabs a bottle of peroxide. More bandages are available for the taking. Upon a top shelf sits an old lantern. Lance eagerly takes it and locates matches for the wick. *This haul should hold us off for a few weeks.* He smiles. However, that expression fades in a flash. A loud sound cuts the sky above. Lance carefully peers out the hallway window. *Helicopters!* His mind panics. Lance's heart races with the grim speculation that...

"The beasts lead them here!" The words fall from his lips.

Deftly, he navigates from the hospital to the empty streets. Lance keeps the helicopter in view. *There isn't much cover towards the church.* He frowns. Lance darts in and out of the abandoned homes. The chopper hovers above the town like a shark circling its prey. Despite his poor state of luck, Lance manages to return to the church. He knocks on the door.

"Daddy's back!" He calls out.

The lock clicks open. Ava stands with her ragdoll in the air.

"Daddy!" She cheers. Ava speaks with enthusiasm. "Found good!"

"Not quite." Lance replies while mistaking her statement for a question. He hurries to bolt them inside. "We have a problem."

Tovi turns towards him with a curious glance.

"There's a chopper overhead." He states while gathering his thoughts. "We may need to flee."

"About that," Tovi replies. He uses the pew for balance. "Ava and I found something interesting."

Lance lifts a brow. His gaze follows Ava approaching the altar.

"Tunnel!" She squeaks.

"Yes." The young man nods. "We can escape."

"We don't know..." Lance's words are interrupted by the sound of gunfire.

Shrieks of the reptilian beasts are heard beyond the sanctuary. *They really did lead those bastards here!* Lance twitches in disgust.

"Let's go then!" He insists.

Beneath the old rug is a cellar door. The trio gather their bearings and make their way inside. The man closes the door above. Lance lights his lantern for the others to see. He then holds Ava closely in one arm. The man provides a shoulder for Tovi to balance. They begin to hear commotion as the fight between the reptilian creatures and officers make way in the chapel.

Once silence ensues, the three feel more at ease. The tunnel leads to another building. Yet, the passage is blocked by a locked door. Lance places his lantern on the ground. *Maybe I can break through.* He surmises. Lance utilizes the dagger as a picking tool. The man has exceptional hearing. In moments the mechanism clicks open.

"Didn't know you were a lock picker!" Tovi exclaims.

"Neither did I." Lance smiles.

The party enters what looks like a bunker. Towards the far wall is a ladder leading to a hatch. On the left rests a table with a radio set. *Good!* Lance beams. There's a bed and a small bucket by the right.

"Here, you can lay down." Lance directs the young man to the cot. He rummages for cans of tuna. "We should eat and rest before we have to move out again."

"Hopefully, they don't find us." Tovi remarks with a sigh. He looks at Ava with a smile. "It's okay. With your dad here, there's nothing to be upset about."

"Right," Ava says.

The little girl's eyes suggest that she isn't buying the other's optimism. *Bad doggy.* Her thoughts cry. *Bad ones.* Ava sits on the floor and spoons out her food. As adrenaline declines two of three are ready for sleep.

"Today was wild!" Lance speaks out-loud. He studies the two with earnest. "You are asleep, aren't you?"

The man begins his work on the radio. Despite his uneasiness, Lance knows they don't have any other choices. *This had better work.* He grits his teeth. As the static clears, Lance cheers. The man finished his task before heading to sleep. However, a loud frequency breaks his comfort.

"Damn them!" He curses. Lance shakes the others awake. "They're in the tunnel!"

"Seriously?" Tovi yawns. He rubs the tiredness from his eyes. "What do we do Captain?"

The address takes Lance off guard. He shakes his head and points to the hatch.

"We fly." Lance directs.

"Scared!" Ava cries. She clings to her father's leg. "Bad dream."

"I'm sorry," Lance replies. He picks her up. "But we must leave now before they catch us."

Lance makes his way to the ladder. Tovi hobbles to the first rung. He goes to pick up his bag.

"Don't bring anything that will slow us down!" Lance remarks with a sharp tone.

"Are you sure?" Tovi asks.

"I'm positive," he replies. Lance pushes the hatch. "I have a plan."

"I take your word." Tovi nods.

The young man follows suit. He stumbles at first. However, after the sixth rung, Tovi finds his pace. *What happened?* He wonders with uncertainty. Still, his confidence in Lance stands strong. As Tovi crawls onto solid ground, the full moon surprises him.

"It's beautiful!" The young man says in awe. "I haven't seen one in so long!"

Lance pats him on the shoulder. A sense of urgency shines in his dark eyes. *Finally, we have some light.* Lance smiles. He offers Tovi his arm. The two make haste for an unknown destination.

"If they find us," Lance states. "Then there's no more hope."

The moonlight flutters across the barren ground. Tovi hears his blood pounding in his ears. *But where are we going?* He wonders. The young man peers to the sky ahead. For a second, he believes that there's metal touching the night clouds. *Are my eyes deceiving me?* As the structure comes into view, Tovi's eyes are proven correct.

"What is that?" Tovi asks while out of breath.

"A radio tower!" Lance laughs. He passes him a mischievous look. "Everything is going to be alright."

The young man adds a bewildered glance. Despite the confusion growing, the three press on. Ava peeks over her father's shoulder. Her eyes widen. A pack of beasts have picked up their trail. Still, behind them are the sounds of gunshots as four military vehicles take pursuit.

"Bad!" Ava's voice shrieks.

Lance's ears piqued to the commotion. *We're going to make it!* His determination grows. If he could carry them both, Lance would. Yet, he must rely on the distraction in between the trio and the authorities. Tension rises and Tovi's breath hitches. The young man's face is flushed from exertion.

"Hang on!" Lance calls out. "Don't give up!"

The party reaches the radio tower. They climb the ladder to its full height. A downward glance reveals a battle between the creatures and footmen. Tovi sits down with his back against steel.

"What can we do?" Tovi's voice shakes with terror. "We're completely surrounded!"

"Tovi." The man kneels down. Lance places his daughter beside the other. "Take care of Ava."

Green eyes stare at him with shock. Lance locks his gaze onto the little girl. *Ava, Daddy has to go.* He says telepathically.

"No leave!" Ava shouts.

"What's going on?" Tovi's words fall frantic.

Lance kisses his daughter on the forehead and hugs the young man. He walks towards the edge of the tower. A loud frequency hovers overhead. Lance points above at a peculiar aircraft.

"They're here." He smiles. Lance begins to fall back. "Farewell."

The others shuffle to the edge. Tovi grabs onto Ava before she could follow. During freefall, the man they know transforms into one of the beasts. Confusion and sadness overwhelm them. Ava screams for her daddy.

In the moonlit glow, the ship beyond the radio tower shoots like a star. *Please, watch over my Ava.* Lance cries. As a beast he falls with nothing else left. As a father, Lance fights in the haze of rage and grief.

Authors Biographies

W.H. Vigo

W.H.Vigo is a Jamaican-Canadian horror and speculative fiction writer based in Switzerland. Their short story *Captured Land* was published in the dark fantasy anthology *Fairy Tales from the Rock* by Engen Books in spring 2023. Their debut novelette *Beneath the Rio Cobre* was published by The Great Lakes Horror Company the same year.

Vigo completed the Horror Writers Association (HWA) Mentorship program for new writers in 2021, and is an active member of the organization. They have been a three-time panellist (2022 and 2023) at Canada"s largest horror event, Frightmare in the Falls, and a two-time panellist for HWA Ontario. Vigo specializes in the academic research and discussion of unconventional or lesser-known folklore, mythology, and urban legends from around the world, with an emphasis on West Africa and the Caribbean. They share these tales on Instagram: @whvigo. Vigo is currently completing a novel-length dark fantasy manuscript.

Odin Mwadows

Odin Meadows is a first-generation graduate with a BA in English from Yale University currently living and working in Central Illinois with his husband and two dogs, not too far from the rural town where he grew up. His work has also appeared or is forthcoming in Mystic Owl Magazine, BULL lit mag, SFWG's Nightmare Fuel Anthology, Litmora, and Breath & Shadow.

Mathew Gostelow

Mathew Gostelow (he/him) is a writer, living in Birmingham, UK. Some days he wakes early and scribbles strange tales. If you catch him staring into space, he is either thinking about Twin Peaks or cooked breakfasts. Mat has written two books: a collection of speculative stories entitled *See My Breath Dance Ghostly* (Alien Buddha Press) and *Dantalion is a Quiet Place*, a novella-in-flash to be released in 2025 (DarkWinter Lit). He has been nominated for the Pushcart Prize, Best of the Net, and Best Microfiction. On Twitter, he's @MatGost

Josh Roach

Josh Roach is a writer and filmmaker born in the aisles of the video store. Raised by the likes of Stephen King and John Carpenter, he grew to become versatile writer. In 2019, his story "In the Details" appeared in the short story collection *Horror USA: Washington* (2019). He worked as a story consultant on the NSI award-winning short STRAIGHT TO VIDEO: THE B-MOVIE ODYSSEY (2015), and then in 2019, co-wrote *Mistletoe & Molly* (2021) for UPtv, as well as the horror-comedy and film festival favourite *THE LAST VIDEO STORE* (2024). He continues to work within genre, crafting stories of menace and the macabre, surviving solely on a strict regimen of Root Beer and buttery popcorn.

Tom Johnstone

Tom Johnstone is a senior gardener with Brighton and Hove City Council, whose stories have lately appeared in more and more publications thanks to the liberal application of organic fertiliser.

His fiction has appeared in *Black Static*, *Nightscript*, *Chthonic Matter Quarterly*, *Terror Tales of the Home Counties*, *The Ghastling*, *Supernatural Tales*, *A Ghosts and Scholars Book of Folk horror*, *Come October, Body shots, Medusa, Shadowplays*, *Infernal Mysteries*, two volumes of *Horror Library*, three volumes of *The Black Book of Horror* and two volumes of *Best Horror of the Year*.

His other accomplishments include a BA in English and Drama and a LANTRA certificate in driving a ride-on lawnmower. He used to buy ice cream from the ice cream van that pulls up on his road but not now. His children are both grown up.

Mia Dalia

Mia Dalia is an internationally published, CWA-nominated author of all things fantastic, thrilling, scary, and strange.
Her stories have been voted top ten of Tales to Terrify 2023 and shortlisted for the CWA's Daggers Awards 2024.

Mia's short fiction can be found: **online** at Night Terror Novels, 50-word stories, Flash Fiction Magazine, Pyre Magazine, Tales from the Moonlit Path, carte blanche magazine.
In print anthologies by Sunbury Press, HellBound Press, Black Ink Fiction, Dragon Roost Press, Unsettling Reads, Phobica Books, Wandering Wave Press, Bullet Points Vol. 3, Critical Blast, Exploding Head Press, Sinister Smile Press, DraculaBeyondStoker Magazine, Mystery Magazine, Headshot Press, Nightshade Press, Off-Topic Publishing, RebellionLIT, and more.
on narrative podcasts at Zoetic Press' Alphanumeric and Tales

to Terrify.

upcoming short fiction appearing in: Jaded Ibis Press, Grendel Press, WritersHive, Dragon Roost press, WonderBird Press, Crystal Lake Entertainment, Dark Matter INK, and more.

Featured publications include novels *Estate Sale* and *Haven*, novellas *Tell Me a Story*, *Discordant*, and *Arrokoth*, and the collection *Smile So Red and Other Tales of Madness.*

Find her online at: https://daliaverse.wixsite.com/auth or https://linktr.ee/daliaverse

Christabel Simpson

Christabel Simpson writes in various genres. She was born in England to parents with a love of romantic poetry (hence the name), but spent her teens in America. She returned to England to study at university and has a BA in English Literature and Dance. She started writing seriously at school when one of her teachers told her she had a flair for it, and has had work published in HEROICA and the HUSH, DON'T WAKE THE MONSTER anthology. Other interests include live performance (seeing and creating), music, ancient Egypt, paranormal research, cosplay and photography. She currently lives in London with her gorgeous girlfriend and their black cat.

L.N. Hunter

L.N. Hunter"s comic fantasy novel, *The Feather and the Lamp*, sits alongside works in anthologies such as *Best of British Science Fiction 2022* and *War* as well as Short Edition"s *Short Circuit* and the *Horrifying Tales of Wonder* podcast. There have also been papers in the *IEEE Transactions on Neural Networks*, which are probably somewhat less relevant and definitely less fun. When not writing, L.N. unwinds in a disorganised home in Carlisle, UK, along with two cats and a soulmate.

Find out more at https://linktr.ee/l.n.hunter or https://www.facebook.com/L.N.Hunter.writer.

Terry Campbell

Terry Campbell recently returned to writing after 20 years away from the keyboard. When he isn't writing, he is playing with his two Chinese Cresteds, road tripping with his lovely wife, or riding his ebike. His work has appeared in Horrors! *365 Scary Stories, Lungers, Lawdogs* and *Legends, and Soul*: A Paranormal Anthology. His first novel, Kindred Feather, is available on Amazon.

Mike Schuler

Mike Schuhler, is an American writer who brings a unique blend of military experience and academic insight to the realm of horror literature. Born in Oakland, California, and now residing in the evocative landscapes of Port Huron, Michigan, Schuhler's writing is informed by his degrees in English and Human Services.

His novella, "*Purgatory*," plunges readers into a chilling world of macabre, while his short story, "*Waiting Out the Storm*," featured in Scare Street's "*Night Terrors, Volume 13*," further demonstrates his talent for crafting bone-chilling tales.

Callum Gracey

Callum Gracey is a new writer from Wigan, England who has resigned from his role as a Police Detective to pursue his dream to become an author. He has always had a passion for writing and, in particular, writing horror. This is his first published work.

M. Legree

Chained to a desk during the day, M. Legree is released at dusk to write genre fiction. Guarded by a pack of savage mongrels, he lives alone in a Depression-era duplex overlooking Brays Bayou in the historical East End of Houston, Texas. Preferring to live in the past, Legree rereads the old tales of Stevenson, Poe, and Wells. His steampunk horror tale "*Victorian Resistance & the Lords Insectile*" appeared in Issue ***9 of **Cossmass Infinities** and his dark fantasy flash fictions "*Dryad Harvest*" and "Feline" are available in the anthology **Tales of Fear, Superstition, and Doom** and online with **Stupefying Stories: Showcase**, respectively.

Khala Grace

What's in a Name? For some a name is as simple as a word. Yet, for others, a name is difficult and important to claim. Ever since finding the name that feels right, Khala Grace continues striving for a life filled with art. Their craft of choice is nonetheless storytelling. Khala Grace is a horror and dark fantasy author with a love for the written word. Once they almost gave up their dreams, but an opportunity to weave Khala's first published book changed the tides. Two authors have inspired their love of stories: J.R.R. Tolkien and Gerald Brom. As time passes, Khala deems to forge their own creative voice. They deem to share tales that not only entertain but provide readers with more room for thought. As stories have always been present in Khala's life at an early age, it only makes sense to create magic from their bittersweet past.